# PRAISE FOR LINDA JAIVIN

## *EAT ME*

'This tossed salad of erotic scenarios charms as few examples of its genre ever have.' *Kirkus Reviews*

'A vivid erotic fantasy…This expertly crafted novel is challenging and hugely entertaining. Its erotic tales and power-play are compelling.' *Everywoman*

'The sexiest thing to come out of Australia since Mel Gibson…And it's funnier, too.' *Glamour*

'Yum…even the steamiest sex scenes…soar into satire. Jaivin never loses sight of her self-declared goal, which is to wrench the writing of erotica from its male practitioners, dress it up with style and sly humor, and restore it to women.' *LA Times*

'Something like *Waiting to Exhale* (or Waiting to Swallow)…You'll enjoy this tasty romp—you'd better, you slave—and you will thank Jaivin for the exquisite pleasure.' *Paper*

'Steamily erotic.' *marie claire*

'The opening chapters of Linda Jaivin's novel *Eat Me* make the famous fridge sequence of *9½ Weeks* look about as explicit as a public information film.' *British Vogue*

'Everybody's talking about *Eat Me*.' *Playboy*

'I laughed out loud at a kiss that goes on for six pages while the participants ponder each other's intentions… very funny stuff.' *Washington Post Book*

'Linda Jaivin's novel will probably do for Lebanese cucumbers what Delia Smith's books did for cranberries. But Jaivin's recipes, revealing the erotic versatility of every piece of fruit and veg on the supermarket shelf, are more suitable for the bedroom than the dining room...The prose is as raw as it comes.' *Observer*

## ROCK N ROLL BABES FROM OUTER SPACE

'Witty and wickedly satiric...The plot is rocket-fueled and the puns almost literally fly off the page. Few writers have skewered the rock and roll world so savagely and accurately and with so much delight.' *Washington Post Book World*

'Linda Jaivin's Tom Robbinsish sex writing gives the story a rapid pulse and gratifyingly sweaty palms.' *New York Times Book Review*

'An erotic romp—no holes barred.' *Elle*

'An outlandishly delightful, X-rated science-fiction fantasy...reads like the insatiable literary love child of Douglas Adams, Kurt Vonnegut, and Susie Bright.' *Sonoma County Independent*

'Her characters are an unorthodox blend of the sharply observed everyday and the sci-fi cartoon...A layered text which navigates the minefield of contemporary gender and sexuality with finesse and humour.' *Sydney Morning Herald*

'Just the right balance of zaniness, hipness and charm... its parody of slacker culture and ufology is a hoot.' *Booklist*

# MILES WALKER, YOU'RE DEAD

Linda Jaivin is a Sydney writer and translator. This is her third novel.

BY THE SAME AUTHOR
Fiction
  *Eat Me*
  *Rock n Roll Babes from Outer Space*
Non-fiction
  *New Ghosts, Old Dreams: Chinese Rebel Voices*
  (co-editor with Geremie Barmé)
  *Confessions of an S & M Virgin*

MILES
WALKER,
YOU'RE
DEAD

linda jaivin

TEXT PUBLISHING
MELBOURNE AUSTRALIA

The Text Publishing Company
171 La Trobe Street
Melbourne Victoria 3000
Australia

First published 1999

Printed and bound by Griffin Press
Designed by Chong Wengho
Typeset in 10.5/14.2 Stempel Garamond by Midland Typesetters

National Library of Australia
Cataloguing-in-Publication data:

Jaivin, Linda.

Miles Walker, you're dead.

ISBN 1 875847 56 1.

I. Title.

823

This project has been assisted by the Commonwealth Government
through the Australia Council, its arts funding and advisory body.

for Tim
who is
for me

ACKNOWLEDGMENTS

This project has been assisted by the Commonwealth Government
through the Australia Council, its arts funding and advisory body. The
Council provided me with a studio at the Tyrone Guthrie Centre at
Annaghmakerrig, in County Monaghan, Ireland, an idyllic environment
where much of the first draft was completed.

I am also grateful to the Eleanor Dark Foundation, which granted me
a three-week fellowship at the Varuna Writers Centre in the Blue
Mountains, to which I've returned many times since; Varuna is my
writing home away from home. I want to thank director Peter Bishop
for his warm support and encouragement.

Thanks also to John Birmingham for the loan of 'Sativa', Jonathan Nix
and Simon Bates for permission to quote from their song 'Plinth' (cred-
ited in the text to 'Nixon Bates'), the inspirational Toronto writer Russell
Smith for passing on the 'ABC' theory of creative genius espoused by
Trimalkyo, and a policewoman—who must go unnamed—for letting
me have a look at her belt and handcuffs. Mandy McCarthy read several
drafts, helped with typing, and offered useful suggestions and support.
Jonathan Nix, Simon Bates and Tim Smith also read and commented on
the final draft, as did my very supportive agent Rose Creswell and
Annette Hughes. Tim loved and understood me through the two years
it took to write this novel. And, as always, I am more grateful than I can
say to my artful editor, Michael Heyward, and everyone else at Text
Publishing.

# Still life (bound and gagged)

My name is Miles Walker. Remember it. I'm keen on immortality. I've got to be. I'm twenty-three years old. I'm the best fucking painter of my generation. And I've got four hours to live.

In a world where millennial hopes collide with apocalyptic expectations, making people just a little bit crazy, where nations go to war to prevent war, where conspiracy theories are rife and bio-hazard a way of life, I should've known that my own career was unlikely to follow a predictable path.

The path I've followed, as you'll see, has led me to a cramped cabin on a cruise ship in Sydney Harbour on what promises to be a spectacular New Year's Eve. But while the rest of the world passes into a new era, I will just pass. To add visual insult to physical injury, I will die staring at beige chipboard walls, a barely double bed with a shiny seashell-patterned coverlet, a vase of dusty plastic roses on a laminate bedside table, and a hideously cheerful blue and white polka-dot curtain obscuring the view from a tiny window that doesn't even have the romantic decency to come in the shape of a porthole.

Though the cabin is minuscule, the *Dinkum* itself is huge. I didn't exactly get the grand tour before I was locked in here, but there's a brochure on the bedside table giving the ship's vital statistics. She's fifty-two metres from bow to stern, has a draft of 1.4 metres and can get up to eight knots. She rents out for harbour cruises, parties, and conferences. In addition to sixty-five cabins like this one, she's got dining 'saloons', lounges, a galley, and a semi-exposed 'disco deck' on top of this one that can accommodate three hundred revellers. There's at least that many up there now by the sound of it. Over the steady doof of the music, which is pumped into the breezeway outside my cabin via a tinny loudspeaker, I can hear a swell of happy voices, shrieked greetings and the clink of glasses.

In one of his chattier moods, my captor, Verbero, told me that our host, the gallery owner Trimalkyo, is costumed in the robes of a Roman emperor, complete with a laurel wreath. But Nero won't get to fiddle while Rome burns tonight. This ship is ground zero. At least I know what's going on. Trimalkyo and his cohort don't have a clue. I'm not sure which is better—to have a few hours to think over your life, or just to go. No warning, no agonising, no regrets. Just one big party and then—boom.

We might be in the middle of Sydney Harbour, but I can barely smell the salt air. This is due to the pall of 'Mist off the Sea' stick disinfectant that sits decaying on the narrow shelf above the bed. ZakDot would appreciate the irony in this.

ZakDot is an irony junkie. His name is short for Zak.com.au. He changed it by deed poll a few years ago. 'It's no longer enough to *have* a website,' he explained. 'I want to *be* a website.' Someone pointed out that he'd become a server, not a website. 'I knew that,' he bluffed.

ZakDot is my best friend by default—de fault of all the sane, normal people in the world for not stepping forward to fill the position. He's got orange hair, tweezed eyebrows, a fake beauty spot, and a tattoo of a martini glass, complete with bubbles, on his arse. I discovered the tattoo under somewhat traumatic circumstances. He smears kohl under and around his eyes, which are brown, and wears satin smoking jackets. 'Decadence is the new black,' he says.

My own wardrobe consists of shapeless maroon and navy blue pullovers, paint-spattered t-shirts and old jeans. I couldn't tell you what colour socks I'm wearing now. ZakDot could tell you what colour socks he had on last week. And the week before that.

Someone once told ZakDot that there was a boy in a Newtown band even cooler than he was. ZakDot laughed. 'The very concept of "cool",' he replied, raising his palms and hooking down the first two fingers of each hand to make quotation marks around the word, 'is so *over.*' Still, I could see that this unnerved him.

Me, I'm in touch with my inner dag. It's a low-maintenance social position.

While ZakDot would love the idea of Mist off the Sea, not even he would recognise the most ironic detail of this whole set-up—the cheaply framed and discoloured reproduction of a painting by Winston Churchill called *Cap d'Antibes* that's hanging on the wall. If Churchill had stuck to politics, then another politician I know might have kept away from art—and artists—and I wouldn't be here tonight. Or dead tomorrow.

If you'll excuse me for a moment, I can hear a key turning in the lock. Friend or foe? Not that there's much to the distinction when even your friends wish you dead. For your own good. I'll get to that story.

It's Verbero. Foe-o-rama. He is wearing some sort of medieval muu-muu with a tasselled belt. My eyes goggle at the sight.

'It's a fancy dwess party, arsehole.' As he slips inside, he lets in a warm breeze. I breathe in the original organic version of Mist off the Sea.

'Well? Thought it over, Walker?' Against the sheen of his pale skin, Verbero's pupils are a dark matt. His chiselled nose and brow look as if they were knocked off from classical statuary. His lips are alizarin crimson. Verbero has evil good looks, like a Hollywood villain, accessorised with a black goatee and diamond nose stud.

He is holding a bottle of Veuve Cliquot and two long-stemmed glasses. Setting them down on top of the brochure, he starts to drop his keys too but, noting my obvious interest, tosses them onto the bed instead. They land on a polyester periwinkle. Without removing his eyes from my face, he extracts a comb from the pocket of his robe and draws it through his neat black hair. 'Well, you little pwick? Weady to play ball?'

I'd answer, but I'm also suffering from a speech impediment. Mine is a recent affliction, known as a gag. The gag consists of a small red rubber ball and two black leather straps, fastened at the back of my head. I saw pictures of gags like this in an exhibition of Photographie Cruelle that Trimalkyo's gallery put on several years ago. In the good old days. Before Destiny. Before the Troubles. When art ruled the world. When all the little children of our little country wanted to grow up to be choreographers and installation artists and performance poets and postmodern theorists. When Gallery Trimalkyo was the trendiest, most happening gallery in Paddington, which is to say Sydney, which is to say, so far as Sydney was concerned, the universe. When collectors like Aurelia Cash fanned themselves at openings with their chequebooks and everyone felt refreshed. When I had the leisure to be irritated by Lynda Tangent's triangle paintings and the impenetrable ravings of Cynthia Mopely. When ZakDot could lie around with a cabbage leaf on his face, call it art, and come away with the class medal. When everything was fine and stupid all at once. When my ambitions were unbound and so was I.

The reason I don't remove the gag and walk out of here is that Verbero has also handcuffed and tied me to my chair. My left eye still throbs from when he punched me—right after that messy incident involving the prime minister's dining room table and immediately before he forced some pills down my throat. They knocked me out even more efficiently than his fist. When I came to, I was in this cabin on this boat—the one place in Sydney I hoped *not* to be on this night.

Verbero leans down towards me and I flinch, but he's only removing the gag. I will tell him of the danger, and he'll surely free me to find my friends and put a stop to this insanity. Three hours and fifty minutes is plenty of time. I am giddy with relief. Verbero's hands shake and he grinds his teeth like he's trying to start a fire with them.

'You ought to cut down on that stuff,' I say, clearing my throat and working my jaw. 'You can lose the use of your nostrils, you know. I once read an interview with David Bowie where he said that—'

'Shut the fuck up, ya stupid pwick.' Verbero lives in a world populated by animated genitals. In addition to those with low IQs or having intercourse there are big ones, lazy ones and bloody ones. When he mistakes you for a body part, it's to your advantage to act in a conciliatory manner.

Verbero walks behind me. I twist my neck to see what he's up to. My back is something I like to keep an eye on when he's around. 'Don't twy no funny business,' he warns, retrieving his keys from the bed and uncuffing me. He sounds like Elmer Fudd doing a Peter Lorre impression on speed.

I don't know how much funny business he thinks a skinny, beat-up artist still tied to his chair can try. On the other hand, the last few months have been chockers with funny business. I shake the stiffness out of my hands and arms.

He hands me a glass. 'Welcome to the hospitality suite,' he sneers. I ping the flute with a fingernail. Crystal.

'Cheers,' I say, as he pours the bubbly. 'Happy New Year.' With the gag out of my mouth, I'm feeling expansive. 'You know,' I observe, 'that bottle is worth more than I was used to living on in a week. You politicians do it in style.'

Verbero is the prime minister's chief of staff. I don't think he likes being called a politician. He narrows his dark eyes.

I take a sip. I study the crystal and, out of habit, imagine how I might represent the sparkling translucence on canvas. Cadmium yellow mixed with lemon and titanium white perhaps. The thought of titanium white makes me smile. There's a story to that as well. I tip the perky golden liquid down my throat and hold out my glass. 'Oh, and I wouldn't mind a ciggie either.' I'm ready to ease into the revelation about the explosive device that, according to my best calculations, ZakDot is helping the fierce and beautiful Maddie to plant on the ship right about now.

'Well?' he demands, cutting into my thoughts. 'Have you thought it over?'

Oh, God, not this again. 'Yes, I have,' I reply. 'And the answer is—no fucken way. But listen, Verbero, there's something—'

He doesn't let me finish. 'Don't you feel the slightest sense of wesponsibility?'

'An artist is only wespons-, uh, responsible to his art. Now, can we leave the subject of Destiny aside for a moment? I really have—'

I don't even see it coming. As he slaps me, the crystal flies out of my hand and shatters against the table.

'Ow. Fuck.' I can taste blood in my mouth. Tears spring to my eyes. I wipe my lips with my sleeve. 'I can't believe you hit me again.'

'Believe it, cawwot-top,' Verbero replies. He jerks my hands away from my face and wrenches them back behind my chair.

'Look, Verbero.' My voice has gone all pathetic. 'I don't want to play any more games. I've something important to tell you. If you don't let me go right now we'll all die. I'm not jo—'

Before I even see it coming, the gag's in. The handcuffs are back on. 'Nice twy,' he says, smirking.

He's split my lip, and my jaw hurts so much I can scarcely feel my black eye. The gag is biting into the corners of my mouth. I'm furious, with myself as much as him, and scared. Why didn't I speak up while I still could?

Verbero goes into the toilet, to do a line of coke, I presume.

I could pray, but I'm not sure if I believe in God. Or rather, my god is Art. Art helps me find meaning and make sense of life. On the other hand, Art doesn't have a great track record in the search-and-rescue department. The police would be more helpful at this point.

The police. The word triggers a pang of longing. I have a funny relationship with the police. But there's no time to meditate on that now. Panic has started to set in. C'mon Miles, I tell myself. You're resourceful. You can figure something out. You survived for years on the government's youth allowance, after all. Do something. Anything.

Summoning all my strength, I rock from side to side, trying to loosen the ropes. It doesn't work. I lose my balance and, together with the chair, crash to the floor of the cabin, hitting my head, and just narrowly missing a fierce-looking shard of crystal.

I feel woozy. My head throbs. Verbero pops his face out of the toilet and laughs his machine-gun laugh. Ack ack ack.

A sharp rap on the door shuts him up fast. He glares at me. Another knock—louder, more authoritative. 'Security. Everything all right in there?'

'Fine. Just fine,' Verbero shoots back.

That voice. It sounds so much like Grevillea's. I must be hallucinating. I'd give anything to see Grevillea Bent just one last time before I die. I close my eyes and fade into a pool of regret.

I'm awash in Eternity. I hate that aftershave. Verbero's bending over me, feeling my pulse. I don't move. My head aches, my eye smarts, my jaw hurts. I'm not getting any more champagne, I'm never going to see Grevillea again, and I'm a dead man. After all these months, after what—a year or more?—of thinking about my death, imagining it, obsessing about it, it's really going to happen.

'Enough of this bullshit.' Cursing, Verbero hauls me upright, chair and all. I let my head flop down on my chest. He pinches my cheek, pulling my face up towards his. I let my eyes roll back. Verbero mutters something under his breath and strides to the window, where he jerks open the curtain. He peers outside and then returns to me. 'Miles Walker, you're dead.'

I've heard that before. I make some gargling noises around the gag, hoping he'll think I'm going to agree to what he wants and remove it. This time I won't waste a moment in telling him about the bomb.

'Did I ever tell you that my wife wan off with an artist? Does that explain anything to you?' His mouth set, his eyes mean, he snatches up the key and is out the door in two strides. The door slams and I hear the key turn in the lock.

He forgot to pull the curtain closed.

Sydney sparkles beyond my window. I now have an unimpeded view of the harbour. That's something most people in this city would die for. Ack ack ack.

The neon logos of the CBD glow seduction indigo and passion red, and the lights of the city wink in the twilight. Masts tinkle, motors hum, people hoot and yell above the music that comes from all directions now. Sydney's a tart and an exhibitionist. Every balcony of every waterfront home, the deck of every yacht, fishing vessel, clipper, dinghy, ferry, party boat, speedboat and tall ship that we pass, and every promenade and walkway and rooftop in sight has been transformed into a stage for the New Year's Eve theatrics of celebration and angst. The Opera House flutters its huge white wings and the giant buttock of the Harbour Bridge moons the night. The lights of the shore cast coloured streamers over the water where they pulsate like electrocardiograms for an over-excited world.

Against the odds, the human race has failed to extinguish itself. Despite burning forests and toxic wastes and nuclear accidents, not all the air is unbreathable, the water undrinkable or the land unliveable. Humanity has somehow survived feudalism, imperialism and colonialism, revolutions, religious wars, world wars, gulf wars and Balkan wars, not to mention Jeff Koons, the end of 'Seinfeld', and even Monica Lewinsky.

Me—I can't even survive my friends.

# Underpainting
## (allegorical,
## large canvas)

A small clutch of party-goers has swept into the breezeway outside the cabin. No one turns to look in the window. They are all gazing out over the harbour, pointing and laughing and chattering. One of them, who is dressed like a clown, puts a paper whistle to his sad red lips and blows it at the others. Over the p.a., Kylie Minogue urges me to celebrate.

Little countries like ours don't often come first in life's track-and-field events. But we go for gold on the New Year's front. I'm sure that Trimalkyo, being an art dealer, takes some pleasure knowing that in this regard, at least, we are ahead of New York and London. We don't just glide first into the New Year, either. We do so with acres of exposed skin, caressed by warm breezes, licking a gelato. Lucky country. Lucky people. Some little patch of New Zealand gets the first sun of the year a millisecond or two before we do, but who cares? You wouldn't want to be there if you could be here, would you?

New Year's Eve. The night when everyone searches for the best, the wildest, the most saturnalian party of all, the Ultimate Bash, the one that's going to change their lives, the one where they'll find the hottest dance music, the truest love. Not that I ever believed that. Unlike ZakDot, I've never been much of a party boy. And the chances that I'm going to meet my true love tonight are slimmer than Grevillea Bent's ankles.

New Year's Eve. The focus of more bullshit and hype than even the art world. The art world. Such as it is. Such as it was. Let me paint you a picture. I've got time—by my best reckoning, some three and a half hours—so I'll do it properly. Underpainting and all. I find a good underpainting helps with composition. It lets you fix the light source and see where the shadows will fall.

Once upon a time, our country, a little country that is also a very big island, lost its way. The way I see it, we were suffering from an existential form of continental drift. Foreigners had never been able to get a fix on where we lived, many of them believing we were either within splashing distance of Hawaii or, due to a fluke of pronunciation, next door to Germany. On account of our colourful Mardi Gras, some people mistook us for Brazil and, because so many of us love to surf, others mixed us up with southern California.

Making fun of this problem, our satirists nicknamed the country 'Strayer'. We 'Strayuns' liked to laugh at ourselves. I think it's fair to say that before the Troubles set in, we considered ourselves the most relaxed, easy-going, fortunate people on the face of the planet.

If we were passionate about anything, it was culture. The streets swarmed with poets and sculptors and film-makers.

You couldn't turn a corner without bumping into public artwork, or lick a stamp without finding a famous artist on the tip of your tongue. People awaited with bated breath the announcements of who'd won the numerous, coveted art prizes, music awards, and literary medals. Some doctors even attributed the prevalence of asthma in our country to this habit of collective breath-holding.

It's no exaggeration to say that our people were mad about culture. Corporations vied to sponsor new works of modern dance and experimental jazz. There were so many literary festivals that municipal governments employed special counsellors to help novelists and playwrights adjust to normal life when the festival season was finally over. Even the commercial television stations dedicated nearly all their prime-time programming to the arts. There were tabloid shows called 'Art/Life' and sitcoms like 'One for the Monet'. Painters and sculptors developed RSI from the effort of peeling off red dots and sticking them to the wall. I was only a student at the time so, unfortunately, this was not my problem. But I was confident that it would be, one day.

We pitied people without any creative potential. Unable to contribute to society, they tended to turn to politics. Once in office, the politicians clamoured for invitations to open art exhibitions; they begged for the chance to launch books. Their parties competed in promising ever better conditions for artists, grander festivals, bigger prizes. The government funded fellowships for, oh, teenage librettists and transsexual ceramicists and three-toed violinists. It even gave artists money to send their work overseas. Not, the politicians emphasised, that their work wasn't welcome at home, but in order that it might gain what was known as an 'international audience' and win glory for the country.

You might find this hard to believe, but there was dancing in the streets whenever one of our films screened in Cannes. Some people did wonder what the fuss was about, believing Cannes to be a small town on the country's north-east coast. Still, we were so proud of our culture that newspapers published front-page reports on such triumphs as our national tap-dancing troupe's European tour. Television stations interrupted their regular programming to run special bulletins on the opening of seminars in Minsk devoted to the art of our indigenous people, or the appearance in a Finnish newspaper of a review of one of our books. For all that, it's my impression that the rest of the world never took much notice of us at all. They simply assumed that every one of our internationally successful playwrights or rock groups or painters had come from somewhere else.

The reason for our invisibility was that our little country was located smack in the middle of nowhere, directly on the periphery of everything. No one ever just 'passed through' or 'dropped in'. Sometimes the fact that we were smack in the middle of nowhere, directly on the periphery of everything, made people despair. They'd get on big metal birds that flew them to bigger, more important countries with fixed locations. Our country didn't exercise much gravitational pull on its people—once they'd flown away, they often neglected to return. We even lost a prime minister once when he swam out to sea and kept on drifting.

It was always a matter of great national excitement when, in an accident of anti-gravity, a foreign sailor meandered into our waters, or when a citizen, having 'made it' elsewhere, decided to come back for a visit.

Still, most of the time, the people of our little country were happy, for the world's strife was far away and not our own and, as the centuries changed over, the world had more than its share of strife. There were holy wars and unholy wars and bombs that went off in the night and weird cults where everyone prayed and died. It was shocking. It was terrible. But it never seemed to have an awful lot to do with us. Watching these events on the telly, we shook our heads and thanked our lucky stars (which were obviously different from other people's stars) that we were safely ensconced smack in the middle of nowhere, directly on the periphery of everything.

Then, one day, all that changed. That day marked the beginning of the Troubles. That day, the citizens of our country woke up crabby and confused. Perhaps it was something in the water—a source of anxiety for some time. Maybe it was a biological version of the millennium bug, or some odd, destabilising ripple in the astrolosphere.

Whatever the reason, that day, instead of saying g'day and humming a few lines from the friendly 'Neighbours' theme song as everyone usually did first thing in the morning—after a spot of tai chi and before their first latte—they began arguing with uncharacteristic ill will. I myself nearly smacked ZakDot that day when he claimed that no painting could match the relevance or spiritual power of a supermarket docket pasted to a gallery wall.

Since everyone was so passionate about culture, there had always been spirited discussions over such issues as whether the judges of the annual portrait competition could tell their arse from someone else's elbow. But now the arguments grew vicious. It was reported that, in the Blue Mountains, fans of heroic couplets took up staves against proponents of blank verse, and that a traditionalist was badly injured when someone hurled a concrete poem. I thought that sounded like urban myth, but I did read in the *Herald* that there was a rise in reported assaults on values and conceptual breakouts. Interestingly enough, the most violent ructions were over the exact location of the little country itself—and by extension the source of its culture.

It's hard to say who started it. There were those who, clutching their cups of fine Bushells tea in one hand and a Sao biscuit in the other, claimed our country was obviously a part of Britain. The critic Jean-Paul d'Esdaigne was one of these. People like him called their homes their 'cahstles' and, when they went out, they said it was to 'dahnce'. They put Promite on their toast instead of Vegemite. They declared that they'd be happy watching Jane Austen re-runs and reading tabloid supplements about dead princesses until the cows came home, and went out, and came home again—and that should be good enough for everyone else as well.

Others insisted that Strayer was a part of Asia. These people waved their chopsticks around as they argued. They pointed for evidence at the popularity of Indian yoga, as well as a recent survey revealing that 87.4 per cent of the population preferred sushi to curried eggs, and cited other statistics showing the extraordinary number of imported dim sum trolleys per capita.

Then there were those like Tony, our local café owner and a concert pianist. One day, I was in the café when he proclaimed, above the roar of the milk-frothing apparatus of his espresso machine, that the little country's soul belonged to continental Europe. 'Why else,' he demanded with Gallic shrugs, 'would half the population stay up all night every night for four weeks just to watch World Cup soccer?'

A customer of Chilean origin leapt up onto the table at this point, spilling his Colombian brew. He shouted back at Tony that the fact we loved World Cup soccer was in fact proof we were part of South America. 'We do the lambada!' he cried. 'We wear big straw hats!'

Not many people seriously proposed that the little country belonged to Africa. Personally, I felt that, since Africa was the cradle of humankind, everyone belonged in some sense to Africa. But what did I know? Quite a few people, including, to my dismay, some of my fellow art students, insisted that the little country was part of America. They said 'yo' and 'd'oh' and wore baseball caps frontwards and backwards to push the point. They took eskies of Coca-Cola with them to the beach, just like in commercials, and never missed an episode of 'Friends'.

The original inhabitants piped up to say they knew exactly where the little country was—right under their feet. Under all of our feet. As this implied that we could define ourselves without reference to anywhere else, it was an even more destabilising concept than the notion that we were smack in the middle of nowhere, directly on the periphery of everything. Lots of people had Aboriginal dot paintings on their walls. They liked to use words from indigenous languages to name their boats and houses. Yet most people had never really listened to anything the original inhabitants had said. They were not going to start now.

Life became one big quarrel. It got nasty. It got violent. The people who wanted to be part of America beat other people with baseball bats, and the people who wanted to be part of Britain beat other people with cricket bats, and the people who wanted to be part of Europe beat other people with stale baguettes. Everyone joined together to beat the indigenous people because their position was deemed the most annoying and provocative of all. The indigenous people, in turn, beat each other for the foolish decision to let the new people into the country in the first place.

Someone burned Tony's café down to the ground. At first police suspected a Vietnamese man whom Tony had attacked with a frozen lasagne in a dispute over the relative superiority of native cuisines. As it turned out, the arsonist was a Percy Grainger fan of Swedish background who'd taken umbrage at Tony's interpretation of 'To a Nordic Princess'.

A popular rock star wrote a ballad called 'The Troubles' about this sad state of affairs. The name stuck.

Like everyone else, I knew 'The Troubles' by heart. But I stayed clear of the turmoil. I was in art school. I believed that art and politics had nothing to do with each other and that true art had a purity that would survive all tests. Of the Troubles, I only knew what I read in the papers, or witnessed that day at Tony's café before it burned down.

I did know that it was a real pity that all this had happened. Strayer was such a beautiful land, with lush green rainforests and scrubby red deserts and long white beaches. It was a country of brightly coloured birds, oddly shaped wild-flowers, giant lizards and blue trees. It had grey marsupials with tiny brains soaked in eucalyptus juice and ants with huge bums full of honey. It was a harsh and dramatic country, prone to flash floods and sudden fires and creeping droughts, the kind of country that made for heroes and legends and riveting weather forecasts. There was always plenty of sky to go around, if never quite enough water, and if the Troubles hadn't started there would have been no better place on earth to live and work and play.

It seemed that our little country that was also a big island was about to go up in a raging bushfire of the vanities. Then along came a woman who promised to save the day, calm the citizenry and make Strayer a nice place, again, in which to live and work and play. She was known as Destiny. How she became known as my Destiny is the rest of this story.

# Futurism, according to plan

The revellers have drifted back to the party. Outside the window, wispy clouds bleed into a darkening sky like watercolours.

Verbero returns. I make urgent noises. 'Gggghhh. Ggggghhh.'

'Forget it, Walker. I'm over your little twicks.' He steps into the tiny bathroom. 'I'm gonna get medieval on yo' ass,' he threatens his reflection in the mirror and chuckles. His chuckle is like his laugh, except backwards: kca, kca, kca. He sees that I am watching him and shuts the door. Through it, I hear him opening the cabinet. There's a soft sound like sugar shifting in a sack. That's impossible. The sack of sugar is with ZakDot and Maddie. Could he have more? I'm dumbfounded. Without another glance in my direction, he departs, cassock rustling.

Medieval on yo' ass. I think, inevitably, of Thurston Tebbit. I'm not sure to what extent, if any, Thurston is responsible for my predicament. At least I can thank him for helping me see the brighter side of it. According to the theories of

Thurston Tebbit, you see, I am about to make an excellent career move.

Thurston Tebbit lives with ZakDot and me in our warehouse in Chippo. Chippo is short for Chippendale. We who live in the little country have a fondness for diminutive nicknames. We like to remind ourselves just how little we actually are. Chippo borders on Sydney's inner west, colliding sloppily with Redfern. The arteries of Broadway and Cleveland Street pump traffic into, through and out of the heart of Chippo, giving it more the feel of a way station than destination. Formerly a leafy working-class suburb with a factory pay cheque in every pocket and a pub on every corner, Chippo has been choppo-ed and changeo-ed to the point where old timers will tell you over a pint at the local that they scarcely recognise their old neighbourhood anymore. The leaves that remain are coated with grime. Even the paperbarks that line our street, a narrow lane running between Broadway and Cleveland, are black with diesel fumes.

At the time we moved to Chippendale, warehouse spaces were plentiful and cheap. You couldn't flick a cigarette butt out the window in Chippo without setting some artist's hair on fire. It's within cooee of two universities, a couple of art schools and Newtown. You can almost smell the cheap pizza and curry places on King Street, and it's only a short walk to the second-hand bookshops on Glebe Point Road and the new cinemas on Broadway. Due east is Surry Hills, with its Turkish pizza, Leb roll joints and artist-run galleries. East of Surry Hills of course is the posh, upstart suburb of Paddington, with its expensive boutiques, four-wheel drives and exclusive galleries. Unlike Newtown, Glebe and Surry Hills, Paddington is not quite within spitting distance—which is probably lucky for Paddington.

The day ZakDot and I went warehouse hunting, I laughed at the name of the old factory building we were about to check out—'Century Dyeing Products Pty Ltd'.

'So "millennial",' ZakDot marvelled. He made air quotes around the word. 'We *have* to live here.'

'Yes, sir,' I said. And that was that.

Our warehouse space was once a storeroom for ball bearings. A slight tilt in the floor doomed that enterprise. We still find them in the corners from time to time. A few incarnations later the space became 'Artha and Marther's Social Dancing School'. There were still how-to-dance diagrams with male and female footsteps stencilled across the floor when we moved in. Tango, cha-cha, fox trot, polka, bootscooting and even rock n roll, a pattern which never made sense no matter how many times we tried it.

The ceiling was all exposed concrete beams, chaotic wiring and piping. Something like the Georges Pompidou Centre in Paris. I haven't actually been to Paris, but I've seen photos. There was a pile of timber in one corner, and scraps of fake fur and velvet: relics of the days when the place was used for furniture-making and costume-design. It was a repository of half-stated ideas, unfinished projects and uncartable dreams. I didn't mind being surrounded by the trappings of failure. They lent me camouflage for my ambitions.

Artha and Marther had put in a small tea-room which the addition of a two-burner and a bar fridge turned into a basic kitchen. They'd installed male and female loos, designated by the same footprints that mapped out the dance steps on the floor. I took what used to be the office for my bedroom, and ZakDot claimed the 'chill-out room', though I don't think it was called that back then. Leaving the central space for a common area, we quickly knocked up two studios along the back wall as well as an extra bedroom. ZakDot set up an old café sandwich-board by the door on which he chalked inspirational sayings: 'Before you decide the sun shines out of someone else's arse, check to see that their jeans fade from the inside' was a typical offering.

Our first co-tenant was a paranoid journo who would pick over the shower curtains for ASIO bugs. Then we got a pair of lesbian trapeze artists prone to violent mid-air stoushes and, after them, a mournful avant-garde music composer named Joy. When Joy moved out, we put an advertisement in the *Herald* for a new flatmate.

ZakDot suggested we accept the seventh caller, no questions asked. That's how we ended up with Thurston.

Thurston looks like the subject of Frans Hals' portrait *The Jolly Toper*. He's got a big, open, meaty face and trusting, lash-less blue eyes, except Thurston's beard is bushier than the Toper's. No sooner had he moved in than people with names like Rodmur and Gwydion started leaving messages on the answering machine about misbehaving Druids and urgent meetings in the Shire of Dismal Fogs, which is, I think, somewhere in the Blue Mountains. Thurston's favourite CD was Hildegard von Bingen's *Ordo Virtutum*, which he played continuously and which I once caught him weeping over. He peppered his speech with medieval words. He spent a lot of time at his computer. He had a habit of knitting chain mail in front of the TV. When he laughed, it sounded like this: nuk nuk nuk.

ZakDot remarked that he didn't think Thurston was actually a psychopath, though one could always live in hope. ZakDot would say things like this, never having met an actual psychopath in his life. At the time, of course, neither had I.

It all started one late spring night not long after Thurston moved in. This was about, let's see, two years ago. Both ZakDot and I were still in art school. The Troubles had started, but we didn't take much notice of them. They didn't affect us, really. So far as I was concerned, the future was a limitless canvas, stretched and primed and ready for me to work my magic upon it.

ZakDot had gone off to his part-time job 'art directing' for the shopping channel. It was a job made for him. You could almost hear the swishing of the air quotes in the title. I also had a part-time job, in my teacher Lynda Tangent's Triangle Factory. Lynda was famous for her paintings of equilateral triangles. They came in three sizes—'travel', 'regular' and 'economy'. She laid on the theory in thick, impasto strokes; the paint itself was thin. 'I want to give the world painting,' she told us, 'yet deny it painting at the same time.' For postmodernist reasons, she never picked up a brush herself, hiring students like me to do the job for her. I hated it, but I switched off and just thought about my own work and the paints I could buy with the money I earned. I had that night off, so I was in my studio, working on a painting that I'd brought home from school.

I'd been at it for some time when Thurston snudged into the doorway. Though I saw him out of the corner of my eye, I was in a kind of groovy pose, leaning back, squinting at the canvas, and dragging on a rollie. I pretended to be so absorbed that I didn't even notice his presence.

'Sorry,' he mumbled after a while. 'Hope I'm not disturbing you.'

'Oh, Thurston! Hello!' Feigning surprise, I beckoned him in. 'What's up?' I stubbed out my cigarette.

Wiping the sweat off my brow with the back of my arm, I watched as Thurston tiptoed through the jumble of old tins and paints and sketchbooks that littered the floor. He looked awestruck at the walls, to which I'd sticky-taped sketches, images ripped out from newspapers and magazines and, since visiting the Brett Whiteley studio in Surry Hills, scraps of paper on which I'd scribbled favourite quotations and profound thoughts. Coming round to where I was standing, he looked at the painting I was working on. 'Wow, Miles,' he sighed. 'That's so *ferly,* I'm speechless.'

I didn't want to break the spell by asking him what he meant. I noticed that his eyes were filling with tears. Embarrassed, I reached down to tickle Bacon, my cat, under his chin.

Thurston asked me, shyly, if I wanted to join him for a beer down the local. The local was just at the end of the street.

I was going in circles with the painting. I knew I had to leave it alone for a while or I'd ruin it. 'Sure,' I said. I was hoping for more compliments on the way.

Like so many pubs in our country, our local provided a highly cultured ambience. The ceiling was painted with fluffy clouds and fat angels like the dome of an Italian church. The back wall featured several naked figures rendered in the classical Greek style. We sat down at the bar near Ionic columns that were shedding chunks of plaster—in a most aesthetic way, of course—and ordered schooners. Across from us, some muscular poets limbered up for a poetry slam that was scheduled for later in the evening and, a few stools over, an old geezer tapped his feet to the strains of the experimental jazz pouring from the p.a.

It occurred to me that I knew almost nothing about our new housemate. 'What do you actually do for a crust, Thurston? If you don't mind my asking.'

Thurston bit his lower lip. 'Freelance statistical analyst and consultant. Sounds pretty boring, hey?'

'I'm not sure I know enough about it to say. What is it that you analyse?'

'Depends. Often it's just stuff like business productivity or market trends. But, about six months ago, this young executive came to me with an interesting project.'

'Yeah?' The words 'productivity' and 'market trends' made my eyes glaze. 'What'd he want?'

'She.'

'She.' Hate it when I do that.

'She wanted, simply, to get to the top. She'd heard about this fellow who fed football data into a computer and worked out what it took for a team to win. She asked me to do something similar for her. It took some lateral thinking but, within a few months of my handing her a game plan, she got herself a promotion and a rise.'

'Far out.' I could feel myself dropping away behind my eyes.

'It gets better,' Thurston insisted. I hoped so. 'Not long after this, she introduced me to a friend of hers, a writer who commissioned me to work out a plan for literary success. So, I collected info about bestselling novels and their creators. I studied the winners of the Nobel and the Booker and the Pulitzer, as well as the Vogel and the Miles Franklin. I factored in a few unusual case studies, Salman Rushdie, Helen

Darville Demidenko and *Primary Colors,* and combined it all to come up with a strategy.'

'Mad.' I was interested now. 'How'd she go?'

'He.'

'He.' You couldn't win.

'Dunno. He hadn't actually written anything at the time. I think he's started now though.'

I laughed.

'Miles. Can I ask you a question?'

'Shoot.'

'What do you want from life?'

Coming from ZakDot, a question like that would've put me on guard. With the guileless Thurston, I found myself answering without hesitation. 'Success without compromise. To be remembered forever for my art.' I *am* the best fucking painter of my generation. It was never my idea to end up being the only person who knew it.

As soon as the words left my mouth, I felt embarrassment flood through me, turning my face and neck the same colour as my hair. My generation isn't comfortable with the idea of success. Our heroes called themselves 'losers', though if you had the t-shirt you were already a winner. The point was, never admit to your ambition. Squinting up at the angels, avoiding Thurston's eyes, I thought about this guy I knew. He loved surfing. He said it was intense, powerful and transforming. Yet you didn't change the ocean or hurt it or leave any sign of your presence. His goal, he told me, was to get through life without leaving a single mark on the world. I envied him. I was so pathetically desperate to leave my mark.

Thurston didn't bat an eye. 'Wow, Miles,' he exhaled. 'Wow.' After a pause during which he shook his head and blew out his cheeks a few times, he asked, 'Were you always this artistic? I mean, were you born this way?'

I shrugged. What could I say? I was the Botticelli of the boxed crayons set, a pre-school pre-Raphaelite. I noticed that the bartender was taking advantage of a quiet moment to work on his novel. I knew it was a novel because I'd once overheard him discussing literary agents with a couple of regulars. I waited till he'd stopped typing to signal him for another round.

'So,' Thurston persisted, 'is your mum or dad an artist?'

'My mum's not an artist. I wouldn't know about my dad. I've never even met the bastard.'

This statement was rewarded with a suitably horrified look on Thurston's part.

'I was born on July fourth, American Independence Day, notable in our family for being the day that my father declared his own independence and split,' I explained. 'My mum emerged from the labour ward to find that he'd vamoosed. Neither of us has seen him since. As it transpired,' I continued, 'he was just the first of a series of Houdinis to whom my ever-hopeful mother chained herself. She's a serial romantic. Unfortunately, the men in her life are just serial.'

'Oh, Miles.' Thurston reached out his hand to comfort me. He pulled it back almost the second it touched my arm, as though he'd received an electric shock.

'Maybe the reason I'm so keen to leave my name to the world is because I'm not sure what it really is,' I admitted, cradling my beer. 'My mum won't even tell me my dad's name. Sometimes I wonder if she even knew what it was. Walker's her surname.'

Thurston cringed. 'At least my dad stayed around long

enough to give us a few memories—and his name—before he split.'

I was only half-listening. Rolling another cigarette, I travelled in my mind back to the house on the south coast where I grew up, with its brick veneer and collapsing verandahs. Home was a clutter of kid stuff and lacteal smells. Oddly enough, there was no art on the walls at all. Not even the sad clowns, big-eyed children and murky landscapes that our neighbours all hung on their walls. My home town was the sort of place where people loved the idea of art but didn't get it.

*My mum's not an artist.* A long-submerged memory floated to the surface. One rainy day, I was rummaging in the attic and came across a stack of paintings. They were quite good, or so I thought at the time. There were several sophisticated-looking abstracts, a portrait or two and a couple of landscapes. I remember asking my mum about them. Her eyes flashed. For a moment, I thought she was going to hit me. 'Stay out of the attic, Miles,' was all she said. When, not long afterwards, I announced my intention to become an artist, mum looked sad. The next time I tried to go up into the attic, it was locked.

In our town, they spoke of people who 'went Away' and 'came back from Away'. I wanted to be in that place called Away. As soon as I could, I fled to Sydney and art school.

Thurston was asking me something.

'Sorry?'

'I was just wondering how you defined success?'

I considered the question. 'According to Freud, the goal of the artist is fame, wealth and beautiful lovers.'

'Is that what you want?'

'Personal satisfaction and the feeling that I'm fulfilling my creative potential are most important, of course. But if I could have the whole shebang, yeah, why not.'

Thurston nodded. 'When you say beautiful lovers…' He blushed.

'I should qualify that,' I said, my voice shot through with heroic melancholy. 'You see, no woman has ever been able to compete with Art for my devotion.' No woman had ever tried that hard either, but I wasn't prepared to admit that. 'I've always permitted Art more intimate moments, more liberties than any woman,' I continued. 'Art, in turn, makes women so jealous that they are ultimately forced to abandon me to her.' Either that or they got so bored with my obsessions that they left. 'You see, my passion for Art makes me emotionally unavailable, and my single-minded dedication to it means I am practically unobtainable.'

The truth was, I was so obtainable it was ridiculous. Though I couldn't have imagined it at the time, I was so obtainable that I'd end up in the arms of a woman who stood against everything I valued. A woman so suspicious of art that she once refused to wear a necklace when she found out it was made from cultured pearls.

Thurston regarded me over the top of his schooner with doe eyes.

'In any case,' I said, 'I've decided to remain celibate for a while.' It was good to make these things look like a matter of choice.

'Celibacy is honourable,' Thurston remarked, nodding. It occurred to me that I didn't know anything about Thurston's own love life. I wasn't sure how much I wanted to know.

'Eventually,' I concluded, 'I'm confident that I'll meet

someone so beautiful, refined, artistic and sensitive that she will break through the barriers I've set up and we'll have a lifelong, passionate and intellectual affair that will be the stuff of legend.'

Thurston forced out a funny little smile and dipped his finger into his beer. He drew geometric liquid doodles on the surface of the bar. With an annoyed expression, the bartender abandoned his Macintosh in order to swipe at them with his cloth, leaving a greasy streak where the patterns had been.

I could see that Thurston was embarrassed. 'What d'ya say? Time to head back?' I suggested.

We staggered home. Thurston had rented a video of an old film called *Knights of the Round Table*, which we watched sitting on the broken-down sofa, our bare feet up on the battered industrial spool that served as a coffee table. 'The relationship between Lancelot and King Arthur is so beautiful,' Thurston sighed when it was over. 'Don't you think?'

I gave the thumbs up. 'Thanks for that,' I said, stretching. 'I'm off to bed.'

As I drifted off to sleep, I could hear the film starting again.

For several days after this, I sensed Thurston working like crazy in his room, banging away at his keyboard. One afternoon, I'd no sooner come home from class than he came flying out, a clutch of papers in his thick hand. 'Well, *you're* excited,' I commented, dropping my heavy satchel of paints. He was wearing a homespun tunic. Just looking at it made me itch.

The front door opened and closed again and ZakDot, who didn't have any classes on Fridays, barrelled into the lounge. He'd been busking in Victoria Park and carried an armful of juggling bats, each of which bore a stencilled phrase: 'artistic integrity', 'commercial success', 'critical acclaim' and 'personal satisfaction'. ZakDot was not a good juggler, but I suppose that was the point. 'Hello boychiks,' he greeted, letting the bats clatter to the floor. He wiped the sweat from his brow with the hem of his t-shirt, exposing his taut stomach with its fine line of blonde hair leading down past the navel. Then he went into the kitchen for a glass of water.

'I've got it,' Thurston blurted the second ZakDot left the room. He was bouncing up and down in his ug boots.

'What? Herpes? Bubonic plague? A winning lottery ticket?' The hurt-puppy look in his eyes made me regret my flippancy. 'I'm sorry, Thurston. What've you got?'

'The formula,' he said, excitement quivering in his voice.

'What formula?' ZakDot had returned. He drank half the glass and poured the rest over his head. It dribbled down over the fox trot.

Thurston glanced at me, as if for permission to speak. I shrugged. I still didn't have a clue what he was on about.

'For success without compromise.'

'Shit! That should be on one of my bats!' ZakDot exclaimed. He picked up a texta from the table and wrote it on his hand as a reminder.

I laughed and sat down on the edge of the table.

But Thurston was serious. 'Remember those analyses I told you about? Well, I've fed in all sorts of data about art and the art world. I've slotted in information on artists who burst onto the scene at a young age and compared them with those who emerged later in life. I've factored in issues like the tall poppy syndrome, photogenicity, and subcultural status, as well as external factors such as the lag between local and overseas trends.'

ZakDot sat down next to me. He looked thoroughly amused.

Thurston took a breath. 'Taking note of the fact that you're a painter, I looked at short, medium and long-term trends in the market for paintings as well as the recent tendency for awards to be given to artists working with very small Styrofoam balls or video games and, well, to make a long story short, I mapped out your optimal career trajectory.'

'My "optimal career trajectory"?' I was so flabbergasted that I actually air-quoted the words, to ZakDot's obvious delight.

Thurston excused himself and came back with a whiteboard, which he propped up in front of the TV. 'Okay,' he said, 'This is the basic plan.' He picked up a blue marker. I was fascinated to see that he wrote in a calligraphic hand reminiscent of illuminated medieval manuscripts. 'One. Put together a solid body of work. Brilliant and original.'

'No worries.' It was, after all, my intention from the start.

'Two. Attract high-level patronage. Three. Engender a controversy. Four. Cultivate an air of mystery. Five. Live dangerously.' He turned and faced us with an eager look on his face. A row of large white teeth found a clearing in the curly brown thatch. His smile was like the rest of him— awkward, out of place, but endearing.

'There's only one small catch. For the formula to work perfectly, you have to die young.'

'Cool!' ZakDot, forgetting that 'cool' was 'over', sat up straight. 'What'll it be then, Miles?' He grinned. 'Murder? Suicide? Or accidental? And can I help?'

He helped all right. They all did. And here I am.

# Romanticism is ultimately fatal

The Monday after Thurston proposed that I die young in order to live forever, Lynda Tangent came through the painting studio at school to check on the progress of our latest assignment, self-portraits. Lynda is a severe-looking woman who is all angles— knife-blade cheekbones, geometric hair, circumflex eyebrows, pointy breasts. A cubist's dream model. It's rumoured, incidentally, that she has a third nipple on her sternum, equidistant from the other two, her own natural equilateral triangle.

Pausing by my easel, she cupped her sharp chin in her hand. After a pause, she uttered the pronouncement, 'Too beautiful.'

Self-consciously, I ran my hand through my hair, which is thick, wavy and red. I have a longish face, full lips, large and hooded green eyes. A girl in my first-year class once told me I look like the engraver Albrecht Dürer in his self-portrait.

Lynda's next comment was completely unexpected. 'You need to live more, Miles.'

What did she mean by that? Sure, I was only

twenty-one at the time but, to the best of my knowledge, I had lived every one of those years. 'And how do you propose I do that?' I fumed.

'Take risks. Expose yourself. Give birth to yourself in each painting and kill yourself, too.'

Kill myself? Could it be a coincidence? Though it was a hot day, a chill ran through me from the very top of my head to the tip of my toes. That day marked the beginning of my paranoia. I dipped my brush in crimson, and painted a jagged red slash across the neck of my self-portrait.

After school, I took the painting home and propped it up on the easel to study it. ZakDot, whose own self-portrait, 'You Are What You Eat', had consisted of a block of chocolate, a dildo and a sex toy in the shape of a vagina, did a double-take when he walked into the room.

'There's something to it, you know,' he remarked, after I told him about Lynda's comments. 'Think about it. Géricault. Keats. Egon Schiele. Jimi Hendrix. Kurt Cobain. They all died young. Legends, every one.'

'There's just one problem, Zed.'

'What's that?'

'I don't want to die.'

'Wowser.'

'Besides,' I pointed out, 'they all had solid reputations by the time they died. I haven't even had an exhibition.'

ZakDot snapped his fingers. 'How's this? You die. Don't make that face, Miles. It's unbecoming. Besides, you've got to work on your aversion to death. It's holding you back. This is the plan. As I said, you die. We'll work out the details later. It will have to encompass all those other things, you know, mystery, controversy, the lot. But the crucial thing is, shortly after you die, I release a press statement describing you as the great undiscovered "genius" of our age.'

I didn't like the way he air-quoted 'genius'.

'I let the interest build to a fever pitch,' he continued, 'gather a selection of your work and put on an exhibition. It would have to be at some place like'—he paused to think—'Gallery Trimalkyo, of course.'

'Of course.'

As ZakDot knew, I'd always dreamed of getting in with Trimalkyo.

I never imagined that it would work out quite as it did. I'm in with Trimalkyo now, all right. In over my neck. And Trimalkyo's in with me. Over his. Even if he doesn't know it yet.

Zak kept going. 'As a result of the enormous success of the sell-out exhibition, there is a tremendous demand for your work. Together with Trimalkyo, I calculate the most advantageous method of dribbling out the paintings to a hungry and eager market. I quit arranging Flying Cow Helicopter Desk Lamps at the Shopping Channel and live off the sales of your work, which continues to appreciate in value, for the rest of my life.'

'Great,' I snorted. 'And what do I get out of this?'

'Weren't you listening to Thurston? Immortality. Success without compromise.'

Recalling that conversation now, I feel goose bumps rise along my arms, which are still tethered behind my back. I wonder if perhaps ZakDot *does* know I'm on board after all. I wonder if Trimalkyo knows. If they're actually in cahoots.

You know how I said I was the best fucking painter of my

generation? Stuff my generation. I'm one of the best painters of any generation who ever lived. I may sound so far up myself that I'm almost inside out, but the truth is I'm major league. The work I've done since that throat-slashed self-portrait would knock your socks off. I'm right up there with Rembrandt and Caravaggio and Titian and Goya and the rest. If I could show you my work right now you'd believe me. There's no question but that it's worth killing for. The question is, is it worth dying for?

What a mess I'm in. And I have nothing to blame but my own talent.

That and the fact I seem to suffer from terminal naivety.

I suppose I ought to admit that it also has something to do with my love life, or rather, my tendency to fall into bed with the wrong sort of woman. Or maybe just *the* wrong woman, full stop. Whatever I told Thurston, I don't really have much experience with women at all. The truth is, they don't come into my life very often. So when they do, I get a little over-excited. I say 'yes' when I should say 'no', and when I say 'no', it's clear that I mean 'yes'. There have been a few occasions, including one this afternoon, when saying 'no' really ought to have meant 'no'.

The boat judders. We're reversing. Another heavy vibration and the Opera House comes into view, in close up. We must be at the Man O'War Jetty. I hear the gangplank slap down, but there's no rush and flutter of guests streaming on board as happened when we docked at Darling Point or Kurraba Road. I suddenly realise that the music has stopped. The conversation level on the sundeck has dropped to a whisper. A band strikes up the national anthem.

It's her. The prime minister. Destiny Doppler. Known to

artists as the Eliminator, the Terminator, the Scourge. A politician who single-handedly led a movement to wipe the smile of culture off the face of this country.

That's my baby.

# Video art
# with anchovies

I remember when I first laid eyes on Destiny. It was the first time she appeared on the political landscape of our little country, also notable for being the day that Maddie moved into our warehouse.

We'd decided to rent out ZakDot's studio. Though his heart belonged to dada, ZakDot was finding it difficult to produce artificial surrealism in a world that already had the Troubles, not to mention the British royal family, professional wrestling, and Dannii Minogue. So, outside of a few projects for art school, he produced nothing. Since inactivity doesn't require a lot of space and we were always skint, it made sense to find another house-mate. We'd just begun the first semester of our final year so we posted an ad on the bulletin board. We couldn't believe our luck when Maddie answered it.

Maddie transferred into our art school from some place in Melbourne. It was rumoured she'd been told that if she left her old school voluntarily they wouldn't expel her or press charges. We didn't know what she'd done, but we were all intrigued.

She was a rare beauty, tall and statuesque, with a shaved head, cheekbones like golf balls, a Maori-style tattoo on her chin and piercings through the top of her nose, lips and tongue. She dressed in heavy boots and camouflage trousers and that evening was wearing a tank top which showed off her broad shoulders, perky tits and serious biceps. She smelled like baby powder. She looked like she could beat the crap out of you.

'I hope you like cats,' I said when she came by to look at the place.

'Yes,' she replied, looking at Bacon and slowly licking her lips. 'Let's share recipes.' I must have looked alarmed, because she added, 'Only kidding.'

Her voice had this flat, almost bored quality that was incredibly sexy.

She told us her surname was @. This gave her and ZakDot an instant connection that I envied.

To celebrate her moving in, we ordered a pizza. While we waited, Maddie reclined on the sofa, her long legs tucked underneath her. She was absorbed in a photocopied tome with the title of *The Anarchist Cookbook*. Without warning, she dropped the book to the floor. She leaned back against the sofa, gripping the cushions. Pelvis raised, she clenched her jaw and let out a series of guttural exhalations.

Thurston chose this moment to appear in the lounge with a large sack full of clanging metal slung over one shoulder. He was holding a broadaxe. I nearly bolted at the sight, for one moment certain that he was coming to give me that little career boost we'd all been talking about. But Thurston wasn't even looking at me. He stopped dead in the middle of the lounge, equidistant between the tango and rock 'n roll, and stared at Maddie. His pale eyes were even rounder than usual.

He swallowed. 'You right?' he squeaked.

Maddie looked up, raising one eyebrow. 'Nice blade,' she commented. Then she began to undulate.

Thurston mumbled something and shabbed out, a bundle of embarrassment and tintinnabulation. Maddie arched her back, moaned, and collapsed across the couch.

It was a source of some satisfaction to note that ZakDot was as gobsmacked as I.

'Kegels,' she proclaimed, after a pause long enough for an elephant to gestate. She got up to let in the pizza guy. We hadn't even heard him knock.

'She's *so* intense,' ZakDot whispered.

Returning with the pizzas, she plopped the boxes down on the table and levered out the biggest piece for herself. She tore off a slab of cardboard from the top of the box for a plate. I'd got up to get a glass of water when I heard her say, 'So, like, what sorta art are you into?' I spun on my heels, eager to grasp even this flimsy straw of her interest only to realise that the question was addressed to ZakDot.

ZakDot was mmm-ing and yum-ing over an anchovy-laden triangle, having been told by a former girlfriend that this was universally understood as a sign that a man was into oral sex. I felt like slapping him. He swallowed and patted his stomach.

'Well,' he began, 'you could call what I do "pre-concep-tual".' I was delighted to see that a small shred of spinach was caught between his front teeth. 'It's an outgrowth of conceptual art,' he elaborated. 'Or ingrowth. Depends how you look at it.'

'Ah,' Maddie drawled, 'a con*cept*ual artist.' I relished the potential for sarcasm that lurked in her voice.

'Actually,' ZakDot continued, warming to his spiel, his fingers making air quotes around every other word, 'I prefer the phrase "ideas man" to "conceptual artist", the inverted commas signifying a parodical-slash-paradoxical attitude towards both "gender" and "imagination". But I suppose the crucial bit is this: by not executing the concepts I come up with, by merely "thinking" of them, I believe I've taken art into a "purer" realm. It's like a state of becoming that never becomes. Rather "Taoist", really.'

'The more common name for it,' I interjected, 'is procrastination.'

Maddie giggled. She had a surprisingly girlish laugh. It was adorable.

I picked up the last piece with anchovies and savoured it.

'Rembrandt here is a *traditionalist*.' ZakDot said 'traditionalist' as if it indicated someone who chewed the ears off live puppies. 'A *painter*.' Painters being the ones who then grabbed the cutest survivors and vivisected them. 'Miles' discomfort with and alienation from the world around him,' ZakDot elaborated, 'has led him to believe that the only way for him to achieve lasting recognition is to die young, but he hasn't yet worked out how best to do this.'

I wanted to kick him. The joke had gone on all summer—long enough. I wanted it buried before I was. I gave ZakDot my I-am-a-dingo-and-you-are-a-matinee-jacket look. 'If you have any ideas,' he continued, 'I'm sure he'll be open to them.'

Maddie looked at me and nodded. I hadn't a clue what she was thinking. I decided not to honour ZakDot's comments with a rebuttal. I noticed that Maddie had a plug of wood stuck through one earlobe. I wondered if she'd stretched out the hole slowly, like African tribal people did, or had somehow punched it all at once, as painful as that would be. I wasn't game to ask.

'How about you, Maddie?' I said, keen to show her who was the sensitive, listening type around here. 'What sort of art do *you* do?'

'Me? I fuck shit up,' she replied. I waited for her to elaborate. She licked pizza goo off her thumb.

'Legendary,' ZakDot commented. Then, after a pause, 'What sort of shit?'

'Oh, you know, just shit.' As though the matter required no further explanation, she reached for the remote and flicked on the telly. '"Baywatch",' she observed, as several pairs of breasts went flying down a beach followed by girls. 'Hubba hubba.'

I felt affronted. She still hadn't asked me about my art. 'I could show you my studio sometime if you like,' I offered.

'Mm,' she replied.

She hit the remote once more and Trixie Tinkles, premier exponent of the dramatic facial reaction school of television journalism, filled the screen with her camera-friendly teeth, auto-cue eyes and tabloid blonde hair. She was interviewing another woman. Despite the distortions of TV, you could see that the interviewee, though in her late thirties or early forties, had flawless alabaster skin. Her eyes were heavy-lidded. She had a long thin straight nose and a small, serious mouth. Her thick brown hair was combed back into a severe bun. Her body looked soft and voluptuous underneath her suit. I found her incredibly sexy. Then again, I found most women incredibly sexy. I was hopeless like that. I also felt like I'd seen her somewhere before. I searched my memory.

'That's it. *Odalisque*!' I exclaimed. 'She's just like the *Odalisque*! By Ingres.'

If ZakDot and Maddie were cognisant of the history of Western art, they did not let on. They seemed absorbed by the program. This would be a first for ZakDot, who only ever watched current affairs shows with the sound off, so he could do his own voice-overs.

'You've heard of Ingres, I take it.' This was aimed at ZakDot.

'Miles, Miles, Miles. Haven't you heard? Painting's dead as Elvis,' ZakDot observed without removing his eyes from the screen.

'Bollocks.'

'The contemporary world welcomes you, Miles. No joining fee.'

I was smouldering. Painting had been declared dead and resurrected so many times in the last hundred years that every other day was Easter in the art world. Even the lecturers in the painting department couldn't decide whether it was a legitimate activity or not. ZakDot passed his last assessment with an empty plinth and flying colours. The only thing that saved my academic career was my tendency to leave one small corner of each work at the stage of underpainting. I think I feared that, once I completed a painting, it would die for me; maybe, like my father, I was just scared of commitment; or perhaps, on some level, I was terrified of the success that I craved. Whatever the reason for it, Cynthia Mopely, our theory teacher, interpreted this tic as a profound statement on the impossibility of closure. This was apparently a good thing. I passed.

This was typical of my experience of art school. My

teachers acknowledged my skill, my mastery of pigment and colour, my sense of composition and the power of my vision. But they fretted right from the start that my attitude might not be sufficiently ironic. Perhaps that's really what Lynda Tangent meant when she declared my work 'too beautiful'.

It was weird. The more the people of our little country valued and cherished art and culture, the more earnestly they argued over its meanings and origins, the more those who created it grew uncertain about its worth and their own motivations. Sitting in front of the telly with ZakDot and Maddie that night, I wondered what it would have been like to have been born in an era when devotion to ideals of beauty, resonance and truth were not seen by other artists as pitiably retrograde. Maybe I was better off dead. Maybe Thurston was right after all.

'What are you going on about?' ZakDot shook his head. 'Or did you not realise you were talking to yourself.' He circled his finger around his ear and tried to catch Maddie's eye.

'Nothing,' I replied morosely. I'd read somewhere that talking to yourself was the first sign of madness. Bacon, sympathetic as always, or maybe just hungry, sloped over and rubbed himself against my legs. I wondered if either ZakDot or Maddie could sense my agitation. Their eyes were riveted to the tube.

The woman with the flawless skin was talking about the Troubles. 'Multiculturalism,' she was saying, popping out the syllables with difficulty, 'is a threat to national surety?'

Trixie Tinkles widened her eyes in a facsimile of shock.

'In fact,' the odalisque continued, 'culturalism of all sorts is a threat to national surety? We see that in the Troubles?'

For all her physical allure, she had one of those inflections where every sentence ended in a question. 'And this government can't seem to do nothing about it?'

That much was true. The government was hopeless. Our leaders, small men with reptilian tongues, paid lip-service to art, but you could tell they didn't know what the word meant. They were a pack of bean counters incapable of grasping any concept that didn't contain a decimal point. The Troubles were way beyond their grasp. Asked for his analysis of the situation, the prime minister, who'd been elected only because voters mistook him for an actor in a respected television drama, thought for a moment and bleated, 'Two point six.' When queried what he intended to do about it, he waggled his finger and shouted, 'One point eight!' His aspirations for the future: 'Ten per cent.'

'There's a lot wrong with the world?' the woman with the long nose was saying. 'Now I can't do much about, you know, Innonesia? Or the Russians? Or that Albaranian thing? But I do know that this country's down on its stumps? And I can get it back up again?'

Trixie glanced down at her notes. 'And how exactly,' she asked, resting one finger against her chin, 'would you do that?'

'I'm glad you asked that, Miss Tinkles?' the woman with the small mouth said.

Trixie Tinkles realised the camera was on her and nodded.

'Get rid of culture? And you get rid of the Troubles?'

This was stupid and offensive. I reached for the remote, thinking to switch channels.

Maddie pinned my hand to the sofa with her palm. A thrill of electricity shot up my arm, into my brain and did a U-turn heading straight for my groin.

The gesture did not escape ZakDot's notice. With Maddie still staring straight ahead at the TV, I smirked at him. She removed her hand. He smirked back.

'Thank you, Mrs Doppler,' Trixie said blankly into the camera. 'We'll be back with Destiny Doppler, leader of Clean Slate, the independent party that everyone's talking about, after this commercial break.' A shampoo ad featuring the country's only artist with clean hair came on.

Maddie turned to me. 'I've actually been into your studio,' she proclaimed, sucking on her tongue piercing. Nervously, I waited for her to go on. She turned back to the TV. The shampoo ad finished and another ad came on in which a well-known composer explained why she preferred a certain brand of tampons. 'First-rate, Miles,' Maddie finally drawled. 'Really like it.'

My heart filled and my head swelled. I wanted the moment to last forever. I wanted to ask her what she liked, to wring out every drop of flattery and appreciation. Destiny's face filled the screen again. ZakDot turned up the sound.

'For all our festivals and exhibitions and—' Destiny paused '—bean-alleys and theatre sports and what have you, in our heart of hearts, the people of Strayer aren't comfortable with the concept? Of culture?'

'How do you mean that?' chirped Trixie. Having accidentally put on her talking-to-happy-mother-of-quintuplets-voice, she struggled towards appropriateness.

A male voice cut in. The camera swung round to frame the speaker, who, it was apparent, had been just off-screen all this time. My first impression of him was that he was handsome, but in a creepy sort of way.

'Think about it, Twixie.' He spat out her name as though it

were a plug of tobacco. 'Look awound you. Don't you think we're all twying a tad too hard? Let's face it, when a citizen of this cuntwee dwags himself off to some wanky little exhibition in which the artist displays his total contempt for his audience by bottling his piss, or sticking plastic bags to the wall, he's in denial. He's in denial of the fact that he's feeling insulted, bored, and angwee. Look what's happened to pubs—you can't go out for a beer or hit of the pokies without finding yourself in the middle of some comedy festival or poetwee weading. It's outwageous. A twavesty.'

'We'll be back with Destiny Doppler and Mister, uh, Verbero from Clean Slate after this break.' Trixie looked into the camera, looked down, shuffled her notes and looked up again. An ad for a cheese snack using the characters from a popular novel came on the tube.

'It's a joke,' I posited. 'Surely.'

'Yeah, but I'd still feel ripped off if I were the author,' ZakDot argued.

'I'm talking about Clean Slate. And Destiny Doppler.'

'Of course it's a joke. I'm sure we'll find out in a moment that she's actually Barry Humphries' latest character.'

'No JOKE!' boomed Maddie. 'Dead fucken serious.'

We were discovering that it was hard to argue with Maddie. We went silent, sitting through an advert for Doomsday-proof bush shelters and then another in which a classical pianist explained how a certain brand of toothpaste had whitened *and* brightened his smile.

Destiny reappeared. 'Let's look at the economics? The statatistics?'

Trixie nodded cheerfully.

'Well...' Destiny glanced down at the pile of papers in

front of her with a panicked expression. A smooth male hand reached over, extricated one sheet and placed it on top of the pile. 'Yes, well, according to these statatistics? The arts and culture of this country is valued at nineteen billion dollars annually, rivalling the road transport and house building sectors? Now this seems like a crime to me? We need road transport? We need houses? While some people still don't own their own houses, why is so much money going into the arts?'

'Uh, Ms Doppler—' Trixie interrupted, frowning with concentration.

'Destiny?'

'Destiny. I believe, now I could be wrong, I'm no economist, but I do believe that those stata-, uh, statistics indicate how much money the arts are *contributing* to the economy.' Trixie tried to raise one eyebrow, failed, worked on the other one.

Destiny knit her brows. 'Let's look at another statatistic then? Foreign visitors spend sixty-five million dollars on Aboriginal arts and crafts? Now, I ask you, couldn't they be spending it on something else while they're here? I mean, shouldn't they be buying things made by our citizens?'

Trixie gulped. 'Uh, I believe that the Aborigines *are* citizens,' she said uncertainly. She turned to the side. 'Polly? Polly? Can you check that for me?'

'Can you believe this?' said Maddie through gritted teeth.

Verbero whispered something in Destiny's ear.

'Well, Trixie,' she began again, 'if the market doesn't have enough demand for artists, if most of them have to survive on something like ten thousand dollars a year, many requiring welfare benefits, then isn't that a sign that we have too many artists? Too much supply? Too little demand?'

Trixie, who looked stunned, shook herself. She grinned at the camera, her head to one side. 'Uh, well, that's all we have time for tonight.'

'Wait?' Destiny cut in as the credits started to roll. 'I just want to say,' she trilled, 'that if Clean Slate gets into power, I will consider it a mandate to cut off all government funding to the arts?' She made a small fist and thumped the table with it, startling Trixie, who was stressing over wind-up signals from her producer. 'I'll impose a creativity tax? I'll cut off the dole for any unemployed person caught using their time to create art or literature or music? I can promise you this—we will wean artists off the public teat if we have to pull the little suckers off one by one? Culture,' she concluded, 'is simply un-Strayun, and that's that?'

The three of us looked at each other. It felt like one of those moments, a JFK-assassination or Neil-Armstrong-moon-landing or Princess-Di-car-crash moment, a future where-were-you-when snapshot in time.

'Damn.' ZakDot was the first to regain his voice. 'I haven't even had a chance to wrap me cakehole round the public teat and she's already weaning me off. *So* unfair.'

Maddie said nothing. She stood up and went to her room. When she came back, she was carrying a gun.

'Holy shit, Maddie. What're you...' She was going to kill me, I knew it.

When I opened my eyes, my ears were ringing and an acrid smell filled my nostrils. Bacon was in my arms. I tried to stand up, but my knees knocked and I sat back down again.

'Have a little fright there, Mi?' ZakDot grinned. I could

see, however, that he'd just got up off the floor himself.

The sorry mess of glass and metal and plastic that spread itself over the lounge-room floor, from cha cha to fox trot, was all that remained of ZakDot's television set. Maddie put down her weapon and rubbed her palms together. 'Anyone for a couple of pots down the local?' I imagined she was going to take the gun down for a few pot shots at drinkers before remembering she was from Melbourne. She was talking about beer. You see, right from the start, I believed her capable of anything. And that was before I knew that she was into making bombs. I can see now that my fright at the sight of her with her gun, like the start Thurston gave me with his broadaxe, was the result of my own neuroses.

I wish I could say the same of my terror at the device she and Zak are setting up on this boat right now.

'Well? Any takers?'

'I never say no to a beer,' said ZakDot, picking a shard of screen off his jacket. 'No telling how it would react to rejection.'

I was too shaken to go anywhere. Staying back with a transparent excuse about having to get up early the next day for class, I swept up. No one had swept the floor for a long time. I found some more ball bearings.

By the time they returned I was in bed nodding off over Robert Hughes.

When I heard the rap on my door, I had a nanosecond of fantasy that it was Maddie.

'Miles?' It was ZakDot. 'You're not sleeping already, are you? It's only eleven-thirty.'

'Fuck off,' I instructed. 'I need my beauty sleep.'

'But Mi. That's what daytime is for.' He pushed open the door.

'Did I say come in?' I rolled over, drawing the pillow over my head.

'What a gal, hey?' ZakDot plonked himself down on the end of my bed. 'What about that *gun*? Scared you, huh? You thought I'd recruited her to the "plan". I could see it in your eyes.'

I pulled the pillow down more tightly around my ears. ZakDot wrestled it off.

'It's only a pellet gun, you know,' he informed me with a smirk.

'Only a pellet gun,' I repeated, trying vainly to hide my mortification. 'You would go telling everyone I want to die young,' I griped, lifting my head to glare at him. 'And while we're on the subject of bullshit, what was that "painting is dead as Elvis" crap?'

ZakDot slipped his hand into my hair and mussed it. 'I was just stirring you.'

'What am I, soup?'

'I love you, Miles,' he said, wrapping his arms around me and hugging me tight.

'Get off me, you fucking pisshead,' I growled and pushed him off. Bastard gave me a stiffy.

A terrible idea has just occurred to me. Thinking about Verbero's movements at the bathroom cabinet earlier, I wonder if perhaps his men went back to the warehouse this afternoon. The gang would have all been there at the time. They'd have been no match for... Here I am, assuming that

ZakDot and Maddie are on board, planting a bomb, when they could be, I dunno, already *dead*. I feel sick.

The ship's whistle has blown. We're moving out into the middle of the harbour again. Verbero dashes in, and snaps the curtain closed. Pointing two fingers at me like a pistol, he dashes out again.

# The last art hero

Somewhere in the third world, the top of a mountain came off like a champagne cork, inundating eight villages with lava. Elsewhere around the globe, tsunamis, hurricanes, and landslides wreaked their havoc. Terrorists terrorised, economies collapsed, children fought whole wars without adult super-vision. Democracy protesters died, dictators didn't. Refugees streamed across borders, the borders shifted and they streamed across them again. Scien-tists cloned themselves, rich people froze themselves, poor people drugged themselves. Cannibalism was making a comeback. There was too much acid in the rain, electromagnetism in the air and poison in the ground.

In other words, nothing had changed in the month or two it took us to get a replacement for the TV. The world scared the shit out of me. I didn't understand it; I didn't want to. Art was the only thing that made sense to me, even when it made me suffer.

'Hello, hello.' ZakDot waved his hand in front

of my face. 'You're talking to yourself again, Miles.' I looked over at him, startled, just as Maddie plopped down between us on the sofa.

'What are you talking about?' She helped herself to the bag of crisps in ZakDot's lap.

'Miles here,' ZakDot explained, 'is the Last Art Hero. He wants to suffer for his art.'

'Excellent.' Maddie nodded.

At that point, Thurston emerged from his room, wearing his tunic, breeches, and the helmet from a suit of armour. With a sidelong glance at us through the visor and a little wave, he walked across the lounge and out the door.

'There goes Ned Kelly,' ZakDot said after he'd gone. 'Off to model for Sidney Nolan.'

'Does something strike you as strange about Thurston lately?' I asked. I had a reason for asking.

'Does something strike you as Catholic about the Pope lately?'

Maddie giggled. 'Oh, here's the news again.' She reached for the remote and clicked on the sound. When ZakDot bought the TV, he made Maddie promise, as a condition for being allowed to watch it, that she wouldn't harm it no matter what came on the screen. Curling her legs under her, she rested her head on my shoulder. Her big sexy feet in their thermal socks were flush against ZakDot's thigh. It was April, and the evenings were growing cool. ZakDot's arm rested on the back of the couch, his hand in my hair. We were one happy family.

I suppose that the fact I was going slowly insane didn't really detract from the general *joie de vivre* of the household. Like Thurston's increasing eccentricity and the slow build-up of sexual tension, it contributed something special to the atmosphere.

'Eccentricity' was ZakDot's word for Thurston's behaviour, by the way. I perceived something more insidious, even diabolical at work. After my alarmed reaction to his formula, Thurston never mentioned it again. His silence perturbed me.

Adding to my apprehension was the way in which his arsenal of medieval weaponry continued to grow. Every other day, it seemed, I opened the door to couriers delivering pole-axes or rapiers from Knights-R-Us. Once, I found him assembling a full-scale catapult in the lounge. I worried about what was behind those long, meditative looks he threw my way when he thought I didn't notice. He took to locking his door when he went out, which struck me as further proof that he was up to something. I began to wonder if the real reason he wore ug boots was to get about in silence, the better to carry out his murderous plans.

'Sh,' ZakDot admonished, ruffling my hair with his hand. I clenched my jaw and tried to focus on the screen. I really had to get a grip.

The local news was on now. ZakDot turned up the sound. The Troubles were getting worse and were spreading throughout the country. Police had arrested a film director in Darwin on shooting charges. There'd been an ugly pub brawl in Townsville over whether *Cloudstreet* should have had a happy ending. The prime minister, licking his lips, appealed for calm. 'Just four point five,' he urged, pulling on his ears for emphasis, 'four point six if possible.' The leader of the opposition failed to come up with a better solution. Somewhere in the backwoods of Tasmania, Destiny Doppler delivered her anti-culture message to a crowd of several dozen cheering supporters. The crowd was small but the cheering loud as many of the people had two heads.

Since that time we first saw her talking to Trixie Tinkles, Destiny had been popping up everywhere.

'You know what Destiny Doppler's problem is?' My voice took on an edge of melodrama. 'She's never been exposed to great art.' The others looked at me, incredulous. 'Seriously. I don't think she even knows what culture is. I bet that if I had just a week with her, I could bring her round.' If I'd only known what a week with her would really lead to. Bringing her round was the least of it.

'I think,' Maddie drawled, her eyes on my face and one finger on her tattooed chin, 'that if you keep saying things like that, Miles, we really are going to have to kill you.'

The following afternoon, she brought home a chainsaw.

I couldn't paint. The noise of the chainsaw was setting my teeth on edge. I was hungry. I'd have gone out to eat if I'd had any money, which I didn't, so I headed into the kitchen.

Where were the pots and pans? I frowned. Then I remembered that Thurston had rigged up a rack and pulley for the pots and pans that morning. It was a device based, he said, on fourteenth century technology. He'd demonstrated it for us earlier in the day. I tugged on the rope that was supposed to lower the rack from its position near the ceiling. I couldn't seem to get it to work.

'NNNZZZZZZZZZZZZZZZ' went the saw from across the warehouse, stripping another layer off my nerves.

With a grunt of exasperation, I wrenched the stupid rope. Pots and pans and woks and ladles and spatulas thundered down around me as I crouched on the floor, my arms wrapped around my head. 'Ow!' I cried as a large colander capped me like a helmet, noisily deflecting all the other kitchenware that came tumbling after.

When the hard rain stopped, I lifted the lid of the colander to see Maddie, Thurston and Zak staring at me. Thurston flung himself at me. I recoiled intuitively. 'Oh, Miles,' he gasped, clutching my shoulders, 'you must be so *thrunched.*'

'I would have been if it weren't for the colander,' I grumbled, pushing him away. I removed the colander and examined the dings in it.

'I think you really should leave the details of the plan to us, Miles,' ZakDot said. 'You're only going to hurt yourself this way.' Maddie, sucking on her tongue piercing, said nothing.

'I found out why she'd been asked to leave her last school in Melbourne,' Zak informed me later, after Maddie had gone out. 'She set off an explosive device that burnt the entire second-year exhibition down to the ground. According to her, she'd only meant it to make a loud noise and a tiny little fireball. She goes,' and here ZakDot imitated her low, lazy tone, '"Sometimes, when you try and fuck shit up, you end up fucking more shit up than you intended."'

I shook my head. 'Delightful.'

'She told me she likes nothing more than blowing things up. Video games, mobile phones, and computers.'

She had yet to add cruise ships to her repertoire.

'Nice hobby,' I said.

'It's got a lot to do with her childhood. She told me all about it the other day. She grew up in Nimbin. Her parents were hippies. Her dad died in a smash-up when his Kombi exploded.'

I made a sympathetic face.

'Yeah, pretty grim. She's been wreaking revenge on "the machine" ever since.'

Thurston passed by the door of the studio, dragging a flanged mace.

'You know the reason Thurston's been locking his door?' ZakDot whispered. 'It's because he's nervous she'll get to his computer.' He would say that. I knew better, of course.

'So what's Maddie doing in the painting department?' I asked.

'Fucked if anyone knows. I overheard Lynda Tangent telling Cynthia Mopely that if Maddie was that keen on the random destruction of electrical appliances, she should be in sculpture.' ZakDot threw his arms over his head and stretched. His jumper rode up, exposing his downy navel. He twisted his head from side to side. The sinews of his neck stood out sharp and defined, as did the lean muscles of his forearms.

What went through my head at that point disturbed me. I scrabbled around in my overheated brain for something else to think about. The face of Destiny Doppler popped unbidden into my mind. All I can say in my defence here is that I really was going loopy.

I think I rather relished this fact. Madness and genius were, after all, intertwined. If I was going to have to die young, at least the full legend would be in place.

I don't think I'm insane any more, by the way. Actual near-death experience does have a way of clearing the cobwebs. In fact, I now think I may be the only one left who is sane. This is not a comforting thought under the circumstances.

'What's *this* then?' ZakDot suddenly noticed the painting I was working on. It was another self-portrait. I won't describe it in detail. But suffice it to say that I had become obsessed with the subject of my own death. After that first cut-throat portrait, I embarked on a series, in which I was killed by various other means, occasionally co-starring my housemates, fellow students and teachers. I had decided to make this the focus for my final year's work. I drew my inspiration from a number of sources, including ZakDot's many creative suggestions. The painting he was now gawping at now, however, featured a device I'd read about in one of Edgar Allan Poe's short stories. I was reading a lot of Poe.

'You're a sick puppy,' ZakDot commented after a long pause. He sighed. 'Sometimes I really envy you, Miles.'

I looked up at him sharply. 'You taking the piss?'

'Not at all. I wish I was as deep and weird and tortured as you.' He held out a hand to silence me. 'No, let me finish. You see, while my efforts at "pre-conceptual" dada represent a kind of "mock-noble" attempt to evoke traditional aesthetic strategies and artistic techniques while simultaneously parodying them and thus "desacralising" the creative act, well, I'm not sure it really "means" a hell of a lot in the "long run".'

I wondered if his fingers ever got tired with all that air-quoting. 'There's a thin line between what you do and what you parody,' I agreed.

I watched, alarmed, as he spiralled down into the beanbag. 'It's true.' He moaned. 'I'm just so, so… *fluffy.*'

I was struggling with the notion that everyone I knew was trying to kill me and he was worried about being fluffy?

'Maybe I should get "political" with my art.'

'What art?' I asked.

There are some people coming into the breezeway. My ears perk up. I swear I can make out ZakDot's voice above the burble of conversation. ZakDot! ZakDot! I'm sorry I took the piss out of you! I'm so happy you're alive!

Then it dawns on me: if ZakDot is alive, then I'm as good as dead.

# Sticky like paint

'Can I interest you in some gustatio?' That's ZakDot's voice all right.

'Gus-what? That a fancy word for horses doovers, is it?' And that's her, Destiny. They must be standing right outside my door.

'It's Latin, actually.'

'Latin like in Latin lovers?' She giggles. Was she *flirting* with him? I am outraged. I strain against my ropes, my eyes bulging.

'I suppose you could say that.' I can hear the amusement in his voice. I want to kill him. Which is kind of funny, if you think about it. I make a hopeless attempt at attracting their attention. 'Nnngh! Wwwwwwhhhh!'

An all-too-familiar voice breaks into the conversation. 'You can leave that tway with us, boy. Now wun along.'

'You're the "boss".' I'm sure he didn't actually air-quote the word. But I can hear it in his inflection.

'Verbero.' She sounds annoyed. I recognise that tone of voice as well. 'You never let me have any fun.'

'Twust me. There's something I need to talk to you about.' He opens the door to the next cabin and, I presume, they both go in. The door shuts. The walls are thin. If I concentrate, maybe I can hear what they are saying.

The breezeway erupts with familiar girlish giggles. The door on the other side of me opens and shuts. Within minutes, there's bodies thumping against the wall, and the bed is creaking. The air is filled with shrieks and moans and strangulated cries. Something crashes to the floor and there's more giggling. There's no way I can hear a thing from the other side.

Bloody Maddie.

ZakDot and I were still lusting desultorily over Maddie when she brought home a girl. Kya had spiky hair and a personality to match. She was also carrying two pairs of scissors for no apparent reason, which she spun on her thumbs like pistols. This is how Maddie introduced her: 'Kya used to be heterosexual but she had a bad experience with men and now she hates the lot of you.' Shears clicking, they disappeared into Maddie's room and, within about five minutes, started to make girl-fucking noises that we could've bottled and sold for Viagra.

'Should've known she was a lezzo,' ZakDot said, turning on the TV and upping the volume. 'It's almost a relief. Don't know if I could've coped with that intensity. Can you imagine?'

'I have. In detail.' I sat down, abandoning any notion of returning to my studio until the worst of it was over.

'Me too. Well, anyway, I read in *Pulse* that "intensity" is out. "Apathy" is in.'

*Pulse* was one of those magazines that told true individuals what they ought to be wearing this season. 'Any particular reason?' I asked. Something landed on the sofa beside me with a thud. I leapt to my feet, and looked around with alarm.

It was only Bacon. He stared at me with round eyes and gave his head a violent shake. I think even Bacon had cottoned on to the fact that I was going crazy. I sat back down as though nothing had happened, scooping him into my lap. I swear he and ZakDot exchanged knowing glances.

'According to *Pulse*'s style editor,' ZakDot continued, acting as if nothing had happened, 'passion is for bogans. Apathy is the only appropriate response of truly cool people to the Troubles.'

'What about your idea of getting more political with your art? You can't be apathetic *and* political.'

ZakDot plucked off his beauty spot, studied it and then put it back on again. He did this whenever he was deep in thought. 'I don't see why not,' he said at last. 'But if I have to choose, I suppose I'll go with apathetic.'

'Because it's cool?'

ZakDot shrugged. He didn't want to admit it, I could tell.

'I thought "cool" was "over".' When I wanted to, I could air-quote with the best of 'em.

'It's back again.' ZakDot looked at the telly, as if he were suddenly really interested in what was on.

So, that explained it. Not the return of 'cool', but the advent of apathy. I'd noticed that lots of our fellow art students had in recent months taken to affecting a complete lack of interest in art. Like the irony which preceded it, their apathy rose in direct proportion to the rest of society's cultural passions. I think they found the excitement of the general public embarrassing. Much as they hated being unappreciated or getting bad reviews, artists tended to interpret negativity as a sign of higher intelligence, and viewed enthusiasm with suspicion. For whatever reason, while the rest of Strayer debated, argued and fought over art, artists simply stopped producing it. ZakDot, of course, was a pioneer in this regard.

On the telly, the smiling blonde host promised, 'We'll be back with episode thirty-eight of the award-winning series, "Peeling Back the Layers: A Conservator at Work", after these messages.' On came an advert for an optometrist whose spectacles 'put the dot back into Seurat!'

I was just about to get up and forage in the kitchen for a snack when a preview came on for a late night news program featuring Destiny Doppler. I was surprised to see that she no longer looked like Ingres' *Odalisque.* In fact, I wasn't sure how I'd ever had that impression at all. She had the same brown hair, staring eyes, long nose, and small lips, but there was a determined set to her jaw that I hadn't noticed before. As she pounded home her message in that high-pitched, querulous voice, two uneven patches of red appeared on her cheeks. I'll give her this, compared with the other politicians, who were so grey that they had to be digitally colourised for television broadcast, there was at least something undeniably real, irrefutably vivid about her. She reminded me now of another painting, one I'd seen in the National Gallery. *Young Peasant Woman* by some French guy. Jean…no, Jules…Jules Bastien-Lepage. That's his name.

'Mr Mumbles?'

Shit. I must have been doing it again.

'Hate to interrupt, but did you notice something else

about Kya?' ZakDot asked. He lowered his voice. 'She was wearing a badge for Clean Slate.'

'Weird.'

'Maybe not. I've noticed a few other people with Clean Slate badges at art school lately. I think it's supposed to be an ironic statement.'

'Of course it is.' I rolled my eyes.

As the months rolled on, there were times when I could see how people might sincerely be attracted to any party offering a solution to the Troubles. I suspected that at first the Troubles were a fabrication of the media, which was starved for any sort of home-grown conflict. The reports of the Troubles then inspired real Troubles. They were beginning to affect our lives as well.

One night, as I was walking home from the Triangle Factory, I was accosted by a gang of boys younger than myself and a lot tougher. They wore the classic homeboy uniform of shiny tracksuit pants, moon-landing runners and hooded sweatshirts emblazoned with the names of foreign art galleries. Their leader, whose shirt advertised Barcelona's Picasso Museum, grabbed me by the collar. 'All right, pretty boy,' he menaced, as his mates leaned in, sneering. 'What do youse think of Barrie Kosky's interpretation of *King Lear*? Reckon he took too many liberties with the text?' Panicked, I searched his face for the required answer. It seemed to be yes. I nodded. His grip relaxed.

Truth was, I actually liked Kosky's *Lear*, but I wasn't going to tell them that. I may have been the Last Art Hero, but I never intended to be a martyr, whatever anyone else thought.

'Fine,' the leader snarled, releasing me with a shove. 'Let this one go.' I scurried off before he could change his mind.

If the outside world was a scary place, the warehouse wasn't much better. One day, without explanation, Maddie sticky-taped an index card to her door on which she'd written, '"A work of art is a dream of murder which is realised by an act"—Sartre.' It was one of those freakishly warm days in August that pop up like previews for the coming attractions of summer, but I shivered as I read the card. The next day, she left gelignite in the fruit bowl. *And* she was teaching the evil Kya how to use her chainsaw. Kya made me nervous. Whenever Maddie had Kya sleep over, I locked my bedroom door.

Thurston, meanwhile, continued to lurk in his ug boots. His friend Gwydion, a frail medievaloid wench who wore velvet gowns even in summer, held urgent, whispered conversations with him over games of Dungeons and Dragons. Whenever I walked past, their voices lowered further and I could feel their eyes burning like brands into my back. Thurston now looked to me less like the *Jolly Toper* and more like Charles Manson. He was always watching me and he followed me around, too. If I was in the kitchen, he'd have an urge for a cuppa, if I was watching TV, he'd conclude it was time for a break. He was overly interested, I thought, in my new paintings.

Our last year at art school was winding up. I was completely absorbed in my self-portraits. I was well pleased with them and hoped they would form the basis for my first solo show, to be held, if all went well, sometime in the following year. ZakDot suggested I call the series 'Paranoia:

Killing Miles Walker'. I think he was being facetious, but I went with it.

For his final project, ZakDot had decided to stick with pre-conceptualism and the empty plinth shtick. To show that he had deepened his sense of self-awareness, however, he covered his plinth with fake fur and called it—what else— *Fluffy*. That resolved, he threw himself wholeheartedly into the task of attending every pre-graduation cocktail hour, party, and rave, on and off campus.

The Troubles intensified. Writers were throwing their words around, and people were getting hurt. A novelist wrote that a certain politician's wife was so un-bohemian as to have been a virgin when she married her husband. She became a laughing-stock, and sued the novelist for defamation. The law courts were clogged with arts-related cases: people regularly sued writers and film-makers when they discovered no reference to them at all in their work. In the visual arts, there was a nasty incident involving a hard-edge painting, though police were refusing to release the details for fear of copycat crimes.

One night in October, the prime minister appeared on the news, all sloping shoulders and shapeless grey suit, a tombstone on legs. Licking his lips, he cited the government's accomplishments to date. 'Seven point three. Four point two eight. *Thirty-six* point nine.' He then denigrated the opposition—'three point six four'—and called an election. It occurred to me that he never blinked.

Soon, the campaigning was in full swing. The opposition attacked the government's record and promised better: 'Eight point five.' Even some of the minority parties began to talk in numbers. Clean Slate could sling statistics with the best of them, but their real strength lay in the fact that they actually addressed the issues. They used the wrong size envelopes, got the street numbers wrong and put the stamps on upside down—but at least they addressed them. That's what one of the commentators on late night radio said, anyway. I didn't hear much more because I switched to a jazz station.

ZakDot, in his relentless search for diversion, began going to all the political rallies, including those for Clean Slate. I asked him whatever happened to apathy. He informed me that apathy was 'last month'.

Despite—or maybe on account of—its loopy policies, Clean Slate was soon ahead in all the polls. I was mildly curious to see what Destiny Doppler looked like in person, because each time I saw her on TV she seemed slightly different, but I really didn't want to leave the warehouse unless I had to. In fact, I didn't even like leaving my studio. The walls were now entirely masked by sketches and clippings and scraps of paper, in some places two or three sheets deep. The floor was so cluttered with paints and tins and rags that even Bacon complained. I still wage-slaved a few evenings a week at Lynda Tangent's Triangle Factory, and attended the few classes that still interested me, but it was getting harder and harder to make the effort to go to either.

I tended to work late into the night, a cup of tea cooling at my feet, my favourite Ashok Roy CD on the stereo. I eventually stopped listening to the radio altogether. There was too much weird news and it was making me nervous. Painting was my world and I had elected to live in it and nowhere else.

Easier said than done, of course.

It was around this time that Kya and Maddie finally split

up. I felt so relieved at Kya's final departure—red-eyed, shirt on inside out, stuffing a dildo into her backpack—that it never occurred to me that worse was to come. Indeed, had I known the problems that Maddie's next lover would help set in train, I might have begged Kya to stay, scissors and all.

I remember well the night he arrived on the scene. I'd been working late at the Triangle Factory. Lynda had instructed me to 'execute' a series of triangles in king's yellow and french ultramarine. I didn't like the way she said 'execute'. Worse, I knew that king's yellow, or orpiment, was actually made of trisulphide of arsenic. *Arsenic.* Could someone have told Lynda about Thurston's formula? How many people knew about it, anyway?

Coming home, I headed straight for the kitchen, intending to drink a whole carton of milk. I'd read somewhere that milk neutralised poison. There, I almost stumbled over a stocky fellow on all fours wearing a leather harness and nothing else. He was lapping water from a saucer while Bacon watched disdainfully from the doorway.

'Gabe?' I gasped. 'Fuck are you doing?'

Gabe was a student from the theory department. His honours thesis consisted of him installing giant red plastic 'D's in public toilets and bus shelters, which I believe he referred to as 'random existential nodalities', and then writing about their inevitable vandalisation.

Gabe looked up, eyes as big as the saucer he was drinking from. Just then, a whiff of sweat and talc tickled my nostrils. I turned to see Maddie, wearing a skintight black PVC minidress and twitching a folded lead against her palm. She winked at me.

'Heel, boy,' she commanded. Gabe withdrew his gaze

from mine. Tongue out, tail wagging, he followed Maddie back to her room.

I laughed. I couldn't help it. How was I to know that was my first mistake?

'C'mon, Mi.' ZakDot came into the studio one evening a few weeks later and stood there with his hands on his hips. 'It's our class party. It'll be good for you to get out and socialise.'

'Why?'

'Because isolation is turning you into a complete loon.'

'I just want to get this one little bit...' I let my voice trail off and raised my brush to the canvas. I was the very picture of artistic distraction.

'Are you really into it or are you trying to prove something?'

'I'm trying to prove something. Satisfied?'

ZakDot peered around the easel. 'Miles, you haven't even begun yet. It's a blank canvas.'

'How am I supposed to get started with everyone hanging around here all the time?' I grumbled.

'Take a break. You need it. Besides, everyone's gonna be there. Even Maddie's going.'

'With Gabe? Great. That'll be fun for the whole family.' I'd put Gabe on my list of people to watch out for.

'Without Gabe. She dumped him.' With his thumbs, ZakDot lifted the lapels of his smoking jacket, a maroon brocade number, and wiggled his shoulders. 'I reckon she's ready for a "real man".'

'Well, cool. Hope she finds one at the party.'

ZakDot left, shaking his head. I heard Maddie ask him

something, then the warehouse door clicked shut behind them.

I never was comfortable at parties, anyway.

I don't think I've ever been quite so uncomfortable at a party as I am now, of course. I'm getting more uncomfortable by the minute. My arms and legs are all pins and needles and my muscles are sending signals like shrieks up and down my nerve paths. My mouth is dry, my stomach empty, my breath shallow and a claustrophobic panic is beginning to over-whelm me. I wish I could let ZakDot know I'm in here. I wish I could open that curtain again. I wish someone would chuck Mist off the Sea into the sea.

I wouldn't even mind another visit from Verbero.

The night of the class party, part of me felt like running out after ZakDot and Maddie. Then I reminded myself that studio time was precious and genius, being random and miraculous, was not for squandering. I slipped Ashok Roy into the player, rolled up my sleeves and selected a small flat brush from an old Farmland tin. Occasionally, bursts of laughter, traffic noise or drunken argument from the street below would drift up into the studio and punctuate the asymmetric rhythms of the sarod. Yet, as I worked, my concentration grew deep and wide, throwing up its barricades against the world. Once an artist set his watch to immortality, Eastern Standard Time held no meaning. Hours flew by like cherubim across some Venetian dome.

At God knows what time of morning, Maddie and ZakDot returned, pissed as newts.

Eventually, I became aware of a noise like crying or

laughter. Maddie's laughter. Beneath the delicious soprano twitter, ZakDot was mewling my name in an oddly muffled voice. I advanced cautiously towards the snuffling and cries, which were coming from ZakDot's room, and knocked.

'Come in!' Maddie's voice rang out.

I was greeted with a martini glass. The one tattooed on ZakDot's arse. His arse was pointed straight at the door. The bubbles rose towards the ceiling. Maddie's feet semaphored his arse-cheeks from either side like the ultimate in air-quotes. His balls were hanging down between his legs and his face was sunk into her muff. His whole body was shaking with laughter.

'Too much information, thank you very much,' I croaked and started to leave.

Maddie raised her head. 'Don't go,' she ordered in her flat, velvety voice. 'We need you.'

'My, uh, eyebrow ring is caught in Maddie's labial jewellery,' ZakDot explained. 'Could you give us a hand?'

'Keep talking,' Maddie sighed. 'The vibrations really get me going.'

'Well, don't just stand there,' Zak reprimanded.

My fingers were trembling, and I took it she liked that as well. The air in the room was close and reeked of sex and sweat. I felt myself flush to my ears. What were they thinking when they invited me in? I was mortified, horrified and aroused. I glanced at Maddie's face, but her ecstatic expression threw me even more, as did the sight of her erect brown nipples. I quickly looked away, only to find myself staring at ZakDot's cock. How could it be that he hadn't been lying about the size of it? ZakDot angled his head as best he could and gave my wrist a slow lick.

Little Miles stood to attention and saluted.

The tremor that ran through my arm coincided with my loosening of their infernal tangle. 'Ta, babe,' sighed Maddie, fixing me with glittering eyes. 'Care to join us?'

'I, uh, c-can't breathe,' I stuttered, flapping my hands around my face. It felt like something was in my eyes.

'Stay,' ZakDot suggested.

'Mmm,' Maddie concurred. She stared at my crotch, a smile growing on her lips.

'I, uh, I need air,' I gasped. Rushing out of the room, I failed to register the peculiar, metallic chunkchunkchunk-chunk that is the sound of someone proceeding across a room in full body armour. And that's when I tripped over the last of the ball bearings and hurtled full tilt into a large figure covered in chain mail and wearing a forged-steel helmet.

'Miles? Miles?' The words, slippery with strangeness, were like pinpricks of light glimmering in a fog.

I fell back into the darkness.

I thought about opening my eyes, but wasn't sure if they were already open. I wondered what day it was, and if I was in Sydney or New York, which is odd, as I'd never been to New York. My eye was stinging but I couldn't hear it for all the hammering. I wished that whoever was doing the hammering would stop it. I thought about this. Could you hear an eye sting?

He'd finally done it. I wanted to say 'good on ya, Thurston', but it came out more like 'gdnyathn'.

'Maybe we should call an ambulance.' This was ZakDot's voice.

With enormous effort, I slowly jacked up my lids, onto

which someone had suspended entire Henry Moore sculptures. Three pixilated blurs gradually clarified into the faces of ZakDot, Thurston and Maddie. Just as I'd suspected. They were all in on it together.

I put my hand to my forehead. It was wet and sticky like paint. Paint. Who said painting's dead? It's the painter who's dead here. I laughed and laughed.

'You're spooking me,' said ZakDot.

I laughed even harder. Maddie and ZakDot exchanged glances. Back in the studio, Ashok Roy continued to pluck at his sarod. The CD was as long as the history of India.

Thurston started to cry. His sobs shook his helmet and the visor slammed shut with a great clang. He regretted it now, did he? Oh, life was too rich. Too wonderful.

I tried to raise myself up on my elbows and noticed I was lying on one of the how-to-dance diagrams. 'Chachacha,' I giggled, gasping for air.

'It's actually a polka,' Thurston corrected, lifting off his helmet and sniffling. 'I feel terrible, Miles. Didn't see you coming.'

'Do you want us to take you to a hospital?' ZakDot's fingertips tugged on the kohl-blackened area just beneath his eyes. He looked like a child pulling a scary face, a caricature of shock.

'Oh no no no.' They weren't taking me anywhere. 'I'm fine, really, although I might need to throw up soon,' I replied cheerfully, unaware that it had taken me a full five minutes to answer the question. Then I passed out again.

# New
## wave

When I came to, I was lying in my bed. There was an icepack on my forehead, trapping the dull throbbing underneath. I opened my eyes. To my left, a looming form resolved itself into the old hat tree from which hung my collection of paint-spattered trousers and shirts. On the floor at the foot of the tree were a smattering of art books, as well as some pre-loved Penguin classics. I kept trying to read books like the *Satyricon* but, after hours of concentrating on canvas, I usually ended up just veging in front of the telly.

Speaking of which, I could hear the theme song for 'Art/Life' striking up in the lounge. That was on at seven in the evening. I must have been out for a whole day. Slowly, I swivelled my head to look in that direction.

'Jesus, Thurston!' He'd been sitting there so quietly I hadn't even registered his presence.

'I'm sorry, Miles, I really am.' He recovered the icepack from where it had fallen and replaced it on my forehead. I beamed the most wan of smiles.

Though he'd startled me, I was suddenly aware of the fact that he no longer frightened me. My head injury, I later realised, had an effect in some ways like a frontal lobotomy. If I was still convinced that everyone around me was trying to kill me, I became remarkably calm about it.

A calm that, I admit, is deserting me at the moment.

I climbed unsteadily out of bed and, trailed by Thurston, made my way to the lounge. I sat down next to ZakDot. He took a squiz at my forehead, cringed, and draped an arm around my shoulder. 'Drama queen.'

'Sex maniac.'

Thurston scuttled off to his room.

'Where's Maddie?' I asked.

'Out. Oh Miles, you don't know what you're missing. You should've stayed.'

'I don't think I want to know.' Well, I did, but that was beside the point. 'Save it for your grandchildren.'

'But Miles,' ZakDot protested, 'you are my grand-children.'

I reached for the remote and turned up the sound. I was smiling, though.

'This evening, we'll look at how theatre companies are handling the chronic problem of over-subscription,' chirped the 'Art/Life' host. 'Also in the show tonight, our roving arts-supplies reporter comes up with some exciting new pigments. But first, let's cross over to guest lecturer Cynthia Mopely at the Museum of the Most Cutting-Edge Art in Sydney.'

ZakDot gave my shoulder two quick squeezes. 'How's that, Mi? Our Cynthia's on the tube. As it were.'

Cynthia Mopely, our theory teacher, was a fretful woman

who always looked like she'd just ingested a handful of dog biscuits. She liked the phrase 'as it were'.

The screen filled with an establishing shot of the MMCEA, across the front of which was slung a banner reading 'This Is Not A Museum'.

'I'll score,' ZakDot volunteered.

Cynthia Mopely stood stiffly next to a brown armchair that, a close-up revealed, was made entirely of TimTams. 'Today we are looking at *Seat of Wisdom* by Annesta Fox.' She cleared her throat. The camera zoomed in on her face. '*Seat of Wisdom* is, as it were, clearly a subverted symbol of the traditional masculine place in the home.'

ZakDot raised one finger.

'The lace antimacassar flung at once casually and yet, para-doxically, so *deliberatively* across the back, meanwhile, articulates both the fragility and the universality of the femi-nine as well as the umbilical debt owed to the ur-mother by the mythic masculine. This magnificent artwork, as it were—'

Another finger shot up.

'—is nothing less than a visual inquisition into the nexus between chocolate, lust and domesticity—or, seen in another way, the tiny chocolate biscuits represent the somatised re-imagination and the amplification of a paradigmatically dysfunctional childhood. As it were.'

Three fingers.

This was the stuff of which our art education was made, and the kind of crap that filled the television screens every day. I'd never have imagined then that, recalling it now, I'd be overcome with nostalgia.

'The existence of celebrity art theorists,' I posited to ZakDot, lowering the sound, 'must be one of the signs of the end of civilisation.'

ZakDot shook his head. 'Quite the opposite. Attaining and maintaining celebrity is the true art of the new millennium. It's a sign that civilisation, having bored itself with such trite entertainments as—'

'Don't say painting.'

'—whatever, can reinvent itself. And civilisation that can reinvent itself is forever young.'

My head hurt. Not just in the spot where it had come into contact with King Arthur, either.

An election ad came on for Clean Slate. It portrayed underwater film-makers getting in the way of jet-skiers, opera singers breaking glasses with their voices and even a few seconds of our old flatmate Joy pulling a bow across an old washing machine. 'That's our Minimatic!' ZakDot cried. 'I wondered where that went.'

'Do you really want culture in your life?' the voice-over intoned. 'Think on it. Better still, act on it. This Saturday, Vote 1 for Clean Slate.' The voice speeded up: 'This political announcement was authorised by Destiny Doppler for the Clean Slate Party.'

'You know what?' ZakDot commented. 'I think I'll vote for them just to see what happens.'

I put my head in my hands. 'You do that,' I said. 'I'm going to bed.'

Over the next few days, ZakDot appeared to be absorbed in his new project of training himself in the art of celebrity. 'What are you listening to these days?' he'd murmur to himself while putting on a CD. 'Where's your favourite spot on a Saturday night?' he'd ponder as he flicked through the latest issue of *Pulse*. 'Juliette Lewis lost her virginity to Brad

Pitt. Did you?' he'd ask the mirror while torturing his side-burns into trendy little points.

Every time I looked at Maddie, meanwhile, all I could see was labial jewellery and brown nipples. I kept wondering if she and ZakDot were still doing it. It was hard to tell.

The bruise on my head went from raw umber with tinges of ultramarine to a sap green, settling finally on yellow ochre.

Saturday came and the people of our little country went to the polls. I voted for the Blues, who were a lot like the Greens, except sadder. They had no chance of getting in. It was a sort of protest vote. I didn't think it made much difference whom I cast my ballot for. The results were always same old, same old. Or so I thought. Boy, was I wrong.

No one anticipated it. But ZakDot wasn't the only one who voted for Clean Slate. That weekend, Destiny Doppler's party secured a narrow majority of seats in the House of Reps—a mysterious, but convincing victory. Clean Slate may have had only one plank in its platform, but it was across this plank that they boarded the ship of state.

I tried to figure out what sort of person had voted for Clean Slate. The bank teller who'd blanched at my paint-encrusted fingernails? The teenager I saw at the bus stop wearing a 'Youth Against Heavy Metal T-Shirts' t-shirt? My own mother, who kept all the artwork in the house hidden in the attic? It had to be more than just a few perverse art students, didn't it?

I didn't get it. Then again, I was an art school graduate. I hadn't a clue about what went on in the world.

With hardly a whisper of protest from the demoralised and splintered opposition, Destiny Doppler did everything she said she'd do. She pulled the plug on all funding of the arts. She whacked hefty taxes on corporate sponsorship, and imposed a forty-five per cent Creativity Tax that applied to sales of books and art as well as ticket prices for dance performances, concerts and plays. She imposed regulations on internet servers so that only over-eighteens would be able to access art-related sites on the net. She turned the MMCEA over to a sports committee, which, after a small mix-up involving an all-expenses paid trip to Bogota, ended up selling it to a Colombian drug cartel.

And this was all before parliament went into its summer recess. As fresh art school grads, we felt like we were in freefall. The notion of leaving school and joining the 'real world' (even I would air-quote that phrase) was scary enough before the changes. Now, it was terrifying.

Though Destiny intended to ban multiculturalism outright, that failed when it turned out no one, even among the experts, was quite sure what it was. But she did dispatch a Rapid Response Team to dim sum restaurants to prevent diners from using chopsticks. There were a few famous cock-ups like when she tried to confiscate computer jaz drives, thinking they had something to do with music. When she attempted to abolish arts degrees, student demonstrators flooded onto the streets in numbers not seen since the time the little country had intervened in the civil war of an even littler country some thirty-odd years earlier.

Despite this, acts of public protest were few—at first, anyway. For one thing, I believe people were too stunned to act. Or maybe they were simply hypnotised by newly prominent entertainments like sports, which were now on the telly all the time and attracting the kind of big corporate dollars that once went almost exclusively to the arts. It's possible of course that people were simply relieved that the Troubles were over. From the day that Clean Slate took office, the Troubles just seemed to fade away.

Having united the country around the premise that the arts were ideologically indefensible, economically untenable and morally unsound, Clean Slate exposed art and artists to public derision. ZakDot stopped wearing his I  Artists t-shirt after he was approached in all seriousness by businessmen in pin-striped suits who snarled, 'Us too. Know any? Let's get 'em.'

One day in parliament, a Democrat mentioned the word 'culture' in a positive context. The Clean Slate member for Upper Black Stump pulled out a semi-automatic and pointed it at the speaker.

We who abided in what was once known as the 'arts community', as though it were a cosy little village with corner shops, bunkered down while Destiny Doppler's policies exploded around us like bombs. With no possibility of my gaining any kind of public recognition, no chance of funding or even of sales, the unlimited canvas that had been my vision of the future appeared to have shrunk to the size of a postage stamp.

But things aren't always what they appear. Clean Slate didn't realise that there's nothing like a dash of repression to spice up a nation's cultural life. It was as if some freak bolt of lightning had struck, leaving the arts charred and smoking but infused with fresh energy and, like the phoenix, rising from the ashes.

On the few occasions that I'd seen exhibitions of dissident art from China and the former Soviet Union and Eastern Bloc, I'd envied those artists their vitality and spirit, their collective defiance and devotion. To my amazement, a similar esprit de corps was forming among my ennui-ridden peers. Artists who formerly appeared to have little better to do than question the purpose of art were suddenly fraught with purpose. It was no longer uncool to be passionate about your work.

There was a new unity as well. Fans of the Morbid Manner had previously refused to speak to advocates of Jenny Holzer-like political interventions. Neither of them had any truck with post-conceptual minimalists or proponents of Neo-Geo. Artists who exhibited in posh galleries like the Prétance in Woollahra, Woollahra being a suburb like Paddington except even more so, had never associated with those shown by the flash Bray Toons gallery in Surry Hills or artist-run spaces like Stoush. The ascendancy of Clean Slate had thrust all artists into the same beleaguered boat.

I'd always worked hard. Now I started painting like there was no tomorrow. Which was probably a good thing. Because for me now, there is no tomorrow.

Clean Slate didn't have to act directly to close the commercial galleries. They'd been foundering for years, ever since artists started scattering pebbles and small pieces of string and torn postcards around instead of making art that you could actually sell. The forty-five per cent Creativity Tax was the final blow. Quietly, one by one, all through the country, the galleries shut their doors.

Yet even as the established galleries shut their doors, new, underground artspaces were opening all over the place. These were typically located in private residences or warehouses. ZakDot, Maddie and I went to the opening of a group exhibition at one of the first outlaw galleries. The artists were all former graduates from our school. It was in one of the derelict theatres at the Opera House. You needed the password to get in. The password on that night was the name of a photo series by Gillian Wearing: 'Signs That Say What You Want Them To Say And Not Signs That Say What Someone Else Wants You To Say'. When we arrived, there was a big bottleneck in the queue at the door as people struggled to remember the password. The bouncer had been strict at first—he was a multimedia artist himself—but after a while he let in anyone who could come up with 'Signs That Say What You Want Them To Say'.

Once inside, I was blown away. The opening had none of the tedium and predictability that characterised such events before Clean Slate came into power. You know the scene—networkers drinking wine, backs to the art, gossiping, bitching, never, ever talking about the art itself. Well, here it was quite the opposite. Everyone clustered around the artworks, voicing their appreciation, analysing influences, spotting trends, debating meanings. Reporters for the samizdat press and pirate radio stations huddled with the artists in an abandoned orchestra pit, capturing their furtive, whispered commentary on tape recorders and video cams while their friends kept watch in case there was a police raid. The police didn't always raid the openings, but the possibility of their doing so lent a frisson of danger to the proceedings. Later, I heard that one artist, whose name will go unmentioned but whose initials are G.A.B.E., actually made an anonymous tip- off to the police himself right before his own opening, just to make sure they came—it was far more exciting that way.

Sales of art weren't too bad, considering. As the art market had now become a black market, everyone switched from red to black dots.

Some people showed their work in the underground clubs that were springing up in similar venues, notably warehouses and places that had once been writers' centres or printmaking workshops. Performing at these clubs were Bulgarian singers, salsa bands, gamelan players and other practitioners of the proscribed multicultural arts, as well as groups like Maddie's own newly formed post-feminist post-punk post-art-school band Cellulite Death. Thai and Indian and Chinese chefs whose restaurants had been fire-bombed by some of Clean Slate's more lunatic followers catered for the clubs, which were patronised not just by artists but gays and lesbians and the indigenous peoples of the little country as well. Being so disproportionately creative had made gays and lesbians special targets of Clean Slate. But the Aborigines were by far the most persecuted. They boasted the longest and richest cultural traditions of any group in the whole country. And having been removed from their land by Clean Slate on account of it being the source of all that culture, they had nowhere else to hang out.

In some ways, it was a lot of fun.

At first, there was talk of organised resistance. Maddie was keen. She'd finally found the enemy she'd been looking for her whole life. But artists are hopeless at organising anything. They could barely put together group shows, for Christ's sake.

Although I liked the outlaw galleries and the underground clubs, I quickly grew bored with the ceaseless ideological breast-beating and ranting and raving of my peers. Speaking of whom, ZakDot had gone right over the edge. He began spending all his time spinning out manifestos. Some days he was so busy, he forgot to paste on his beauty spot. He even stopped putting air-quotes around everything. I was mystified by the transformation until it occurred to me that, forbidden to do what he had never managed to get around to doing in the first place, ZakDot was happy as Larry. He told me that if I ever told anyone he'd voted for Clean Slate, he'd kill me, and this time he meant it.

I wasn't worried. It had occurred to me some time ago that, if ZakDot couldn't move beyond the pre-conceptual in art, he was hardly going to do much better with murder.

'Haven't heard you interviewing yourself lately,' I observed. I missed the old ZakDot. 'What is your one essential cosmetic?' I prompted. 'Have you ever had a secret eating disorder? What is the most embarrassing album in your collection?' He looked at me askance.

'Irony is so over,' he informed me.

Gabe and Maddie got back together. He started wearing an old Mao suit he'd found at a trash and treasure in China-town. He'd read how, in the Chinese Cultural Revolution, Red Guards would write the names of their political enemies upside down as a visual pun signifying 'overthrow so-and-so'. Struck by the possibilities presented by Destiny Doppler and the fortuitous coincidence of his red plastic 'D's, he tried turning the letters on their heads. Unfortunately, an upside-down 'D' looks exactly like a right-side-up one. He considered switching to another letter, but then the impact would be lost. He tried placing them backwards, to make a statement on the effect of her policies but, as they were three-dimensional, all you had to do was walk around to the other side and they looked right. He asked Maddie her opinion and she said, 'Blow 'em up.' So puppykins was over at our place all the time, downloading bomb recipes off the net.

I felt safer than I had in a long time. If the people around me still had murderous impulses, they were directed at the prime minister. Nobody seemed interested in blowing me up anymore, which should have been a relief. To be honest, one part of me, maybe not the healthiest part, missed the drama and the attention. Still, I was over it. Let Clean Slate do their worst. I didn't care. I'd just go on painting. I concluded that all I had to do was ignore politics and politics would ignore me.

In the infinite wisdom of my twenty-three years and from the enormously clarifying vantage point of my nearing-death experience, I can now see that I had a hopelessly naive view of the world.

# Our
# very
# own
# Medici

The sound of an explosion makes me jump, or want to. It's hard to jump when you're tied to a chair. More explosions follow. The first set of fireworks. It must be nine o'clock. How time flies when you're having fun. Now I can hear someone making a toast. It sounds like Cashie. I suppose it's only logical that she'd be here tonight. I feel really sad. I'm fond of Cashie, and I don't want her to die.

Aurelia Cash entered our lives in a big way during that first summer of Destiny's government. She was a property developer, one of that mob who, in the old days, way before Clean Slate or even the Troubles, gentrified the slovenly boho suburb of Paddington, taking it from the artists who'd colonised it and turning it over to the dealers and collectors, forcing the artists to head for the hills. Surry Hills to be precise. Then, they did the same thing to Surry Hills, buying up the warehouses and sending the artists scurrying like cockroaches after a

Mortein bomb to suburbs even further west, to Chippendale, for instance. It was around that time that ZakDot and I moved to Chippo. Soon they'd be putting the squeeze on Chippo, but that's another story. The thing is, Cashie made a bundle.

The acquisition of wealth gave Cashie her ticket into society. When she got there, she discovered that—at that time, anyway—culture had greater cachet in society than money. It became stingingly obvious to Cashie that there was a chasm between culture and herself so wide you could string a cable car over it. The commercial gallery owners made it their personal mission to help her overcome this problem, while relieving her of some of the burden of her wealth. Even the price tags at Gallery Trimalkyo didn't faze Cashie.

She became a fixture at every exhibition, even the student shows, and that's how we all got to know her. At first people were a bit wary, especially since she decked herself out in expensive gear that she thought made her look boho, but which no real boho could afford. Double Bay at the Primavera Ball: silk turbans and caftans and hand-painted beads. It didn't take us long to cotton on to the fact that her relationship to wealth was that of a guileless infatuation requiring frequent public displays of affection. I'm not saying she was a fool, but she was easily parted from her money. This suited most artists down to the ground.

On the other hand, she wasn't a total pushover. I remember this one group show. I'd gone to the opening because there were several painters involved whose work I liked. Cashie was there and the gallery owner was amping her to buy a painting by Finn, not one of the artists I liked. The painting in question depicted a bull being fucked up the arse by a large mouse standing on its hind legs. A speech bubble filled with Egyptian hieroglyphics extruded from the mouse's bum. In the background was a nuclear explosion spewing limbs, electric toothbrushes, the Venus de Milo and Sydney 2000 logos into the atmosphere. Clever, predictable fin-de-siecle, épater la bourgeoisie sort of thing. Funny thing about trying to shock the bourgeoisie—the more you try, the more they love it.

In this instance, Cashie was neither shocked nor loving it. 'Do you really think it's Finn's best work?' She sounded dubious.

'Oh, absolutely, darling,' the dealer replied, lying through his capped teeth. 'It's so *now.*'

'Well, I like it, but,' Cashie said, twisting her gold bangles over her plump forearm and chewing on her bottom lip, 'while I appreciate the, uh, *vivid palette* and the, er, *creative deformation* of the, um, *prevailing paradigms,* well, I just don't think it's me.'

The gallery owner blinked twice. 'You're obviously not ready for it anyway,' he sniffed, walking off.

Taking a sip from her wine, Cashie turned to Maddie and confided, 'I've just had my lounge suite re-upholstered, actually, and I'm quite sure that painting would clash. I'm looking for something in a sort of Atlantic blue. You understand, don't you?'

Maddie didn't understand at all and told her so. She told the rest of us later that she'd like to set off a paint bomb in Aurelia's north shore mansion. A green paint bomb. 'Blue and green,' she explained, 'must never be seen—unless with gelignite in between.' Gabe talked her out of it. He was hopeful of getting Cashie to bankroll some 'D's and he didn't want Maddie to blow it. In every sense.

I did like that about Gabe. His art was ludicrous, but at least he was honest. I didn't know anyone else who'd admit to wanting to become some rich woman's pet, although I know I secretly did. Isn't that what everyone did in Renaissance times? Besides, he already had the collar and lead.

When Clean Slate came into power, Cashie was as devastated as the rest of us. It was like she'd just bought her ticket to Disneyland and they closed down the Matterhorn. Since it coincided with the time we were graduating, she did this amazing thing. She bought the warehouse that we lived in and presented it to us. She said she'd be happy to receive the occasional artwork in lieu of rent. So, we all became her pets in the end. I don't recall hearing anyone turn the offer down out of principle, either.

A veritable Medici, our Cashie.

A journalist got wind of her act of generosity and wrote it up. The day the article came out, parliament erupted. Clean Slate members howled like wolves. But they couldn't do anything about it. It was still legal for consenting adults to make art in the privacy of their own home, so long as no children were involved.

It was like a great big party at first. Everyone moved in, even our former lecturers Lynda Tangent and Cynthia Mopely. The only space not taken by artists was right next door to us, a largish place that had been converted into the local parish meeting hall of The Church of Our Princess Diana. Like the Hare Krishnas and the Salvos, the members of the church gave us the occasional feed, though they never seemed to eat anything themselves.

By now, Destiny's rules were really kicking in. There were

no more grants, no more festivals, no more 'bean-alleys'. Some of the big names in the art world, as well as some of the no-name brand of artist, fled overseas, preferring chaos and danger to the absence of public applause for their work. The planes would scream overhead, concussing the windows and filling our ears with their dreadful roar. Clean Slate made sure the planes flew over the suburbs with the most artists, musos, film-makers and writers. We in Chippo copped a fair share of the noise along with Glebe, Balmain, Newtown and Darlinghurst. For a while it seemed I knew someone on every flight. As I stroked away at my canvas, I'd imagine them staring out the window as first the cities with the red roofs and then the red land itself disappeared from under them. Me, I still called Strayer home.

It was great, actually. I liked the feeling of being left behind after evac. For one thing, and this is the shameless admission of a young and ambitious artist, it helped clear some of the old, dead wood from the scene.

For another, I'd finally acquired the cred I'd always deserved. My devotion to art, previously viewed as loopy at best and suspect at worst, was now seen as admirable, prescient in fact. Even Maddie became interested in what I had to say about glazing techniques and pictorial planes. It seems I had gone from being the Last Art Hero to just Hero. Everyone, including Cashie, took to hanging around my studio, which I cleaned up a bit.

Cashie was there the day that Destiny made the announcement that changed my life.

# Expressionism yourself

I'll get to the announcement. But there are a few things you should know first. Like how *Cap d'Antibes* enters this story.

Although Clean Slate marched into power over a single-plank platform, it soon became evident that they couldn't govern by it. Clean Slate's 'econonomists', as Destiny called them, had argued that their policies of cultural taxation, slashing arts subsidies and selling off creative resources for hard cash would put the country in the black. They proved just as stupid as the economists who'd told previous governments that the answer to all the nation's problems lay in taxing apples and oranges or that 'work for day care' would give toddlers a sense of responsibility. They were all wizards of Oz, sitting behind their curtains, pulling levers and blowing smoke.

The rest of the world took time out from its wars and disasters, natural and unnatural, to protest what Destiny was doing. It was particularly vexed by her proposal to tear down the Sydney Opera House and turn the space into a shopping mall for the people living in the household appliance-shaped apartment buildings erected along Circular Quay. After all, when people in other countries needed a respite from their own calamitous existence, they liked to come to our little country for a holiday. As the Opera House had long been the very artistic symbol of our very cultured nation, the first thing they did when they got here was take a photo of themselves in front of it. If Clean Slate was going to knock down the Opera House, they might as well go to...to...to somewhere else that was as warm and sunny and beautiful and peaceful and relaxed. They couldn't think of any place off-hand, but they'd come up with something.

Speaking to Trixie Tinkles about the issue, Destiny said she couldn't understand what the fuss was about. She smoothed back her dark hair defensively and pursed her serious little mouth. 'The developer will take into account the fact that the Opera House is one of the architax- architextual wonders of the world? He'll build a replica of it that'll be the centrepiece of the mall?'

As Trixie Tinkles raised one eyebrow, accidentally wiggling her ears at the same time, Destiny noted that the replica would be even better than the original because it would offer opportunities for state-of-the-art, back-lit advertising displays on each of the shell-like roofs. Also, unlike the original, none of the tiles would fall off, because they'd only be drawn on. There followed a pregnant pause while Trixie attempted to get her ears under control and Destiny pondered the suspicious phrase 'state-of-the-art'.

Not long after that, Destiny announced that she intended to cut funding to scientific research. She explained that she had it on 'reliable sauces' that scientists were involved in 'growing cultures in pea-tree dishes'. Besides, she said, like other native plants, pea-trees should be reserved for industrial wood-chipping.

She also decided to shut the 'liberries' because someone told her that 'a little knowledge is a dangerous thing', and that the liberries were where they stored it. 'I promised to make this country a safe place to live in,' she explained, 'and there's no safety in danger?' Apprised of a report that recent immigrants had found the process of acculturation relatively easy, she ordered her ministers to look into ways of making it more difficult, and not just for migrants.

The jokes flowed; the knives came out. Destiny found herself on the back foot. In parliament, the newly unified opposition hammered her with questions neither she nor her ministers could answer. Her backbench began to grumble and her frontbench to squirm and there were constant rumours about leadership challenges. Clean Slate had only managed to swing the election on marginal seats and preferences—and because the voters, clever little dicks that they were, wanted to teach the other parties a lesson. And, I suppose, because the people of the little country love a ratbag, and Destiny Doppler certainly seemed to be that.

But if there's one thing the people of Strayer love better than elevating a ratbag, it's cutting down a tall poppy. It wasn't long before the papers began running headlines that suggested Destiny would be a one-term wonder. 'Pundits Predict: Doppler a One-Term Wonder.' 'Destiny Doppler—Comin' a Cropper?' Cartoonists portrayed her rubbing herself out with a blackboard eraser—her party's symbol.

As her political life looked like it was about to be cut short, very short, Destiny's thoughts turned increasingly to my favourite subject. Immortality.

I didn't know this at the time, of course. If you'd told me I'd be hearing it from the horse's mouth, I'd have laughed. If you'd told me the circumstances under which I'd be hearing it, I'd have cried. Laughed and cried.

And look at us both now. Wanting to live forever, scheduled to die in just over, what, two hours? Would you laugh or cry?

Destiny's a funny old thing.

From the day she had leapt into the political arena, she was single-mindedly focused on the gaining of power. Now that she had it, she saw that power could never be more than a fragile compromise, a balancing act. Power was a temporal art, like a piece of improvised music that, once played, was gone forever. I'm not saying she thought in those terms; at the time, I'm quite sure, she didn't know what improvised music was. But she was distressed.

She began to feel her own mortality creeping up on her. I know the feeling.

I've always wanted to leave something to posterity. Destiny just wants to be left. The leaver and the left, that's us.

What would people remember her by? What would she leave behind? She later told me, 'I wasn't completely out of touch with reality?' She understood that she hadn't really managed to banish the arts, or put an end to culture. She knew she'd merely driven it underground where, her spies told her, it was flourishing.

She also knew we were mocking her. 'And that hurt?' Rock bands with names like Culture Clubbed played exuberant gigs at the underground venues beneath the banner 'Not Our Destiny'. Artists sent protest work abroad to be exhibited in New York and London galleries, where Strayer became the oppressed flavour of the week. Well-meaning people all over the world sent angry letters to our embassies, demanding the government restore artistic freedom, release all cultural prisoners and lift the ban on chardonnay. They didn't always get their facts straight but they meant well.

Some people, meanwhile, had been pushed to the edge. Following the abolition of the 'liberries' and the raising of the tax on fiction to eighty-five per cent, one novelist became so desperate that he made an attempt on Destiny's life. He was a comic novelist, so predictably, it was a laughable attempt. Not having worked out the logical flaws in his plot, the ending didn't turn out quite as he'd anticipated. He got a long sentence.

Destiny became exceedingly anxious about the possibility of dying. She obsessed about what her funeral would be like, and wondered who would come and mourn. She tried to imagine great elegies being read, but then she realised that great elegies required great poets. It occurred to her that, if there were any great poets out there, they probably loathed her.

As the long winter rounded the corner into spring, the treasury produced a confidential analysis of the impact of Clean Slate's anti-culture policies on the economy showing them to have been disastrous. Someone leaked the report and both the opposition and the press screamed for her resignation. Destiny called a Cabinet meeting. Entering the room, she sat down at the long table. The table had been crafted to look like a tall ship with a cut-out in the centre shaped like a longboat. There were pictures of native birds on the wall. She felt uncomfortable in this windowless room with its boats that would never sail away and birds that would never fly out of their frames. She told me all this later. When I was *her* flightless bird.

Soon the meeting was in full swing. Pressing the buttons underneath the table for the official messenger like disgruntled airline passengers summoning stewards, Destiny's ministers ran him ragged racing between them and their harassed staff. They bounced up and down on the sheepskin-covered chairs like children, and worried the orange leather armrests with their overheated palms. The shouting grew so loud that it shook the bulletproof doors.

Destiny could see her empire collapsing before her very eyes. She made several stabs at drafting her elegy on the margins of a briefing paper. She stared at the marquetry over the table, trying to pick out the three insects some joker of a craftsman had worked into the decoration of this bug-swept room. She considered making an 'if you are watching this, then I am already dead' video. Then she remembered what happened to the last person who'd tried that. No, Destiny wouldn't follow in those footsteps. She was smarter than that.

Tuning back in, she announced to Cabinet that she would hold a quick press conference. Soon the bell trilled in the press gallery and the house journos descended on her office like vultures onto carrion. She watched from the window of her office as they gathered in the courtyard. At the back of the courtyard flowed an artificial waterfall. Attendants turned on the waterfall when she was there; this thrilled her at first, for it was a symbol of her power. Now all she could think was that they'd turn it on for the next prime minister's benefit, and the one after that.

In her office, she paused before the one painting that remained there—*Cap d'Antibes,* by Winston Churchill. She'd given the other pictures, the Nolans and Streetons and

Cossington-Smiths, their marching orders long ago. She had nearly got rid of *Cap d'Antibes* as well, but something had stopped her. Destiny liked history, so long as it stuck to the facts. She knew that Churchill had been a great statesman, that he was remembered by posterity much as she would like to be. Besides, it was kind of pretty, with its ship and lighthouse and sea. She looked at this painting and a thought nagged at her. She pushed it to the back of her mind.

She went back into the small antechamber behind her office to freshen up. I can see her splashing water on that flawless skin, powdering her fine nose and re-applying her lipstick to those serious, little lips. She returned to the courtyard, now despoiled by the untidy tangle of camera leads and the journalistic scrum. The journos threw questions at her all at once, questions that barely concealed their own mocking disdain, questions that she couldn't answer, questions she didn't want to answer. She imagined that even Verbero, her chief of staff, who was observing from the side, held her in contempt.

When the ordeal was over and the press had fled back to its warren, Destiny returned to her office and slumped in one of the doughnut-shaped orange chairs there, the garish awfulness of which she found oddly comforting. In an act that only amplified the Troubles, a previous prime minister had banished them, ordering in a new set of lounges that he felt went better with Sao biscuits and Jane Austen re-runs. Destiny vastly preferred the orange seaters: they had no cultural connotations whatsoever. So she'd rescued them from the storeroom.

She swivelled her neck and peered at *Cap d'Antibes*. Nice boat. Nice lighthouse.

Verbero knocked and entered with a sheaf of papers in his

hand. I can easily imagine the smirk that would have been on his face. 'No west for the wicked,' he announced, sounding almost delighted to be able to tell her yet another crisis was looming, this one over the rise in youth unemployment following the disbanding of the national and regional youth orchestras and young people's theatres. 'I think it's a beat-up,' he commented. 'I mean, weren't actors and musicians chwonically unemployed anyway?' He cleared his sinuses in what seemed to Destiny to be a prolonged and deliberately annoying manner.

'Can you leave me alone for a bit?'

Verbero raised one eyebrow and, she presumed, disappeared into the private secretary's office, where he could observe her movements on the video monitor. She needed to think. It was dusk. She wandered out of the office and down the corridors, and eventually found herself in the Members Hall, where the Historic Memorials Collection was hung. The collection consisted of the portraits of all the previous prime ministers, as well as governors-general, presidents of the Senate and so on. On taking power, she'd ordered most of the 3000-odd piece parliamentary art collection returned to the Art Bank, but she'd overlooked the memorials.

On this evening, looking at the portraits, she felt her unease growing. It occurred to her that their subjects would live forever. Not because they'd been in the papers. Not because they'd been on TV. By the close of the twentieth century, nearly everyone had been on TV at least once in their lives. And if someone hadn't been on TV, they certainly had a website. ZakDot's enthusiasm for the concept notwithstanding, the currency of celebrity devalued faster than the Brazilian real. The American talk show host Sally Winfrey

Lake had even done a special program about people who were upset that MY FIFTEEN MINUTES OF FAME WAS MORE LIKE FIVE AND A HALF; she gave them exactly four minutes of screen time each.

'Those men and women in the pictures?' Destiny told me later. 'They'll live on because they were part of art?'

'You're not wrong,' I replied. 'After all, who remembers Whistler's father?'

She didn't get the joke.

I'm running ahead of myself.

The point is, she saw something for which she'd been searching for a long time. She saw immortality. And, though she didn't know it at the time, she'd seen my name on the bottom right-hand corner.

Looking at the Historic Memorials, her heart thumped, her cheeks flushed and she sat down heavily on one of the hall's curvilinear benches of silky oak and beefwood, which embraced her generous bottom like cupped hands. The more she stared at the portraits, the more convinced she became that the faces on the wall were laughing at her, even the unsmiling ones.

Fleeing the Members Hall, she was nonetheless loath to return to her office and the suspicious looks with which Verbero was sure to shower her. At the last minute she changed direction and headed for the North Wing. She took a lift up to Room 108, the Meditation Room. The Meditation Room had three 'thinking cells', designed, like everything else in the nation's capital, on an open plan. Poking her head over the dividing wall, she ascertained that all were empty, as usual.

Politicians didn't have much time for thinking of any type, much less meditative.

Choosing the middle chamber—she'd always been suspicious of both the left and the right—she recoiled at the sight of a large stain soiling one of the cushion covers. Recalling that it was forbidden to eat or drink in the Meditation Room, the thought came to Destiny, not for the first time that day, that politics was a grubby business and, herself aside, didn't always attract the best class of people. Sitting down at the other end of the bench, she stared at the khaki hills that lay darkening beyond the roofs of parliament.

After a long while, it came to her. She knew what she had to do. Have all the portraits taken down and destroyed.

Unfortunately, the little country was still a democracy, and there were some things that even a prime minister couldn't do. She breathed a sigh of relief at this, surprising herself. Her mind turned, with increasing and finally unstoppable enthusiasm, to a better solution.

Strayuns were no more suited for culture than koalas for water-skiing. She had done the right thing in suppressing the arts. The nation was better off without them. On the other hand, maybe she ought to make an exception for portrait painting.

Portrait painting wasn't really art or culture, she rationalised. It wasn't like those other artworks that looked like shelving or aquarium filters, or which were made of matchsticks or garlic skins. The ones which always seemed to come with a silent soundtrack in which the artist was laughing at you for not getting it.

The truth was, Destiny hated art because she imagined art hated her. She sped back to her office.

'Get off the bloody phone, Verbero.'

He mumbled something into his mobile about a pick-up and ended the call.

'I don't like the sound of it. Once the dykes are bweached, all hell will bweak loose. It won't end with just poor twit painting, you know,' he warned. 'Give an artist an inch and he'll take a mile. And besides, how will you find one you can twust?'

This stumped her. Then it came to her. Boats and light-houses. If Churchill could do it, so could she. She would paint her own portrait.

It wasn't as crazy an idea as it sounded. In the little town she grew up in, it was considered that she came from an artistic family. Since at the time practically everyone regarded themselves as artistic, this was hardly surprising. Her father Davo Doppler, a retired sausage stuffer who joked that he was the original snag, would sit her on his knee and tell her the story of how he used to play the piano accordion when he still had all his fingers. Destiny's mother, Sadie 'Bubbles' Doppler, who was renowned both for the sexy, cockatoo-shaped birthmark on her neck and her festive slices, had once rendered Mona Lisa in crosspoint from a kit. She changed it slightly so that the Mona Lisa didn't look quite so sad. She had planned to do one of Degas' ballerinas as well. When the Degas kit arrived by mail order, Sadie saw that one of the ballerinas had got cut off at the edge, so she sent it back requesting a new one. The company, infuriatingly, simply delivered an identical kit. After a frustrating flurry of corre-spondence, Sadie gave up needlepoint for macrame, and covered the walls in owls.

When Destiny was seventeen, her local council sponsored

an art fair. She went along. While admiring the pretty pictures of roos and waratahs and farmhouses and waves and penguins, she overheard two women talking. They, too, marvelled at the art on display. 'You know, I could never do that,' said the one with the polka-dot hat, pointing to a water-colour picture of the sun setting over the desert. 'I couldn't draw a cork out of a bottle.'

Her friend shook her head sympathetically. 'I know what you mean,' she said. 'I can't even draw a straight line!' This stuck in young Destiny's head. Bubbling with excitement, she skipped all the way home, sat down with some paper and pencils and, scarcely daring to breathe, drew—a perfectly straight line. She held it up to the light, and checked it against a ruler. She did it again. I can see her tongue sticking out of her mouth, beads of sweat forming on her smooth schoolgirl forehead. Within an hour, she had a formidable collection of what she called 'line drawings'.

She enrolled in a private art school. When she told me this, I asked her how it was that no one knew she'd once been an art student. 'There was a, you know, prolification of art schools? There were always ones opening up and closing down? Records got lost?'

She was keen as mustard. The teacher, Colin, was young and handsome, and on the first day of classes he gave her such a searing look that she clutched at the neck of her blouse as though fearful the fabric had been burnt straight off. She fantasised that they would run away to Paris, France, or maybe just Perth, which was the nearest big city, and live in a garret. She wasn't entirely certain what a garret was, but she imagined it to be a nice little fibro with lots of roses out front. They'd paint and show their pictures in art fairs just like the one that inspired her to become an artist.

The first problem came when Colin tried to instil the principles of perspective. 'You want us to draw everything round but I see the world as flat?' she complained. Then things got worse. He introduced concepts like *gestural brush strokes,* and *painterly effects,* and other things that didn't make any sense to her at all. When he showed slides of work by Max Ernst and De Chirico and then, more alarmingly, by people like Jackson Pollock and Andy Warhol and Dinos and Jake Chapman and Bill Henson, she grew upset and confused. Although she worked very hard at art school, she never quite got it. She sensed that she was becoming the butt of jokes between Colin and the other students. This was very painful.

Art school wasn't working. She chucked a u-ee and embarked on another path entirely. Accounting was good. There were problems and there were solutions. Numbers retained their shapes no matter how you pounded or crunched them, no worries at all, and this was deeply comforting.

Like a spurned lover, Destiny Doppler turned her fury on art itself. Art became the classic ex: a bastard now, a bastard then, with no redeeming features. She couldn't even bear to hear the word.

Following a whirlwind romance involving funny little Valentines sent in July and the purchase of single roses from vendors in restaurants, she married an accountant from another firm and set up house with him. But things started to go wrong when he began calling to say he'd be working late and she'd discover that he'd actually snuck off to the theatre or ballet. Soon, he was unapologetically spending hours glued to the television, watching art program after art program. Divorce followed swiftly.

When the Troubles began, Destiny, who'd had a lot of time alone to think about things, felt called to public life. From the start, she made her position clear. Culture had to go. Art was for poofs and malcontents and Aborigines. If they didn't like it, they could go back to where they came from.

Having said—along with so many other people over the years that gallery walls echoed with the words—'a child could paint that', she now faced her moment of truth. She ordered Verbero to buy her materials. He was surprised to discover the art-supplies shops had been doing a roaring trade ever since Clean Slate's policies had made art the single most fashionable thing to do for rebellious youth. And all youth were rebellious. Besides, they didn't have anything more pressing to do. They were youth.

He came back minus the prime ministerial petty cash and with a great swag of brushes and paints and pens and inks, pastels and charcoals and sketch pads and putty rubbers and stretchers and canvas, which he dumped on her desk. 'I hope you know what you're doing,' he snarled.

Destiny informed her private secretary, a doleful woman whose husband had been decapitated by a large, badly anchored public sculpture that fell over in a windstorm, that she was not to be disturbed except in the case of national emergency.

There was little chance of national emergency. Now that the Troubles were over, our country was rarely disturbed by emergencies of any kind. In other lands, religious groups that faced east when they prayed declared holy wars on groups that faced west. Wealthy terrorists ran around with bombs in their Louis Vuitton bags and poor terrorists cut off the ears of hostages with old butter knives. As the headquarters of strange new cults went up in flames, the heat caused the seeds of even more nutty theologies to germinate. The new Christian inquisition burnt down all the libraries in the American Bible Belt and people calling themselves 'pro-lifers' committed a murder a day. The rich got richer and went out with supermodels and the poor got poorer and went out with mudslides and floods and tidal waves.

The people of the little country that was a big island, meanwhile, just went out to dinner.

Behind closed doors, Destiny propped up her best make-up mirror from home on the big, jarrah-wood desk. With occasional glimpses up at *Cap d'Antibes,* she studied herself for a long while. Then she sketched and drew and painted, with brushes and paints and pens and inks and pastels and charcoals, on sketchpads and canvas. She napped on the lurid orange sofa and had her meals delivered to the private dining room adjoining the reception area of her office. She ate at a long table fashioned from blackheart sassafras with a marble centre. While eating her solitary meals, she frequently paused, fork halfway to her mouth, in order to stare at her even, plain features in the mirrors on either end of the room.

After ten days, she touched up her make-up and her hair, re-applied her lipstick and straightened her clothes. She threw all of her efforts, along with the brushes and paints and pens and inks and sketchpads and charcoals and putty rubbers and stretchers and canvas into the bin. She lit a match.

Toxic smoke billowed out, triggering the alarms. All twelve thousand speakers of the public address system in the parliament building crackled into life and bright red fire engines raced up the bright green hill towards the bright white building. Destiny, meanwhile, strode with a calm sense of purpose into Verbero's office, where she found him bending over a small mirror, razor blade in hand, oblivious to the general commotion. She told him to get ready to fly to Sydney that night. First, she instructed him, he was to inform the media that she was going to make a very important announcement that evening. She wanted it televised live to the nation.

# Painting is

# dead

At the time, I didn't know any more about this than anyone else, which is to say, I knew jackshit. All I knew was, following Destiny's 'Fifty Days Reform' and the birth of the underground, the world seemed to me a more benign place. Occasionally, lying in bed trying to concentrate on Ovid or Dante, I'd still fantasise about ways of doing myself in. Not in my wildest dreams did I imagine that I might become collateral damage in a political assassination, the victim of what I believe is called 'friendly fire'.

I finished my 'Paranoia' series—well, as much as I finished anything. I was ready to move on. The afternoon preceding Destiny's address to the nation, I was doing a pastel sketch of Thurston. The sketch was a study for a group portrait paying homage to Gustave Courbet's *Interior of My Studio, A Real Allegory Summing up Seven Years of My Life as an Artist.* Mine would be called *Interior of My Warehouse, A Real Allegory Summing up Three Years at Art School and One in the Underground.*

ZakDot and Maddie were hanging around,

waiting for their turns to pose. ZakDot was sprawled on the beanbag chair flipping through an old copy of *Art + Connections* and Maddie was doing biceps curls with a pair of barbells in the doorway. She was wearing a tight grey Bonds t-shirt and trackies. I snuck glances at the perspiration marks spreading out from her armpits towards the swell of her beautiful breasts. As the weather warmed up, Maddie had taken to hanging out in greater and greater degrees of undress.

Cashie was going to be in the painting as well. She'd commissioned it, in fact. Thank God for Cashie. I needed the money.

Shortly before Clean Slate came into power, I'd got myself sacked from Lynda Tangent's Triangle Factory. I'm not sure if it was a response to the king's yellow scare or a sign of my general lack of balance, but one evening I just flipped. I laid a fat, expressionistic slash of defiance across the unpainterly surface of the triangle I was working on, and then on every triangle in the room. Lynda fired me, but you know what? The critics loved them. Crapped on and on about 'crypto-conceptual breakthroughs'.

Even Cynthia Mopely, who was working on a critical biography of Lynda, called to thank me. 'I've almost run out of philosophical references and symbolic interpretations and even synonyms for the number three, as it were,' she confided. Breathing into the phone, she whispered, 'I had a dream the other night in which Lynda unveiled a new series of paintings featuring rhomboids. In it, I rushed forward and bit one of them. When I woke up, there were saliva stains on my pillow. I think I was just anxious to get my teeth into something new. As it were.'

Every piece sold, by the way. Lynda apologised for

sacking me and asked me to come back to work, but then Clean Slate got into power and that was that.

I went on the dole. But Clean Slate put into effect its strict policy of cutting off benefits for anyone caught using his or her time making art. My case manager at JobLess, the government agency overseeing unemployment benefits, was a man with small pink eyes like a bull terrier and a tired mouth. At my last meeting with him, I caught him staring at my hands, which, I realised too late, were covered in paint.

If they cut me off, I'd be fucked. Three years at art school doesn't even qualify you to drive a forklift. Commissions were more my style. Well, I'd always believed that, anyway. This group portrait was actually my first.

'How much longer do you want me to hold this pose?' Thurston asked meekly.

I'd been daydreaming.

'It's just that, uh, it's a wee bit hot in this gear.' His cheeks had coloured bright pink, beads of sweat clung to his brow and he looked like he was about to pass out. It was a hot day for a suit of armour. 'Of course,' he hastened to add, 'I'll stand here as long as you need me to.'

'Oh, sorry, Thurston,' I said. 'Take a break. I'll get Maddie to pose for a while—if that's okay with you, Maddie.'

Maddie sat on a stool, long legs angled. She held up her arms and flexed her muscles.

The door was open and Cashie called out from the foyer in that singsong voice of hers, which betrayed her not-so-distant past as a real-estate saleswoman from one of those suburbs where lattes come in tall glass mugs with handles. 'Halloo?' she trilled. 'Ha—loo—oo! I have arrivée!' Cashie liked to throw in a bit of French.

'Halloo!' ZakDot trilled back.

'Hi there dudes,' she greeted, waving a bottle of gin. In her other hand was a bag with tonic and limes.

She moved about the studio, bussing the air a few centimetres off everyone's cheeks. You could see Maddie just tolerated the affection, and only because Cashie had become a 'comrade'. Examining my sketches, Cashie clapped her hands with delight, sending her bangles jingling down her arms.

Returning with a clutch of glasses, ZakDot made us all G&Ts and put on the Verve's *Urban Hymns*. It was a cosy scene. I liked to think, at times like that, that we lived in a world that was beautiful and bright and insulated from the rest of society. I didn't like to dwell on the fact that police were storming the clubs and underground galleries, or stories like that of the bestselling novelist who had literally to eat her words when the cultural vice squad came pounding on her door.

That day, I was feeling particularly buoyant. After all, I was the focus of attention, the master, the hub of our little social axis, the Artist, the Hero. And no one, to the best of my knowledge, was trying to kill me. By the end of the night, I would be amazed that no one had succeeded in killing me, but I'm getting ahead of myself.

'Oi, guys.' Julia popped her head in the studio. Julia was a photographer in her early thirties. She lived downstairs. Julia was easy on the eyes, a petite little thing with olive skin, long dark hair and a quirky line in op shop clothing. She shared her warehouse space with Gabe and a poet who emoted at length about her neuroses to audiences that demonstrated their appreciation by taking off their sandals and slapping them against the tables. 'Doppler's making some big announcement in fifteen minutes,' Julia informed us. 'Come to my place and watch it on my TV if you like.'

Julia sold a lot of photos to magazines and owned the best television set in the building. One of those big screen jobs.

I never watched television anymore. Clean Slate had introduced changes to media ownership laws which allowed a wealthy and reclusive dwarf to buy all the newspapers and television networks. He forbade coverage of anything that smacked of culture, even yoghurt. Pulling all the arts programs, he replaced them with shows like 'Most Appalling Home Videos', and 'Morons Say the Stupidest Things'. The McNews reached depths of irrelevance, superficiality and bad taste to which previous owners could only have aspired. Neither of the state broadcasters ran any news programs at all; their budgets had been slashed to the point where they could broadcast only Slovenian comedies and second-run New Zealand police dramas.

'Boring,' I said without looking up. Julia was spoiling my tableau.

'She *is* the prime minister,' Julia insisted.

'Blow the bitch up,' muttered Maddie, with a gorgeous snarl. Our own Enyo, goddess of war. Penthesilea, Queen of the Amazons.

'Look, suit yourselves,' Julia replied, sounding hurt. 'I just thought I'd tell you guys. If you don't want to come, that's cool.'

Now I felt bad. Julia was a nice chick. Her heart was in the right place, even if her other bits frequently went astray— most recently with ZakDot. He'd been spending a lot of time down at her place. He said her fridge always had stuff like smoked trout and the kind of pasta that came in sealed pouches in the refrigerator section of the supermarket.

ZakDot was holding Julia's hand and swinging it in a big arc. 'Uh, I might go along to Jules' place, Mi, if you don't mind. Could I model for you some other time?'

I shrugged. 'Whatever.' I looked at Maddie and was about to make a stroke on the paper when she made a 'T' with her hands. Time out.

'I'd better see this, Miles,' she said. 'Could be important.'

I looked at Cashie. She screwed up her face apologetically. 'Fine, fine, fine,' I said, 'just piss off, everyone. Don't mind me. I'm just trying to create art.' I looked for my packet of Drum, fearing even it had deserted me.

'Well, Art Hero, you're invited too, you know.' I wished ZakDot wouldn't call me that in front of other people. My mood, so happy just moments earlier, grew blacker than a gallery full of Ad Reinhardts.

'Be there or be square,' piped up a voice from behind Julia. It was Gabe. 'Hey, Miles. How's it hanging?' Everyone always asked painters that. It was supposed to be funny.

'Woof,' I replied.

Gabe blushed. 'Fuck off.'

I looked at Thurston. 'Feel free,' I said, making a shooing motion with my hands. 'Everyone else is abandoning me.'

'I'll stick with you, Miles,' he said.

'You don't have to.'

'I want to,' he replied, a touch too ardently.

I sighed. 'All right, all right,' I said, putting down my chalk.

114

We all quickly freshened our G&Ts. I made mine a double. Just as we were about to leave the warehouse, this girl I'd never seen before marched in, a swag over one shoulder. She was chewing on what appeared to be a slab of raw meat. A thin trail of blood dribbled down her chin. She dabbed at the blood with a finger and sucked it with the inborn intensity of really skinny people. Then she threw the swag down on the floor and exchanged high fives with Maddie.

'Guys,' Maddie said, 'Sativa. My cousin. She's from Queensland.'

'Oh, *really,*' we all exhaled. Queensland was a state in the north-east of the little country. Since Clean Slate came into power, our city had received a lot of refugees from Queensland, even more than usual. An almost mythical land of golden beaches and giant pineapples, Queensland had been an intermittently difficult place for artists even before the Troubles. Destiny Doppler had grown up in a small town out west, but, as she put it, 'I consider the north-east my spirchal home?'

Sativa had the same flat, bored voice as her cousin. It was weird. Enthusiasm and vivacity were clearly more desirable traits in a friend or, you'd think, a girlfriend, but there was something about languor and ennui and dangerous eccentricity that I was having trouble getting past. Besides, so far as I was concerned, any potential diversification of the gene pool was tantamount to an incitement.

As we ambled down to Julia's warehouse, our voices ringing in the stairwell, I manoeuvred my way to Sativa's side. 'So, what do you do?' she asked in a tone of voice that implied she couldn't care less whether I answered the question.

'I'm a painter.' I smiled in my most debonair fashion. I could see myself having a short-lived, passionate but ultimately tragic affair with Sativa. You know, the sort that would suffer from my greater devotion to art, but would entail a lot of vigorous sex and leave us both exhausted and full of bittersweet memories.

'Oh God,' she said, shaking her head in disbelief, as if I'd told her I liked to pick up hitchhikers near the Belanglo State Forest and then bury them. 'But, like, conventional two-dimensionality is *so* over.' She bore into me with her cat-green eyes. 'Know where I can get a bowl of sugar?' she asked. 'I'm ready for dessert.'

Life was so fucking difficult.

Julia's place was stocked with the usual artsy mix of scavenged furniture, old signboards, industrial spools and twister mats. A couple of claw-toed bathtubs filled with pillows served as lounges. There were already lots of people there, all twittering excitedly. I even recognised a handful of famous artists, including Immense Miller and Tiny Harmonious, who were chatting with one of Julia's friends, a chick called Philippa who apparently had written some scandalous novel a few years ago under a pen name. Sativa disappeared into the crowd.

A performance artist approached Thurston and me, holding a glass of milk. Pulling a breast out of her shirt, she dipped it in the milk. 'Do you think I'm outrageous?' she asked.

Thurston looked as embarrassed as I felt. 'Uh, Miles, do you mind if I go back upstairs?' He grimaced apologetically. 'I've got to be up at graking.'

As he shuffled off, the performance artist smirked. I felt intensely self-conscious. The scene brought me straight back to the first day of art school. I'd so looked forward to that day. Moving away from the south coast, I expected to find my true community in Sydney. Instead, I felt like a total hick. The other students all seemed so sophisticated and fashionable with their pink and silver dreadlocks, funky hairclips and retro frocks—and that was just the boys. Well, that was ZakDot, actually.

It took me a while to realise that, for most of them, their first-day costumes would come to represent the pinnacle of their artistic careers. Shyly, I followed the assembly into the auditorium for the welcoming speech by the head of school. He told us that he didn't buy into the 'cult of technique' and that individual genius was an outmoded concept. He assured us that he would not put the values of the academy in the way of our 'creative fulfilment'.

I was outraged. I'd always known that alienation was a typical response of the artist to his environment, but it hadn't occurred to me that art school would be the most alienating environment of all.

Now I relived that feeling. What the fuck was I doing there anyway? Did Leonardo da Vinci rush out of his studio every time the Duke of Milan handed down some new decree?

I turned and was about to head for the door when a strong little hand grabbed me by the waistband of my jeans and pulled me back and into one of the cushiony bathtubs. Sativa. We were thigh and thigh. Maybe it was true love after all. I decided to stay.

She offered me a spoonful of sugar. I shook my head. It suddenly occurred to me that I was a little tipsy from all that gin.

Destiny came on the tube. She was wearing a simple brown frock the same colour as her hair, which was pinned up. It accentuated her pretty rounded shoulders, small but firm breasts and long, pear-like body. She was in good nick for someone her age. She looked into the camera and smiled. I don't think I'd ever seen her smile before. Her cheeks dimpled. When she began to speak, some people hissed. Others shushed. Everyone leaned towards the television, as if a few inches could make whatever she was about to say more audible, if not comprehensible.

'My fellow citizens? I have an important announcement to make?' She looked down at her notes and then up at the camera again. 'I've decided that it is in the national interest to encourage certain types of cultural activity?' She cleared her throat. 'For example, I think that certain realistic types of painting should be okay? Like, if you draw apples and they look like apples, right? Or you draw a person and it looks like that person?' She blinked. 'It's like taking a photograph or something?'

Julia groaned and put her fist in her mouth. 'No,' she begged, 'don't talk about photographs.'

'I mean, painting in a realistic manner isn't like chopping the heads off stuffed animals or making videos of people eating their breakfasts, or throwing scraps of yarn into piles on the floor, or putting, I dunno, *yoo-rine* in bottles? It's like, *real* art?'

I threw my head back, threw my arms in the air and whooped. At last, *someone* was talking sense. 'Yes!' Sativa looked at me as though I'd just announced I had the ebola virus. Clearly, I was alone in my enthusiasm. Around us, the uproar was immediate. Decapitated teddy bears rained down on the screen. Maddie grabbed the first thing she saw—a videotape of Gabe eating his breakfast—and pulled back her arm to throw it at the television but Julia grabbed her wrist just in time. Destiny ploughed on, looking almost radiant. Though I strained to hear what she was saying, the abuse drowned out the sound of her words.

ZakDot leapt to his feet, skidded on a pile of yarn, and recovered his balance by grabbing onto one of Gabe's plinths. A 'D' shuddered at the impact and tumbled off, just missing a row of urine-filled bottles. ZakDot scrambled up onto the plinth. It swayed dangerously under his feet. Someone shrieked and soon the entire attention of the room was focused on him. As the plinth settled, he struck a dramatic pose, one fist raised, the other clenched by his side. 'Painters of the world unite,' he declared in his most theatrical voice. 'Lay down your brushes. Let's call a strike.'

The cheers were deafening.

'I shall be the first to put aside my brush.' His voice quavered with emotion.

This was a bit rich, if you asked me. The only time ZakDot had handled a brush in three years of art school was when he dropped one into a vat of acid as a statement on the transmogrifying nature of art.

'Who will follow me?'

Another roar.

I'm thinking, this can't get any sillier. Then it did.

'As a gesture of solidarity, I'm cancelling all commissions for paintings,' Cashie declared to general approbation. She scanned the crowd for me. 'It's just a matter of principle, Miles. Nothing personal,' she explained.

'Fuck it,' I retorted ungraciously. 'I'd rather work on my

own stuff anyway.' I tried to haul myself out of the bathtub but the pillows kept sliding around underneath me.

'You're not, like, going to keep painting?' Sativa prodded. I didn't answer. She gave me a push—to emphasise her point or give me a hand, it wasn't clear, but I finally cleared the rim.

'Art will save the world,' someone shouted out.

'Art will save the world!' the others chorused.

It was getting worse by the minute.

'Where are you going, Miles?' Gabe challenged. 'Aren't you gonna to stay around and help plan the strike?'

'Actually, Rover, I'd love to but I've got some paintings to work on.'

Gabe glared. 'Paintings? Guys, will you listen to this? Guys? Miles here has to go home to work on his *paintings.*'

The commotion died down and everyone turned to stare at me.

'How could you?' demanded Gabe. His tone was contemptuous. 'You've always been an irrelevancy, Miles. Now you're in danger of becoming a sell-out. Do you realise that you're just playing into their hands?'

My face burned with humiliation. Irrelevancy?

'Do *you* realise,' I spat, 'that if your cock is long enough to reach your coit, you can go fuck yourself?'

Gabe asked me to repeat myself.

'I'd rather not,' I replied. 'I prefer taking on new aesthetic challenges with every work, unlike certain conceptual sculptors I know.'

'Careful, Miles.' He stepped in front of me.

'What are you going to do?' I taunted. 'Bite me? Bark at me? If you get hungry, stop over for some Pal, okay? Now, if you don't mind, I'm going.'

'You're being very stupid, you know.'

'I'm stupid?' I snorted. 'When your IQ reaches 60, Fido, you should sell.'

Julia stepped between us. 'Aren't we all on the same side here?' she wailed. 'I mean, why can't everyone just be nice?'

At this point the poet stepped forward and cleared her throat.

'NICE,' she bellowed.

Like everyone else, I was distracted by this interruption.

'Nice is what Costner copped from Madonna.
Nice is what people don't mean when they say good onya.
Nice is the colour of your girlfriend's hair.
Nice is the slides you took Over There.
Nice is a film you thought was shit.
Nice is a fuckwit a bogan a twit.
NICE IS FOR NANNAS WITH PROZAC BREATH.
NICE IS ACTUALLY SOCIAL DEATH.
NICE IS AN EMOTIONAL PALLIATIVE.
NICE IS A SEDATIVE EXPLETIVE.
I SAY NICE WHEN I MEAN NASTY!
I SAY NICE WHEN I MEAN NASTY!
NASTY NICE! SUGAR & SPICE!
REDBACK VENOM ON MY THUMB,
COME AND TASTE IT EVERYONE.
IT'S NICE! NICE! NICE!'

When she concluded her recitation, I turned towards the door again. My nose ran straight into a freight train that came in the shape of Gabe's fist. I heard a sharp crack like a bull-whip. It was starting again. People were trying to kill me, this time not to promote my career but to put a stop to it. I took a wild swing back at Gabe, missed by about a mile and sat down with a thud, holding my nose and swearing. I was astounded to see him hit the floor immediately afterwards. I was certain that if I connected I'd have remembered. A long pair of legs in tracksuit pants planted themselves in front of me. I looked up to see Maddie slapping her palms together, as if to indicate a job well done.

There followed what I believe is referred to as a melee.

# Surrealism

ZakDot and Maddie dragged me upstairs. I should have just called it a night, gone to bed and sulked. Instead, I shook them off, stomped into the studio, grabbed my palette knife and attacked the canvas on which I'd begun to work in some of the figures and background. Unfortunately, it being a commission and all, the canvas was first-rate, twelve-ounce, and the knife just bounced off it.

They observed my tantrum in silence. Finally, ZakDot spoke. 'You know what the most brilliant thing about calling a painters' strike is?'

I was scrabbling on the floor for my Stanley knife and didn't answer.

'No one would notice.'

'Ha, ha.' I wasn't laughing. I released the blade and attacked the painting. The sound of the ripping canvas sent Bacon fleeing for the security of the lounge-room sofa.

I saw Maddie raise her eyebrows at ZakDot. 'You're a dickhead, Miles,' she said, 'but I'm fond of you. Look after those cuts and bruises. Now, if you don't mind, I'll leave you to it. I've got unfinished business with Woof Woof.' She patted me on the bum and split.

ZakDot looked at me as if he were minister for tourism and I was a koala who'd pissed on a visiting dignitary. 'You're not really going to keep on painting, are you? It's embarrassing.'

'Pretend you don't know me then.' I hated the world. I tore some sketches down from the wall and crumpled them up. Still, the little censor in the back of my brain stayed my hand when it came to the better ones. The ones I could see framed and much admired and studied in the sort of major retrospective of my work I imagined galleries would be putting together in fifty years or so.

'Don't try to stop me,' I raged at ZakDot, hoping he would. He stepped aside. I stormed out of the warehouse.

The Church of Our Princess Diana had just concluded its evening mass or whatever it was they celebrated. Lack of mass perhaps? To reach the stairs, I had to negotiate a clutch of faux-princesses twittering in the hall. During the course of the evening's merriment, I had lost the collar of my shirt, and acquired the imprints of fists and feet on various parts of my anatomy. A small cut above my eyebrow was producing a steady trickle of blood down my face. My nose was swelling. At my appearance, the Dianaoids went silent. Before I knew what was happening, they were fluttering around me in a collective dither.

'Are you—a *landmine victim*?' asked one, barely able to contain her excitement. The others held their breath, waiting for my answer.

'Jesus fucking Christ,' I said, thoroughly vexed, shaking off their hands. Feeling suddenly faint, I crumpled to the floor, my stomach heaving.

'A sick child,' one of them suggested in a tremulous whisper. 'Maybe he's a sick child?'

I confirmed this speculation by throwing up on her shoes, which had inexplicably loomed up in front of my face. They were made, I noticed, of shiny pink satin. They looked expensive. Dabbing at them with the corner of my sleeve, I mumbled an apology into her ankles. I realised that I was clutching her knees with both hands.

Her reaction was no less fierce for being delayed. By the time I escaped the now frenzied pack of princesses by crawling into the stairwell and locking the fire door, I possessed a brand new set of abrasions and contusions that had yet to be inventoried. A cursory glance down at my clothing made clear that the attack had done nothing for my sartorial dignity or general well-being. I felt hideously sober. I realised I was clutching a blonde wig. I detached the rhinestone tiara from the synthetic tendrils, put it on my head and ventured forth into the world.

I stumbled towards Broadway. As I made to cross the road, I had to leap out of the way of a limo with tinted windows that had neglected to signal its intention to turn. 'What is this?' I cried, as the limo slowed to a halt. 'Indicator exemption week for fat bastards in big cars?'

The driver lowered his window and hollered, 'What're your eyes—painted on?' Then he frowned. He appeared to be listening to someone in the back seat. He pulled over, but I wasn't worried. What was he going to do? Beat the crap out of me? Frankly, I didn't think there was any crap left for the beating.

The driver stepped out of the car. He was in uniform. He held open the back door for another man, who stepped out with a wry smile on his face. He looked weirdly familiar. But where would I know someone like this? He was a study in masculine elegance, from the silk-weave jumper hanging off his coat-hanger shoulders down to his pressed chinos and boat shoes. The sculpted lines of his torso were visible even through the loose fitting linen of his shirt. His dark hair sprang away from his high forehead and curled towards his collar. His goatee was too neatly trimmed. A stud sparkled in his nose. He looked me up and down. 'You an artist?' he asked.

Bloody hell. What was his game?

'You've got paint all over your skin and clothes,' he observed. 'You also look like you don't have a lot of friends at the moment.' I stared at him sullenly, suspiciously. I still couldn't work out where I knew him from. I could feel my skin trying to sneak off somewhere safe.

'Give me a call,' he said. He flipped open a small silver case, extracted a business card, and held it out towards me. 'I could be your friend,' he offered, in a voice so oily you could've sold it for eight dollars a tube.

I figured he was a rich pervert who liked to fuck dirty-looking boys, and I was certainly one dirty-looking boy. I took the card and, without looking at it, flicked it into the gutter. 'Fuck off,' I said.

His eyes darkened and he shook his head. 'Your choice, of course.' He got back into the car and was gone.

The card blew away.

Heading up George Street, I passed the hock shops, video game parlours and the tapas bars. I found myself in the middle of the movie strip. My brain was aching and I needed a diversion. Hollywood films were exempt from the culture tax; Doppler's advisers concluded that they didn't really count as culture. *Apocalypse Then—the Hale Bopp Story* was playing, as was *Babe 3—Pig in Parliament* and a couple of films based on video games. Others starred giant monsters, aliens, natural disasters and Gwyneth Paltrow. I dug into my pockets but only came up with $5.30. Not enough for a ticket, even with a concession card. I smiled bitterly to myself, thinking of Gabe's accusation that I'd sold out.

Yes, I thought, jangling my precious little cache of coins, you can say whatever else you will, but you can't say I've sold out.

Selling out. What does that mean anyway, for an artist? In my experience, when artists accused others of selling out it simply meant that the people they were criticising were selling more artworks than they were.

It occurred to me that passers-by were giving me a wide berth. The artist's plight was to be marginalised and misunderstood, but this was ridiculous. I started to laugh.

A bloke with one squint eye and a vivid scar on his chin who'd been slouching against a poster of Mel Gibson reached out and patted me on the arm. 'Got a ciggie for an old painting teacher?' he rasped. I gave him the last of my Drum and rollie papers, and on impulse the $5.30 as well. 'Conquer Olympus, my lad,' he said.

Close to midnight on the deserted Pitt Street mall in the business district, I encountered a dozen people wearing aeroplane life jackets and oxygen masks strutting up and down the empty mall. They were holding blank placards and chanting 'bumbumbum beebumbumbum beebumbumbum'. I stood there watching them for ages but couldn't work out if it was a protest demonstration, surreptitious performance art or if they were just wackos.

This was a general problem, I found, of millennial life.

In Hyde Park, I came upon a fellow wearing an old-fashioned suit and bowler hat and holding up an apple, just like in that Magritte painting. Upon spotting me, he put down the apple and, from a pile of paper at his feet, picked up a reproduction of a Juan Devila with one hand and a Cezanne with the other. He flapped them about like wings. 'When the Apocalypse comes,' he intoned, 'life under Clean Slate will look like *Dejeuner sur l'herbe*. There will be fatwahs for all. Fires and no sale. Fahrenheit 452 is the temperature at which art burns.'

An old bum prodded me in the ribs. 'Got any spare change?'

'Sorry,' I replied, turning out my pockets to show him. 'I'm an artist.'

'*I'm* sorry,' he said, his hard old face dissolving into sympathy. He scrounged in his own pockets and came up with fifty cents. 'Here,' he said, 'go buy yourself some new clothes.' Then he handed me a flask. 'By the way. I like the tiara. Nice touch.'

I'd forgotten about the tiara. I searched for something to compliment him on. 'Groovy medallion,' I said at last. It looked rather classy, even if it was hanging around his filthy neck by a piece of frayed twine.

'That's me Strayun Literary Society medal,' he said proudly, fondling it with his blackened fingers.

It turned out he was a well-known writer. His books had been part of my high school curriculum. He'd been hit hard by the new taxes, but the final blow had been the abolition of writers' festivals. Despite the awards and two books on the bestseller list, he'd been homeless for years. Thanks to the festivals, he survived on per diems and long subsidised stays in five-star hotels. 'And book launches. Not much food but there was always free piss. Those were the days.'

I can't remember how long I sat with the writer under that big Moreton Bay fig, drinking and talking about life. Eventually, he nodded off. I eased his jacket up over his slumped shoulders and placed my tiara on his head. There was no one else about except a few optimistic Mormons and a lone pickpocket, whom I recognised with a shock as Tony, the former café owner and pianist. He didn't seem to recognise me. I wandered down William Street as evil-looking smoke-glassed casino buses streaked past. Clean Slate encouraged gambling—it kept people from doing art.

At King's Cross, a section of Sydney too adult to be given a diminutive nickname like Paddo or Chippo, a spruiker pinched my shoulder and intoned the strange mantra, 'hamburger and pussy, pizza and anal.'

The world was making less and less sense.

'Wanna lady?' A trannie flaunted her breasts at me.

'Wanna get on?' whispered a dealer, raising an eyebrow.

'Wanna punch in the face?' snarled a man in a hooded sweatsuit, upon whose territory I had, it seems, inadvertently stepped.

'No thanks,' I replied, 'already had one tonight.'

A Hare Krishna offered me wisdom. I turned it down.

A Scientologist offered me a personality test. I was afraid of failing.

A Christian marching band offered to save my soul. I asked how much they wanted for it.

On the corner of Bayswater and Darlinghurst, a super-annuated arts bureaucrat hissed for my attention. He flashed a tattered Strayer Council ID. 'Uninformed police patrol this train,' he said. He handed me a small bag of pills and powders just as he passed out, sliding down the window of Condom Kingdom, his sparse but oily hair leaving a streaky trail on the glass.

I was not very good at taking drugs. The next thing I knew I was splayed across the pedestrian overpass to Paddington, with my hands clamped over my ears to prevent my grey matter from leaking. I noticed the road below, decided to make some grand pronouncement on art and instead spewed over the rail onto another one of those Stygian casino buses.

# Bellus homo

It was morning. My back was stiff, my hands were cold and my face was pressed into an iron rail. Lifting my head, I rubbed my cheeks and could feel tracks that the rail had made. My eyeballs throbbed and my stomach was curled up around my Adam's apple. I looked around and was shocked to realise that I was sprawled on the front steps of an elegant terrace house in what appeared to be the heart of Paddington.

For artists, visiting hours in Paddo were traditionally six to eight in the evening, when galleries had their openings. I don't think I'd ever been in Paddo in the morning. The garden was full of strelitzia and other alarmingly vivid flora. The day was by Brett Whiteley but my brain was one of Dale Frank's swirling, psychedelic canvases. I squeezed my eyes shut to keep the colours at bay.

Someone giggled. 'And what do we have here?'

I willed the violent rotation of the earth to a halt.

Slowly, I opened my eyes and twisted my face around. My neck wasn't working very well. I found myself looking into a pair of brown orbs that expressed concern and amusement in equal measure. Large and pretty, they were sexed up with a touch of mascara and a hint of eyeliner, and complemented by a prominent nose, sensual mouth and high forehead.

A very high forehead.

It was, it turns out, a rather sensitive point, that high forehead. Its owner did not like the idea that he was going bald.

I buckled over and retched into the strelitzia. 'I'm sorry,' I mumbled, mortified. 'I'll clean that—'

'Oh stop,' chuckled my new friend. 'It's probably very good for the rooty-poots. We just won't tell the Big T, will we?'

I smiled uneasily. The Big T? Who was he talking about? If any bells were ringing, they were in a steeple far, far away. Where was I anyway? He looked familiar, yet I couldn't work out who he was. This was happening to me a lot lately. I recalled the man in the limo. Had that really been the previous night? As a visual sort of person, I never forgot a face. I just had a hard time recalling who it belonged to. Whoever he was, I thought it might be a good idea to stand up.

My legs disagreed. I didn't even reach mid-point before I collapsed again. A discreet throbbing in several parts of my face and a sharp pain in my ribs reminded me that I was cut and bruised as well as filthy. I must have looked a total dero. 'I, uh, had a bit of a night.' It occurred to me that I couldn't have begun to explain what had happened. Bashed for sticking to artistic principles? Kicked by clones of a dead princess? And that was only the start of it. 'I really should be going.' I felt desperately shabby next to this fellow in his trendy-as casuals and embarrassed about soiling his garden.

'You are *so* cute,' he said. 'You're an artist, aren't you?'

Grinning, he extended a hand and helped me up.

The question sent me into a tailspin. I was outraged that just because I looked like a walking disaster area everyone assumed I was an artist. Clean Slate had popularised jokes like: 'What do you call an artist without a girlfriend?' 'Homeless.'

'Well, aren't you?'

Being an artist is at the core of my identity. Yet I always felt put on the spot by the question. There was this sense that I had no right to lay public claim to the title until I had an exhibition, or won a prize, or earned some sort of critical recognition. As if that was even possible anymore. On the other hand, if a tree falls in the forest and no one sees it, it still falls, doesn't it? So if an artist paints in his studio, even if no one ever views his work, he's still an artist, isn't he? Still, it seemed like such a pretentious statement—'I am an artist.' Irritated beyond logic, I lapsed into silence.

'You're wondering how I knew.' He smiled. I noticed that he seemed to be wearing a light lipstick. 'For one thing, the blue and orange pigments streaking your auburn locks are reminiscent of a Fred Williams landscape. They complement the dark smudges Rothko-ing your maroon jumper, the speckled Seurat of your jeans, and the Jackson Pollock-like masterpieces that are your workboots. The blood stains are a bit worrying, and it does look like you tried to signal the 380 to Bondi with your face, but even that, on you, is all a bit, *comment dire,* fauvist. Yes, an artist you most certainly are.'

He laughed at my astonishment. 'You see,' he explained, 'I am, or rather once was, an art dealer. The name's Oscar. Oscar Bone.' He held out his hand. I shook it dazedly.

'Uh, Miles. Miles Walker.'

'Miles Walker. Of course you are!' He stepped back and

slapped one hand against his cheek, his mouth forming a perfect pink doughnut of recognition. '*Love* your work, darling, love your work.'

'You love my work?' I was incredulous.

'I saw it at the last graduate exhibition, the one before all the art schools closed. It was stunning, girlfriend, absolutely magnificent. We were *very* interested, but by the time we got around to making inquiries, well, that dreadful woman got into power and we all know the rest of the story.'

He was an art dealer. An art dealer who'd seen my graduate exhibition and wanted to pick me up. I was filled with elation, then panic—that was a whole year ago. I'd progressed so much since then. I clutched the railing to keep myself upright.

'All this Clean Slate business is such a shame,' Oscar continued. 'Thank God we made such a killing off the artists we represented in the past, otherwise I don't know *what* we'd be doing now.' He pulled a pair of garden shears from a clay pot next to the doorway and decapitated a hydrangea. 'Mmm.' He inhaled its scent and passed it to me.

Oscar shook his head. 'Here I am prattling on,' he reprimanded himself, 'while you, my dear boy, look like you're about to expire. Like anyone else in this town, I'm not ungrateful for the occasional spectacle of famous artists perishing extravagantly—acts of fatal dissipation, rare tropical diseases, romantic gestures of opiate abuse and, of course, motorcycle accidents, which are my personal favourite. Death is a bit wasted on inconnus, don't you think?'

'Depends,' I said, thinking of Thurston's theory.

'I must say, those are some *mighty* impressive wounds. Can I ask?'

I grimaced. 'In the wound the question is answered,' I quoted.

'Caravaggio.' He clapped his hands. 'What a divine film. Well, girlfriend, I won't ask you more than you want to tell me. But why don't you come inside and freshen up?' He opened the door and beckoned me in. 'I was just about to make some coffee. I can do espresso, or cappuccino if you prefer. If I say so myself, I'm very good with the frother.'

I hesitated for a moment but, the truth was, I was in desperate need of comfort and comforting and it looked like Oscar was offering a bit of both. *An art dealer!* I followed him inside. The foyer was clean, light and uncluttered, an alternative universe to my own.

As he chattered, Oscar broke the hydrangea up into florets, which he dropped into a shallow ceramic bowl filled with water. 'Now,' he said, 'let me show you the bath.' Oscar led me upstairs. I couldn't help stopping for a better look at the framed drawings and paintings on the wall by the stairs, recognising them as the work of Strayer's most celebrated artists. At the doorway to the master bedroom, my progress was brought to a dead halt by the sight of a garish painting over the bed.

I remembered seeing it in the Archibald Prize exhibition several years back. It was a portrait of the art dealer Trimalkyo. The Chinese emigre artist Hu Lüexin had depicted Trimalkyo as a one-man history of modern art. In the painting, Trimalkyo, draped in velvet, reclined Rubenesquely on a chaise longue. A melting watch crawling with ants sat upon his wrist. His head was a study in photorealism, his torso neo-expressionist, his knees cubist, his toes minimalist. In the background hung one of Lynda Tangent's trademark triangles and on a shelf over the chaise longue laughed three jolly Chinese-style gods wearing sashes that identified them as Cobber, Lucre and Luck. It was hideous.

'It is a bit hard to sleep under,' Oscar conceded.

Why would anyone try? I nearly asked, then it occurred to me that the Big T to whom Oscar was referring was probably Trimalkyo himself. This was his house. Oscar was his partner.

I barely had time to digest this fact when Oscar led me into a massive bathroom, about the size of my bedroom. He hung a thick terry-towelling robe on a hook. 'Take your time,' he said fluttering his fingers at me like Liza Minnelli in *Cabaret* as he left, pulling the door shut behind him.

The bath was the size of a wading pool. On a shelf above the taps was an array of salts and oils in jars and bottles. *Trimalkyo's things.* I poured some into the steaming water. My teeth felt like they were wearing unwashed jumpers. Opening the cabinet, I found a spare toothbrush still in its packet. By the time I finished brushing, the bath was ready. Because of my cuts, I entered the water gingerly, but soon sank into it like sleep.

I felt all the heaviness inside me lift. I was Henry Moore reincarnated as Alexander Calder. I scrubbed the traces of the night off my skin with a big loofah. *Trimalkyo!*

My thoughts turned to ZakDot and Maddie. I would have liked it if ZakDot had tried to stop me from leaving, but what did I expect? And Maddie—she'd fought for my honour. I wasn't sure what I'd done to deserve such friends. On the other hand, you couldn't be too careful. ZakDot did incite that whole painters' strike thing, after all. And Maddie returned to see Gabe right afterwards—what was all that about? As for Thurston—he disappeared from the scene a tad too conveniently, if you asked me. Lifting my hands from the hot water, I watched vapours rise from my fingers like smoke. I lay back and closed my eyes.

After a long while, I opened them again and sat up. The water sucked at the sides and dribbled over onto the floor. I felt light-headed. My skin tingled. I'd gone pink all over and my fingers and toes were puckered like an old man's. I smelt like boronia and ylang ylang. My hair, which I'd washed, gave off a whiff of marshmallow. I stepped out of the bath and wriggled my toes in the bathmat's deep pile. Wrapping myself in one of the fluffiest towels in world history, I felt like the subject of one of those Orientalism paintings. I only required a Nubian slave to help dry me off. Clearing a little circle in the steamed-up mirror, I peered at my face. With the crusted blood washed off and a few Elastoplasts in place, I looked almost normal. I glanced at the stinking pile of rags that were my clothes. Unable to cope with them for the moment, I slipped on the terry-towelling robe and emerged into the hallway. My clean feet squeaked on the parquet as I made my way to the kitchen.

'I *knew* there was a person under there,' cooed Oscar, handing me a steaming cappuccino. I felt as warm and fuzzy as one of Kathy Temin's duck-rabbit problems, and just as weird.

I followed Oscar into the lounge. The room was cool; an air-conditioner hummed quietly in the background. The furniture was all polished surfaces and elegant lines, like something you'd expect to see in a Tanguy painting, moon-landing furniture, lounge suites for flying saucers. Oscar gestured for me to sit down on a chaise longue and disappeared back into the kitchen. I obeyed, then jumped up with a yelp. It was made of aluminium and felt like a big ice cube under my thighs, which were naked under the robe. I spread the spilt coffee around with my toes on the polished floorboards until you couldn't see it.

'Everything okey dokey in there?' Oscar trilled from the other room.

'Fine,' I answered. This time I made sure that the robe was positioned between my skin and the hard cold surface. The lounge had obviously been designed for small alien beings with no bones in their arses. I shifted about, trying to get comfortable.

Oscar reappeared holding a platter heaped with pastries. 'While you were in the bath, I nipped out to this marvellous little bakery down the road, Le Petit Con.' Gratefully, I selected an almond croissant. The combination of caffeine and sugar did its work instantly.

Oscar perched himself on what looked like an enormous white staple, one foot of which had been bent forwards and the other back. It didn't look much more comfortable than the chaise longue. He informed me it was David Star's *Stool for the Gallery Sitter.* He warned me not to try and balance my cup on the nipple-shaped coffee table, designed by someone else I'd never heard of, as the mound in the centre caused things to slide off.

'Isn't that silly?' I asked. 'I mean, for a coffee table?'

'Oh stop,' Oscar giggled. 'Of course it's silly.' He looked around, as though checking that we weren't being overheard, and whispered, 'This whole place, if you ask me, is silly. The bathtub is the most comfortable thing in the entire house. And that was my decision. The Big T picked the rest of this stuff.'

The Big T. I couldn't wait to tell ZakDot. If he was still talking to me, that is. I hoed into another pastry, too hungry for either regrets or apologies.

'I do love a starving artist,' Oscar commented, clapping his hands with glee. 'Now. You must tell me all about yourself, Miles Walker.'

'Nn.' I pointed with embarrassment to my mouth, which was full.

Oscar smiled, a distant look in his eyes. 'We used to meet artists all the time. It's all too rare these days. Most of our stable has fled overseas.'

Stable. Such a funny word, as if artists were animals to be groomed and watered and trotted out from time to time and then retired when they passed their prime. On second thought, it was rather appropriate.

He chattered on, apparently forgetting all about his intention to ask me about myself. I reached for another pastry. They were very more-ish.

'It's funny,' he said, 'I mean, before all this distasteful Clean Slate business, I used to complain about artists all the time. Artists can be *so* difficult.'

True. If it weren't for a certain degree of difficulty on my part, I wouldn't have ended up on Oscar's doorstep. I nodded and sucked on the soft centre of a buttery *pain au chocolat.*

'For one thing, they can be so bitchy. Worse than poofters, don't you think?'

I wasn't sure how to respond. I didn't want to agree too heartily, for fear of causing offence.

'I mean, every time you organise a dinner party you have to make sure no one is seated next to anyone they might be tempted to stab with a fork—but honestly, darling, if you're going to worry about that in the art world, you might as well have dinner parties for one.'

I heard the front door open and someone come in, but Oscar was so caught up in his rant he didn't appear to notice.

'And then, of course, they're such prima donnas. We'd do *everything* for them and it was never enough. We showed their works in our beautiful gallery, which, quite frankly, looks perfectly fine without anything at all on the walls. We sent out the trendiest little white cards printed with the trendiest illegible white ink inviting everyone and their dog to the launch. On the night, we'd hold their hands and assure them they were more brilliant than anyone else we'd ever shown. We gave all their scruffy, freeloading, gasbagging non-art-buying friends as much wine as they could drink and then, with any luck, sold their work for them and never, ever, took more than sixty per cent commission in return. And of course, who got famous? They got famous. Did we resent that? Not at all. But who did all the real work? We did.' He exhaled a little sigh.

It occurred to me that I might have felt offended, but I was having mixed feelings about artists myself. Besides, I liked Oscar. I still do, despite everything that's happened. Happening.

'And all they can do is whinge, whinge, whinge,' he continued. 'There's an itsy bitsy scuff mark on the wall and Finn starts screaming, there's a wee little typo on the date and Tobias Gerbil snaps my head off. One bad review and we're peeling Lynda Tangent off the pylons of the Harbour Bridge.'

'Ooscar, eef you don't shut oop, I am goink to eat my own 'ead.'

An older man stood in the doorway of the living room with

his hands on his hips. *Trimalkyo!* I'd never seen him close up before, only across a room. He was tall, about my height. He had hooded eyes that I felt I'd looked into before. He was quite striking despite the fact that his gingery hair was mixed with grey and age had begun to claw its lines into the soft skin around his tired-looking eyes. He smiled politely.

I put down my half-eaten Danish and tried to swallow inconspicuously. For the third time in twenty-four hours, I was struck by that odd, nagging sense of familiarity, though this time it made no sense. After all, I knew who Trimalkyo was.

I could have sworn that some kind of recognition flickered in his eyes as well. 'Do I know zees gentlemoon?'

'This is Miles Walker. Miles, Trimalkyo.'

'May-alls Vucker. May-alls Vucker.' Trimalkyo's eyebrows shot upwards and then nudged down again.

His accent was the weirdest I'd ever heard. The voices of Amsterdam, Bolivia and half a dozen Latin cities appeared to cry out amongst the tortured vowels and mangled consonants of his eccentric diction. There was even a hint of the Transylvanian, though I suppose all art dealers have a touch of the vampire about them.

'Mek yourself at hoom.' He motioned Oscar to step outside for a moment. They closed the door behind them. I quickly stuffed the rest of the Danish into my mouth. When they didn't return immediately, I had a look around. On a side table lay a book with the title *Natural Healing for the Apocalypse*. With restless fingers, I flipped through it. It had a section, dog-eared, I assumed, by Oscar, that gave tips for protecting your hairstyle from the effects of atomic wind.

I heard the door open and close once more. I wondered if I hadn't overstayed my welcome.

Oscar returned. 'He wanted to know *all* about you. Pardon my directness, but you are straight, aren't you, girl-friend?'

I was taken aback by the question. Sexuality was a spectrum, and I wasn't totally certain what my hue was. On the other hand, I hadn't had sex of any kind for so long it felt like a past-life experience. I struggled for the *mot juste*.

Oscar interpreted my awkwardness as an affirmative.

'No need to be embarrassed.' He patted me on the shoulder. 'It's perfectly normal for a certain percentage of the population to be straight.' He sighed. 'I'm afraid the old boy gets a little jealous.'

'Oh, no. I hope…I mean…did he say…'

Oscar held up a hand. 'No, dear boy. But to tell you the honest truth, sometimes I think he's looking for an excuse to dump me.' He slumped over the table, just missing the plate of pastries. I pushed the platter to the side and patted him on the arm.

Oscar's shoulders juddered. 'And if he did, who would have me? I'm nearly forty.' He sat up. 'Too old to be a catamite, too young to die. All the anti-ageing, collagen-boosting, free-radical quashing, triple Alpha-Hydroxy fruit acid peels and aloe vera-and-vitamin E potions in the galaxy can't stop my hairline from retreating, or my gums from receding. I can't even stand up at a urinal any more. Years of sporting a Prince Albert—you know,' he elaborated, noting my puzzled expression, 'a cock ring—have left me peeing like a garden sprinkler.'

I didn't know *where* to look.

'Dear boy, before coming home to discover you collapsed on the front porch, I'd spent two hours in Salon Salon getting, let's see...' He ticked the list off on his fingers: 'Manicure, pedicure, deluxe facial, shoulder wax and purifying seaweed and mineral mud body wrap. You've heard of Salon Salon?'

I shook my head.

'Of course you wouldn't. You're still young and beautiful.' He cocked his head. 'Rather like Trimalkyo when he was your age. Not that I knew him then. But I've seen pictures.'

He clutched at my arm like it was the last life raft on the *Titanic*. 'Once, I asked the Big T if he wanted to turn me in for a younger, prettier model,' he confided.

'What did he say?'

'He replied *"res petricosa est*, Oscar, *bellus homo"*.'

'All Greek to me.' I shrugged.

'Latin, actually, girlfriend. It's an epigram by Martial. "A pretty fellow is a waste of space." I wasn't sure how to take it. Trimalkyo is like a club where there used to be a table reserved just for me but now the doorman demands to see my ID every time.'

The caffeine and sugar completed their circuit through my body and began gnawing on my nerve endings. A yawn fought its way out of my jaws.

'This must be boring you,' said Oscar.

'No, no. I'm just a little tired. I ought to be going. I should get my clothes.'

'You don't want to be putting those back on for the moment, girlfriend. Come with Uncle Oscar.'

We went back upstairs and he led me into the walk-in closet, which was roughly the size of my studio. Every immaculately folded or neatly hung item of clothing in the entire closet was black, white or grey.

'This is you,' Oscar said, handing me a slate crew-neck

pullover of cotton woven so finely it felt like silk. I hesitated.

'I don't know. I feel a bit funny.'

'If you don't like it, then there's plenty of other choices.'

'No, it's just that it doesn't feel right. Taking your clothes. You've done so much. You're like a fairy god—' I clapped my hand over my mouth.

Oscar laughed. 'Yes, I am your *fairy* godfather.' He handed me a pair of charcoal linen trousers. 'Try these,' he suggested. They were a perfect fit.

He picked up a hairbrush. 'Trust me,' he said, 'I'm a hairdresser. Used to be, anyway.' I felt kind of silly, but I sat down at the dressing-table and let him smooth my hair back. He added a dollop of sweet-smelling goo. I looked at my reflection. I couldn't think how I usually wore my hair.

I stood up and peered into the full-length mirror. I looked like an artist as imagined in a Mills & Boon romance. 'All I need now is a beret,' I observed.

Oscar plunged into a drawer and came up with two.

'Just joking.'

When I finally left Oscar, it was late afternoon. I clutched in my hand a David Jones bag with my old clothes in it. I promised to return in two weeks, bearing slides of my work. 'Just for old times' sake,' he said. 'I used to love looking at artists' work, so long as it wasn't too vaginal.'

I assured him my work was not too vaginal.

'I'll speak to Trimalkyo about whether we could seriously consider putting on another exhibition. Now that the rules have changed a bit. You never know.'

You never do.

# Classical Greek

I arrived home to find ZakDot in the lounge, positioning his camera on a tripod facing the sofa. 'Where were you?' he demanded.

'Do you care?'

'Not really.' He pressed his eye against the viewfinder. 'It's just that after you didn't come back last night, I was tempted to call the police and report your brain as missing. Which reminds me, Thurston's out looking for you.'

I rolled my eyes. 'Where's Maddie?'

'I think she's got a band rehearsal. Either that or she's starting work at the catering service today.' The shopping channel had sacked ZakDot when they discovered him inserting anti-Clean Slate slogans into a Moo Cow Family Alarm Clock and Magic Motorcycle Wall Hanging arrangement. He then got a job with Dinkum Catering as a waiter. Dinkum Catering was a subsidiary of Dinkum Fair, a tourism conglomerate that specialised in package deals for foreigners who needed a break from their wars and strikes and natural disasters.

The ship I'm on now is actually Dinkum's flagship.

If only ZakDot hadn't suggested to Maddie that she try and get a job with Dinkum as well, I might not be in quite the mess I'm in now.

But maybe I should stop trying to put the blame on everyone else. It wouldn't matter who ZakDot and Maddie worked for if I hadn't cocked everything up in the first place.

I watched ZakDot fiddle with the knobs on the old manual Canon. 'Did Maddie come back last night?'

'Nup.' ZakDot shook his head. 'My guess is she was bumping uglies with Gabe.'

I made a face. 'Is it totally over between you two?'

'Where have you been? It was over before it started. We agreed that it wasn't really good for flatmates to fuck. More than once, anyway.'

'What are you doing?' I pointed to the camera.

'I've found out about this retreat in the Swiss Alps that gives fellowships to foreign artists. Switzerland is just about the only place in the world besides Strayer that has yet to go up in flames, and I never had the chance to try for a grant here before they were abolished. I thought I'd give it a go.'

'So what's the deal with the camera?'

'You have to document your work.' ZakDot was now peering into a hand mirror and plucking his eyebrows. 'They need a dozen slides. I thought I'd take some photos of myself thinking of projects. I don't think I'm over irony after all. I felt a little silly after last night. Earnestness doesn't suit me, to tell you the truth.'

This, I suspected, was as close as ZakDot was going to come to an apology.

'Now, what do you think? Is it this one?' He held up a

burnished gold paisley smoking jacket. 'Or that one?' Laid out over the sofa was a red silk Chinese robe with four-toed dragons and bats and curly silver waves.

'I'd go the Chinese.' I felt a surge of affection for him. 'They probably all have smoking jackets like that over in Switzerland.'

He fiddled with a setting on the camera. 'Mind just sitting there for a tick so I can check the focus? Ta.' He looked up from the viewfinder, as if seeing me properly for the first time. 'Holy shit, Miles, classy threads. Where'd you knock those off from?'

I had my story ready. As tempting as it was, I didn't want to tell anyone about my encounter with Oscar and Trimalkyo. I knew the revolutionary masses would view me as a collaborationist for even thinking about putting on an exhibition. Better to keep it my little secret for now. I had no idea that I'd be keeping a much bigger secret before long.

'After I left here last night,' I fibbed, 'I hopped the train down the coast to see my mum. She took me shopping in Wollongong.'

'Liar, liar, pants on fire.'

I did my best to appear offended.

'Well, it's just that your mum called this morning.'

Oh shit.

'She hadn't heard from you for a while and wondered how you were going. I told her you'd thrown a complete and irrational spac attack in front of everyone we knew, then, after getting the crap beat out of you, you went huffing and puffing off into the night to lick your festy wounds.'

'You didn't.'

'No, I didn't, actually. But it was tempting. Instead, I made something up about you visiting a friend, said I wasn't sure when you were coming back, yaddayaddayadda. She asked when you were going to get a real job. I assured her I was concerned as well and would encourage you to do something useful with your life.'

I gave him my you're-a-little-cockroach-and-I'm-the-Flick-man look. 'And what did you tell her *your* real job was?'

'Actuarial scientist.'

'Jesus, ZakDot,' I said, prior to slamming my door, 'sometimes you give me the shits.' I flopped face down on my bed.

He pushed the door open. I didn't look up. 'If it's any consolation you give me the shits more, Miles. In fact, with friends like you'—he jumped on my bed, straddled my arse, and poked me hard in the ribs with his fingers—'who needs enemas?'

As I lay there squirming and gasping for breath, he curled his body down towards mine. 'Miles, Miles, Miles,' he said softly, his hands on my shoulders. 'You know, I worry about you, you stupid little bugger.'

'I worry about me too,' I conceded.

We lay like that just a second or two too long, a second or two in which I became aware of ZakDot's musky scent, of the heat and shape of his body next to mine.

'I love you, Miles.'

'I love you too,' I mumbled into my pillow. I recalled Oscar's question—*you are straight, aren't you, girlfriend*—and considered the unspoken tension that had informed my friendship with ZakDot ever since that night I had to disentangle him from Maddie, though, if I was to be honest, that tension had existed long before Maddie ever came into our lives.

Lying very still, I listened to the sound of our breathing. I could feel his cock swelling against my thigh. He kissed the side of my neck. His mouth was softer than I'd imagined a man's could be. My heart beating madly, I twisted my face towards his. He pressed his lips onto mine. I felt his tongue slide inside my mouth. His stubble grazed my cheeks and chin.

My nerves felt like they were sandpapered back. When he felt under my shirt for my nipples and scratched them lightly with his nails, I jumped like I'd been electrocuted. I had a raging hard-on.

ZakDot tugged my new jumper over my head. Feeling self-conscious, I folded my arms over my chest. ZakDot checked out the label on the jumper. He whistled, impressed, and looked as though he was about to say something. I covered his mouth with my own.

'Ouch!' ZakDot had grabbed my thigh right where it had been turned black and blue by pink princess shoes the night before.

'Sorry.' ZakDot moved his hand up towards my groin. What did this mean for us as friends? Was I gay? Bi? How did this fit in with my vision of the future? ZakDot's hand slid over my fly. I imagined him folding his hand over my cock, twisting round the head, bending down and licking it. He stroked me through the fabric, and Little Miles strained up at him. I closed my eyes. Two images popped unbidden into my brain: Caravaggio's young Bacchus and Destiny Doppler. I was one confused boy.

'I…I need time to think,' I panted.

ZakDot, who was pressing his face into my crotch, looked up and raised one tweezed eyebrow. He went to stroke me again, but I grabbed his hand and held it away from me. He took a deep breath. 'And I was going to show you how the guards used to do it.' Rolling onto his back, he stared at the ceiling.

We lay there for a while, both of us on our backs, our knees up and touching. Little Miles settled down reluctantly to await further instructions. I grew aware of sweat stinging me wherever I was scratched or cut, which was just about everywhere.

I broke the silence. 'What are you thinking?'

Zak removed his beauty spot, stared at it, stuck it back on. 'I want to spend the rest of my life everywhere, with everyone, one to one, always, forever, now.' I couldn't believe he was quoting Damien Hirst's book title at me. He knew I hated Damien Hirst. He rolled over in my direction and leaned on his elbow. 'Where *did* you get those duds, anyway?'

'Wouldn't *you* like to know?' I sat up.

'Where you going?'

'To the studio,' I replied. At which point, the blood rushed out of my head, I keeled over, moaned and fell sound asleep. I didn't come to till nine o'clock the next morning when Bacon, hungry for breakfast, roused me by nibbling on my toes. I was alone in my bed.

'How's it going, you little faggot?'

Who's calling me a faggot? I open my eyes. I didn't even hear him come in. Must have been daydreaming. He pinches down over the tip of his nose with his thumb and forefinger a few times as he observes me straining and struggling.

'Uhhuhhuhhaw!' I cry.

'I guess you're cuwious how I knew.' He starts doing a Marvin Gaye imitation, snapping his fingers, wiggling around in his cassock and pursing his lips. It's painful to watch. I hate it when middle-aged men start trying to get all groovy. Besides, he's got the words to the song wrong. Even a post-seventies kid like me could tell him that.

Then I focus on what he's saying. What does he know? He couldn't know about the bomb, could he? There's no way. Only ZakDot, Maddie and Thurston know about that. I rack my brains. He must mean…He's not going to start in on me for what happened this afternoon with Destiny, I hope. 'Ahhahahey,' I whimper. I can explain. I can't, actually, but it seems like the right thing to say.

'You can thank your fwiends. Kca kca kca.'

But they didn't know about what happened today. I'm puzzled. I'm more than puzzled. What the fuck is he talking about? 'Heephhahihaho,' I plead.

Ignoring me, he pecks out some numbers on his mobile, goes into the toilet and shuts the door. I can just hear him say, 'It's snowing in the Bwindabellas.' The cabinet door opens and closes. Verbero emerges, winks and leaves.

# Let's make a deal

Almost immediately after our little liaison, ZakDot took up again with Maddie, pissing off Julia, devastating Gabe, and leaving me at loose ends. I thought they'd agreed that flatmates shouldn't fuck more than once. I felt, to be frank, a fraction jealous.

I was also worried. I knew that, even though they had defended me, both he and Maddie disapproved of my behaviour the other night. I suspected that they'd be thinking of ways to keep me from painting. Painting was my life. Keeping me from painting was tantamount to—killing me. Sativa, meanwhile, moved in, staking out the lounge and observing me with what I grew convinced was malicious intent. The paranoia returned.

When no one was home to overhear, I called Oscar and made an appointment to show him and Trimalkyo slides of my work. He seemed especially interested when I mentioned that I was very much into doing portraits.

It took me a full day to make a good selection of my paintings and document them. I'd have liked to have asked Julia or even ZakDot for a hand. But politics aside, I wanted to keep the whole thing to myself. I wouldn't have been able to bear the humiliation if Trimalkyo rejected my work.

Genius is commonly overlooked or undervalued in its own time. It's always been within the bounds of possibility that my extraordinary gift might escape the notice of my contemporaries. That the spotlight under which my work is destined to shine may, in my lifetime anyway, take on the appearance of a dim torch.

Yet until the moment came to show my work to Oscar and Trimalkyo, this knowledge was hypothetical. I was beside myself with anxiety. I don't know if you've ever seen any of Jean Tinguely's sculptures, all cogs and wheels and bits and pieces of suspended, rusting junk, which he called 'self-constructing and self-destroying works of art', but that's what my stomach felt like—Tinguely. I put on the trousers and pullover that Oscar had given me, felt like too much of a suck, and discarded them for a pair of paint-stained cords and one of my own skivvies instead. I did attempt to back-comb my hair the way Oscar had. Then, I mussed it up again. They could have me as I was or forget it.

As I walked towards Surry Hills, I reflected on the fact that Trimalkyo had always exhibited artists like Lynda Tangent, Finn, and Hu Lüexin, a dour fellow prone to declarations like 'I have felt oppression, I know the Tao' and whose work, with the single exception of that execrable portrait of Trimalkyo, consisted of gum leaves dotted with sperm.

I was wasting my time. People had stopped appreciating true artistic talent well before the collective hallucination that produced Clean Slate. Maybe ZakDot was right when he claimed that, since the—airquote—'meaning of life' was a moot—airquote— 'construct', it made no sense to search for it in art. Perhaps Maddie was right too, carrying out her project of destruction, so that a new culture could arise from Ground Zero. Maybe Clean Slate was right, but not for the reasons it thought it was.

'It's called "Gaea", darling. You've heard of the designer Simone el Phulia? No? She was in the last issue of *Black & Blue*, posing in barbed wire with that gorgeous little Thai chef? No? Anyway, it's Trimalkyo's latest acquisition. Go on, try it, it's actually more comfortable than it looks.'

I sat down tentatively on the green plastic excrescence. It looked liked something Godzilla had sneezed into a hanky. Oscar was wrong. 'Gaea', the designer stool, was actually *less* comfortable than it looked. Before I had a chance to make my excuses and shift to something else, Trimalkyo entered the room, rolling a cigarette. He did it one-handed, just like I do.

'Ah, you like za new seating implement-o?' He looked pleased.

I nodded helplessly, thinking that 'implement' was an excellent word for the furniture in this place.

'Vere'd you say you vere from?' Trimalkyo asked.

'I grew up on the south coast,' I said, 'but I was born in Wollongong.'

'Vullengoong? Really?' Trimalkyo settled his bulk into the only comfortable-looking chair in the room, an upholstered swivel chair with a high back split down the middle like an unzipped frock. 'Charles Vilson designed this.'

I knew as much about Charles Vilson as I did Simone el Phulia, but I nodded politely.

'Vullengoong's a nice leetle town,' he murmured, as though to himself.

I was not interested in discussing the merits, such as they were, of Wollongong. My mind was very much on the box of slides in my hand. I handed it to Trimalkyo.

'Let's see vat you huff brought me, hey?' He fed the slides slowly into the projector, which was set up on a table next to his chair.

Winking at me, Oscar went off to make the coffees. I could feel my legs shaking, though I wasn't sure if it was the jitters or if Gaea was pinching a nerve in my thigh.

'Zo,' Trimalkyo began, still feeding in the slides, 'Tell me somesink more about yourself. Vat motivates you. Vy you are an arteest-o.'

My mind went as blank as a Robert Ryman painting. The topic of myself, my motivation and my art was something to which I devoted much—some might even say excessive—thought. But, for the life of me, I could not at this moment imagine what conclusions I'd drawn. I stared at him, panic-stricken. Up close, his smooth, fair skin had the finely wrinkled quality of a deflating balloon.

Oscar spared me further embarrassment by entering with a tray on which were three thimbles of espresso and a plate of pistachio biscotti. As Trimalkyo reached for his coffee, I noticed the square, spade-like shape of his hands, not unlike mine, which I supposed explained our common ability to do one-handed rollies.

'Let me tell you somesink. Zere are three types of talent-o.' Trimalkyo stared hard into my eyes as he spoke. 'A, B und C.

Ze As are za geniuses. Zey know zat, everyone else know zat. Bs are good, but zey are not As. Zey know zat, everyone else know zat. Cs, zey are not so good. Problem is, zey are only ones who don't know zat. Zey sink zey're As.' With this observation, or caveat, or whatever it was, he held up the projector's remote control and pressed the button.

Trimalkyo's little speech had done nothing for my self-confidence. With the first *ca-chink* of a slide dropping into the little bay, my stomach rose into my throat and then pushed its way towards my ears. Looking at the colourful images projected on the screen, all I could see were glaring errors of shading or proportion, inadequacies of composition. I wanted to drink my coffee but I was afraid I'd be unable to swallow. My cup clattered back down on the saucer. *Ca-chink.* I saw how hopelessly self-referential my art was. *Ca-chink.* Projected on the screen in this room, the subject matter of death seemed trite. Christ. What was I thinking?

More relevantly, what were Oscar and Trimalkyo thinking? I could scarcely bring myself to look at their faces and, when I did, I found Oscar's brow furrowed in what looked to me like dismay. Trimalkyo's expression was unreadable. *Ca-chink.* I couldn't take it anymore. I was a C who thought he was an A. I leapt to my feet with the intention of leaving, taking with me a few final shreds of dignity. Hasta la vista, baby, and all that. I was out of there.

In my haste to decamp, I neglected to take account of Gaea's topological terrain. Designed to resemble the stump of a tree, it featured low twisting roots that dribbled away from the base. As I strode out, my foot connected with one of these, and I flew forwards, my arms reaching out just in time to break my fall. My palms landed like miniature aquaplanes on a sea-green scatter rug which rippled forward over the floorboards. I thus found myself stretched out on my stomach with my face to the floor and my arms extended in front of me, fingertips just inches from the tips of Trimalkyo's shiny Italian shoes, in the classic supplicant posture of the kowtow.

'Very moofing gesture, but most unnecessary.' Trimalkyo sounded amused. 'I like your verk very much. I'd like to invite you to 'ave a show mit us as soon as ees feasible. Perhaps eef you vill recover za vertical, zen we can talk bees-knees. Are you eenterested?'

Giggling, Oscar offered me a hand. 'You tickle me with *feathers*, girlfriend.'

I winced. The skin of my palms stung and my face was hot with embarrassment. I scrambled awkwardly to my feet. 'I...I really don't know what to say.'

'Well, "yes" would be a good start,' prompted Oscar. 'I told you he was fab,' he said to Trimalkyo, clapping his hands in delight. 'And *I* discovered him.'

They looked at each other and then back at me. Trimalkyo nodded at Oscar.

Oscar bit his collagen-enhanced lower lip and cleared his throat. 'There's just one condition...'

Trimalkyo and I shook hands, and Oscar gave me a peck on the cheek. He slipped me an envelope that rustled when I took it. The door closed behind me and, as I strolled up towards Oxford Street, I breathed in the calming scents of Paddington's rampant gardens. Wisteria, jasmine, roses and chocolate...I was passing a specialty cake and truffles shop. The window display consisted of an edible version of the Book of Nostradamus and a caramel asteroid crashing into a mint chocolate earth. I found some change in my pocket and, adding it up, realised I could either catch a bus or buy one handmade chocolate.

I chose a truffle with a dark and bittersweet centre. Just like me.

As I turned up Burke Street towards Surry Hills, I paused for a moment to consider the sign on a pub door: 'The Judgment Bar.' That'd be right. I'd be judged, for sure. 'Just one condition...' I needed a drink, but I had no more money. Then I remembered the envelope. By the time I came out of the bar, it was dark.

Fuck doubt. Fuck what other people thought. The world was changing. I was going to have an exhibition. It was going to be brilliant. The critics would love it. I was going to be famous. I was going to achieve, at last, the recognition I craved. Success without compromise? Not quite. But at least I'd be around to savour it.

I visualised the exhibition. The paintings would be hung just perfectly, a dozen or so large canvases anchoring the show, counterpointed by smaller studies and drawings.

The opening would be first-rate. None of that cask wine in plastic cups. Proper wine. In bottles. Proper glasses. There'd be collectors with fat chequebooks, beautiful women in sleek black dresses, cute young girls with sparkles on their cheeks, and critics like Jean-Paul d'Es-daigne. My breath caught. What would the reviews be like? Would they be able to perceive the eternal narratives in my work, the wry classical references, the way I interrogate tradition even as I draw on it, the sophistication yet playfulness...

Brakes screeched. The red-faced cab driver was leaning out the window and shaking his hammy fist at me. 'If brains were Vegemite, mate,' he spluttered, 'you wouldn't have enough to part yer hair.'

'You're mixing metaphors,' I pointed out, cocky from the great imaginary reviews I was receiving.

Another car honked. 'Multiculturalist!' the driver cursed.

Hurrying up Cleveland Street, I returned in my mind to the opening. My friends would be there too of course, scruffy and attitudinal and drinking all the free piss they could—just the way Oscar described them that first day we met. Or would they? Despite the balmy evening air, I felt a chill.

All my daydreaming about the exhibition, I realised, was a way of avoiding thinking about the rest of the bargain. Tomorrow wasn't very far away.

I needed to talk to ZakDot. He'd understand. Either that, or he'd dissuade me from doing this crazy thing before it was too late.

Pushing open the door to the warehouse, I was greeted with the sight of Thurston flapping his arms and dancing about the lounge in a tunic made of overlapping tabs of leather. Around each row of tabs was tied a strip of cotton. He was gritting his teeth and chanting 'dretch dretch dretch dretch dretch'. He didn't notice me come in until I was practically on top of him, at which point he treated me to a grin so cheesy I could've grated it.

'Thurston. What are you doing? If you don't mind my asking.'

'I'm shaping my klibanion,' he replied, with a peculiar

mixture of pride and embarrassment. 'It's hot,' he added, puffing with exertion. 'Just hardened the lamellae in the oven, so they're still a bit warm.'

'Right.'

'I know you must think I'm a bit of a knar,' he said, his feet now still but his hands fanning away.

'Nar,' I said. 'Where are the others?'

'Maddie's band's playing at Club Apocalypso. ZakDot and Sativa went along as well. Didn't they tell you about it?'

I'd forgotten about Maddie's gig. I'd promised to go. Maybe I could talk to ZakDot there. I tossed my stuff on my bed and raced out the door and back to Surry Hills.

# Performance art (with police)

Lynda Tangent opened the underground Club Apocalypso after she closed the Triangle Factory. She didn't have any more teaching to do, as we were the last class to graduate before Clean Slate closed all the art schools. She funded the club with the money she'd earned from those triangles I'd slashed.

I will give her this: she put a lot more effort into the club than she'd ever put into her art. She covered the walls with wallpaper patterned to look like a cityscape. Then she ripped and scorched the wallpaper and onto its scarified surface painted the shadows of burnt trees and melted bicycles.

Artwork leaned against the wall here and there or lay tossed in corners as though abandoned by fleeing refugees. The imagery was sexual, decadent. Not a triangle in sight. It complemented the smell of sweat and sex and cigarettes that swept over me in waves as I made my way through Little Hiroshima to Hieronymous Hall (the names of the rooms were written in neon) and towards the

Armageddon Room, where Cellulite Death were thrashing away at their instruments.

In Hieronymous Hall, Titian McLesion, the rumpled master of hard-edged abstraction, leaned against the wall pontificating to a dewy-eyed young groupie, one of the sort that flocked to clubs like this hopeful of picking up artists, not believing their luck when it happened, not realising just how easy it was. It always had been very easy to pick up artists. Titian taught me for one term at art school. I waved, but he looked straight through me. I thought that was weird until I noticed he was wearing a badge with the symbol of the painters' strike: like a no-smoking sign, except there was a paintbrush under the red slash. The strike had been a wild success. Call me cynical, but I think most of my fellow painters embraced it as the best excuse for not working they'd ever come across. As I've mentioned, painting had a credibility problem long before Destiny came along. If my peers were going to snub me for not joining the strike, fuck 'em. I was moving on.

I remembered what I'd come for. Where was ZakDot?

I searched the dimly lit room. In one corner, the comedian Mannick de Press slumped in a chair picking at his fingernails while Cynthia Mopely talked at him with excessive brightness. As it were. In another, a baseball-capped fellow with a video camera interviewed some Koori elders. I was momentarily distracted by the sight of a striking Asian woman holding forth to a gaggle of young artists while wearing nothing but clingwrap and a few Christmas decorations. I recognised her from photos. Kaneko Itedaku: the post-zen, post-scatter artist superstar whose work consisted of raking gravel over the lawns of modern art museums or standing naked in dark rooms while sushi menus and Japanese porn flicks were projected on her body.

Before the arts had been driven underground, few famous international artists like Kaneko ever bothered visiting our country. Now they flocked here to thrill at the illicit atmosphere of clubs like this one and to experience vicariously the thrill of persecution. We were particularly popular with artists from countries that used to be communist, for whom there was an added element of nostalgia. Wherever they came from, they'd raise glasses filled with our excellent beers and fine wines, making toasts to artistic solidarity, and fly out again feeling good about themselves. Their concern for our plight could be predicted to grow to a near-frenzy from November to March, when the climate of the little country was particularly welcoming. It was early December now, high season for the tourists of oppression.

I spotted Sativa, looking sensationally bored even as she held a brace of visiting French post-trans-avant-gardists in her thrall. I passed, unnoticed or ignored, through Hieronymous Hall and into the Armageddon Room. A big presence on the small stage, Maddie stomped her feet and slashed at the air with her hands as she bellowed out the lyrics to Nixon Bates' 'Plinth'. Nixon Bates was another classmate of ours; last I heard, he'd become a punk rock star in the Czech Republic.

> Klimt's extinct and Dali's gone and Picasso can't
> be found
> And the only way that you'll find Klee is digging
> in the ground
> Ad Reinhardt to the artists that are never coming
> back

> He's finally found a place to rest that's very
> square and black

Girls in skimpy summer gear pogoed in front of the stage, tits jiggling, heads bouncing as if on springs. Boys in t-shirts and pants, either so tight they were endangering the future of the species or so baggy they were hanging halfway down their cracks, jumped about punching their fists into the air. ZakDot was in the midst of it, platform boots giving him an even greater advantage in the height stakes. I watched him dance with something that felt like longing. I was terrified of losing his friendship once I told him what I had agreed to do.

> No longer missed misogynist Willem de
> Kooning
> Georgia O'Keefe is underneath the graveyard
> flowers blooming
> No more exists the Dadaists and fish bowl final
> score
> Magritte is beneath our feet and Warhol is no
> more

Fishing out a beer from the tub filled with ice by the door, I rehearsed my case. Saying no to Trimalkyo would mean forfeiting my only chance to exhibit in the gallery I'd always dreamed of showing in. Eventually, of course, I wanted to have shows in places like New York and London, but I didn't want anyone to say I couldn't make it at home first. I'd be foolish to throw away this opportunity. Wouldn't I?

> Lichtenstein liked comic books and Pollock was
> just messy

164

But they got respect and healthy cheques from
    Mr Jean Paul Getty
    Mr Jean Paul Getty...

Sweat was running down Maddie's face and neck and plastering her t-shirt to her chest.

The song evoked an era that was, as ZakDot would say, 'so over'. I was launching myself into the era that was about to be.

And if you say you haven't heard about the
    semiotic word
And exactly what it means in this postmodernist
    dream
And if you don't know where you stand
And if you find blank canvas bland
Then you just don't understand
You just don't understand

It's hard to believe that all this happened only about a month ago. Looking around me that night, I felt weirdly sentimental, as if I knew that it would be the last time I'd ever see most of these people, or be part of the scene.

As if I had ever truly been part of it. I mean, *I* didn't understand blank canvas.

I could no longer wait. I made my way across the dance floor to ZakDot, bouncing a little on my heels so as not to seem too out of place but too self-conscious to let loose and dance. 'Hey, Miles.' He shouted over the din of the band. '"Boogie on down".' I was relieved to see he air-quoted this phrase.

'I've got to talk to you.' I shouted in his ear. ZakDot slugged back the rest of my beer as he followed me to the other end of the room. 'What's happening?'

The guy with the video camera loomed up. 'Yeah, what's happening?' he repeated.

'A private conversation.'

'All discourse is public,' replied the video-meister, his finger still on the record button. 'In a sense.'

'Fuck off,' I said. 'In a sense.'

'That's good,' he said. 'Mind repeating that? I want to get a close up.'

'How many times,' I growled, 'do we have to flush before you go away?' Young Antonioni shrugged and moved off to where Kaneko Itedaku was slowly unwinding her clingwrap.

'I love it when you talk tough,' ZakDot purred. He was still bouncing to the music.

'ZakDot. I need to talk to you. It has to do with painting.'

ZakDot blew out his cheeks. His eyes flickered back towards the dance floor. 'I mean, sorry, Miles, I know the whole world revolves around the application of pigment on canvas, but this is a party.' He started to do his John Travolta imitation. Then he stopped and stared over my shoulder in the direction of the band with a funny expression on his face.

'You don't understand, ZakDot,' I pleaded. 'This is important. Look at me.' ZakDot's eyes were glued to the room behind me.

'You're not even listening to me.' My shrill complaint rang out into what I noticed was a sudden hush. I swivelled around.

The members of the band, along with everyone in the room, stared at the foyer. About a dozen police stared back, their hands on their gun holsters. A raid. One of them prodded an artwork with his toe, a knitted vagina fitted with dentures. The dentures chattered; he drew a bead on them. My hair stood on end.

'PIGS!' Maddie broke the silence. Everyone wheeled about to look at the stage. Satisfied she had the complete attention of the room, Maddie reached into her boot and drew out what looked like a Colt .45. Within an instant, the police were ranged around her, Smith & Wessons aimed at her head. Their leader told her to lower her weapon. My breath caught in my throat and my knees slammed together. The next few seconds seemed to stretch out into infinity. The only sound was a just-audible whimpering of some theoreticians and the slight hum of the amps. Maddie laughed her beautiful laugh, raised her head and drew her gun in an arc until it was pointed at the ceiling. She fired, shooting out a thick stream of water and letting it splash down on her upturned face and into her open mouth.

Some of the girls started to ululate and the boys whooped and hooted. The cops looked around, uncertain what to do next, when the video guy bounded up to them and started filming. They shook their heads and tried to escape him at first, but he was persistent, and in the end they were mugging for the camera, striking James Bond poses with their guns. Kaneko Itedaku knelt in front of them begging to be handcuffed. Mannick de Press leaned on their shoulders, making donkey's ears above their caps with his fingers. Gabe worked a 'D' into frame. It was all rather jolly, really, until Maddie let off the smoke bomb.

In the coughing and screaming and general confusion that followed, I saw Gabe take a hopeless swing at a policeman with his D, following which he was pounced on, handcuffed and led out. I could just make out Lynda Tangent arguing with the sergeant. I was disoriented, my eyes were watering and my lungs felt like they'd been tarred and feathered. Someone placed the fans near the windows and the smoke began to disperse. I cast about for Maddie and ZakDot, but both seemed to have disappeared.

I was still coughing and wiping my eyes on my sleeve when a hand tapped me on the shoulder. I turned to look straight into the eyes of a small policewoman with dark, freckled skin, a tough, sexy mouth, uptilted green eyes, a nose broad but not coarse and, I couldn't help but noticing, great tits holding up her sky-blue uniform blouse. Girdling her tiny waist was a black belt of woven leather. Over her right hip was slung a holster with a pistol and over her left was another black leather pouch in the shape of an upside-down pear. 'Talk to you a minute?' She indicated the corner of the room under the window with her chin, into which was pressed the faintest of dimples. I saw other cops leading those of us who were left—there were surprisingly few—into different parts of the room for interrogation.

I didn't see that I had much choice. We sat down side by side on a springless couch. She took off her hat and placed it in her lap, shaking her head slightly as she did so. A few shiny brown curls escaped her loose plait and fell down around her pretty face. She pushed them back behind her ears. She crossed her legs under her navy culottes; they rode up, revealing choice little knees. My eyes were drawn to her ankles, not only because they were fine and shapely, but because above the left one was an exquisite tattoo of Botticelli's *Venus*. Her shoes were no-nonsense black leather tie-ups.

'The name's Senior Constable Grevillea Bent.' Her surname made me smile. She smelled nice, like lavender; I got a comforting whiff of her perfume through the acrid air. She pulled a small notebook and pen out of her back pocket. 'You understand that you're not obliged to say anything unless you wish to do so?'

I nodded, wondering about the tattoo.

'But anything you say might later be used as evidence.'

I nodded again. My eyes were still tearing from the smoke. She offered me a hanky. I dabbed my eyes and handed it back.

Flipping open the notebook, she stared at me from under the thick curtain of her eyelashes. I swear there was a sparkle in her eye, though it may just have been the effects of the smoke.

'Name?' she demanded, her pen poised above the paper.

'Miles Walker.'

'Artist?'

I nodded.

'Can I see your artistic licence?' she asked.

I blinked. 'I…'

'That's a joke.' Her mouth twitched. Her lips were made for mischief. 'Look, Johnny. Uh'— she glanced down at her pad—'*Miles*. I'm just doin' me job.' Sighing, she leaned forward. 'Between you and me and the wall,' she confided in a low voice, 'I reckon all this is going too far. I mean, I don't know much about art, but I know what I like, and I've always'—here her voice reduced to a whisper—'been right fond of Fiona Hall's parodical transformations of the detritus of consumer culture, as can be seen in her Coca-Cola can and sardine tin sculptures. And I don't mind Lynda Dement either, particularly the way she breaks down the boundaries between quote-unquote acceptable and unacceptable representations of female sexuality. Of course, call me old-fashioned, but I like oil painting most of all. Nothing like oils to convey subtleties of light and depth and intensity of colour, eh?'

I swallowed, entranced. 'Yeah, well…I'm an oil painter myself.'

'*Are* you now?' She didn't sound like she was taking the piss. 'What sort of painting do you do then?'

'Is this for the record?'

She laid her pad down on her lap and folded her neat hands over it.

I explained my work as best I could.

'Remember that Biennale a few years back?' she mused when I finished. 'Title was "Art is Easy"?'

I laughed. 'False advertising.'

She smiled. For a moment, I forgot entirely where I was or why I was talking to this woman. All I knew was that I wanted to talk to her for a very long time. I wanted to release those mahogany curls and kiss that tattoo, and untie her shoes slowly.

She picked up her pad again and cleared her throat. 'You know, I've seen a lot of bad art, but I wouldn't arrest it. We should be concentrating on the real criminals. You know, economists, bankers, commercial television programmers, talk-back radio hosts, lawyers.' She sighed and glanced down at the pad. 'Are you personally acquainted with Ms Madeleine, uh, Ms Madeleine @?'

'Maddie's my flatmate, actually.' Oh shit, I wasn't going to say anything about that. My mind was churning with desires and propositions. 'Can I ask you something?' I blurted.

Her eyes lit up.

What was I thinking? I scrambled for a question more acceptable than the one dancing on my tongue. 'Uh, what's in that pouch?' Trying not to blush, I pointed to the oddly shaped case over her left hip.

She unsnapped the lid and popped it open to show me. There was a clutch of surgical gloves in the top part and a pair of handcuffs in the bottom. I stared dumbly, unsure what to say.

Her eyes twinkled. 'Kinky, eh?' she observed.

That did it. I flushed red to the roots of my gingery hair. When I finally got the courage to look at her again, she had composed her features into an expression of professional cool, though the twinkle hadn't left her eyes. 'Look, Johnny. Miles. Let's just get straight to it, all right? Could you tell me please what's going on here?'

'I don't know about you, officer,' I blurted out, 'but I think I'm falling in love.'

She smiled, biting her lip. 'The facts, Mr Walker. Let's stick to the facts.'

# Installation

I slept fitfully that night. My dreams were erotic and seemed to involve Senior Constable Grevillea Bent and her collection of rubber gloves. I had gone from desiring my best friend to fantasising about the prime minister to obsessing about a policewoman, but if these were signs that I needed therapy it'd have to be some other day.

When I woke up it was already noon. I had no time to lose. I splashed some cold water on my face while mentally composing a list of the things I needed to do. First I had to get to the art-supplies shop. I'd got out the door before I remembered that the envelope with the money that Oscar had given me was still in my room. At the shop I ran through my checklist twice to make sure I had everything. Back home again, I packed up my gear, organised stretcher wood into bundles, which I bound with gaffer tape, and threw a change of clothes rescued from the laundry basket into my rucksack. *Satyricon*. Why not? I shoved that into my bag as well. I remembered my toothbrush. As I was doing a final check of my paints box, I pulled out a tube of viridian and showed it to Bacon. 'This is the colour of Senior Constable Grevillea Bent's eyes,' I told him. He yawned and licked his armpit.

I found Sativa sitting on the spool-table, spooning baby food out of a jar. She said she was waiting for a lift to Melbourne, adding, 'Like, thanks for having me stay.' She shrugged when I asked if she knew where her cousin might be. Sativa had slept in her room; Maddie had definitely not come home that night.

My watch. Where was my watch? I searched for it in my room and then the lounge, scrabbling through piles of magazines and junk, and knocking a pile of CDs to the floor as Sativa looked on. Thurston appeared. 'Hey Miles,' he said. 'How was Club Apocalypso?'

'A blast,' I replied. 'You haven't seen my watch, by any chance?'

Thurston shifted in his ug boots. 'Uh, Maddie took it the other day. Said she needed it for a timing device in a detonator.'

'Great.'

It just occurred to me that the bomb that Maddie is planting on this ship may be using the works of my watch as part of its detonator. This is not a comforting thought. My watch is about as reliable with the time as Picasso was with women.

'You can borrow mine,' Thurston offered.

'Ta.' I realised with a start it was later than I thought. 'Gotta run.'

Thurston noticed my pile of stuff. 'Where are you going?'

'Out.' I hated it when people gave me that sort of answer, but I didn't have time to think of anything better, kinder to say. It was nearly 2.30 p.m. Refusing Thurston's offer of help, I gathered up all my gear and moved as quickly as I could out the door. The lift was stuck on another floor, as usual, so I took the stairs.

'G'day, troublemaker.' Julia's voice made me jump. With a little twitch of her shoulder, she slid the strap of her camera into a more comfortable position. She was wearing one of those see-through tops. Her small, apple-like breasts were visible through the fabric. I tried not to stare. I thought, if nothing else, what I was about to do should at least get my mind off sex for a while.

'Where you off to?'

'Uh, nowhere. Out.' I wasn't too bad at keeping mum, but I was a hopeless liar. I broke out into a sweat. It was turning out to be a very hot day.

'Out?' She looked interested. I could do without Julia's interest. She had a big mouth and she knew everyone. Julia had become friendly towards me once she realised that the brawl I'd sparked had attained legendary status. Two poets penned epics on the subject, a multi-media artist was working on a series of computer animations, and foreign documentary makers hung out at her place every night in the hope that something equally thrilling would happen. 'C'mon, Miles,' she persisted, 'you can tell Auntie Julia.'

'There's nothing to tell.' Perspiration stung my eyes. 'I'm just off to a, mm, friend's studio.' I shifted the pile of wood from one arm to another.

She looked at me suspiciously. It was a well-known fact that I didn't actually have that many friends, and that I lived with most of them. I decided to switch tactics. 'Thought you'd be at Club Apocalypso last night. ZakDot was looking out for you,' I said.

'*Was he?*' She brightened. 'Was he really?'

The topic of ZakDot took us down the rest of the stairs.

I don't know what I expected. The sight of a limo parked on our street was already astonishing; recognising it as the same one I'd encountered that surreal night on the town was even more of a shock. The man whose card I'd chucked into the gutter now leaned against the car. He was puffing on a cigarette and looking up the street with narrowed eyes while muttering into a mobile.

Julia did a double take. 'There goes the neighbourhood,' she hissed. 'You know who that is, don't you?' She didn't wait for me to answer. 'Verbero. The infamous. Brain behind the no-brain. Controller of Destiny. Creep-o-rama. What's he sniffing round here for anyway?'

I now knew why he'd looked so familiar—I'd seen him on the tube that night when Destiny Doppler was being interviewed by Trixie Tinkles. I needed time to think. I spun on my heels with the idea of dashing back inside. My movements were clumsy. Several lengths of wood escaped their bundle and clattered to the pavement.

Verbero strode over as I was gathering them up. 'So. It's you.'

I didn't say anything. I still thought he looked like a rich pervert, and he clearly remembered the insult of the tossed name card.

'Got him,' he barked into the mobile before folding it away and reaching out for my bag.

I made a half-arsed attempt to pull away from him but

now the fat bastard driver was on me as well. Julia watched the whole scene, her eyes round and her hands flattened against her cheeks in an almost comical imitation of Munch's *The Scream,* as they efficiently relieved me of my gear and chucked it into the back of the limo and shoved me inside after it. Verbero jumped in after me, slammed the door and we were off. Through the darkened windows, I could see Julia still standing there, frozen to the spot.

'Jesus fucking Christ,' I spluttered. 'And g'day to you as well.' The air-conditioning chilled the damp fabric of my shirt. I pulled it away from my body and flapped the cloth to dry it. I was furious, hot and humiliated—and, now that Julia had seen me go off with Verbero, I was convinced that none of the few friends I had left would ever speak to me again.

Verbero observed me coldly. He glanced at his watch. 'We're late,' he said. As the limo manoeuvred into the city traffic, he extracted a small silver case from his pocket. We were sitting across from each other on seats upholstered in what felt like kid leather.

Between us was a table, upon which he sprinkled a line of white powder from the case. With a silver razor blade, he chopped the powder and scraped it into neat lines. The blade went back into the case and out came a small silver straw. He snorted and leaned back. His eyes danced like a poker machine hitting the jackpot.

We turned down a side street at Sydney airport and parked outside a demountable building that was part of an air force base. This time, neither Verbero nor the driver offered me a hand with my stuff, which I struggled to lug into the building.

No sooner had we sat down than the pilot and copilot approached and shook hands with Verbero. He stood up and followed them out and I trailed behind with my gear. There on the glittering tarmac stood an alarmingly small plane, the VIP, which I later learned was nicknamed the 'vip' to rhyme with 'zip'.

Greeting us at the top of the stairs were two male attendants in formal if somewhat dated uniforms of royal blue. Verbero settled himself into one of four pale grey leather armchairs at the front of the tiny plane. He didn't particularly look like he wanted me to join him. I glanced around. Farther back in the cabin there was a table with sofas on either side, and then two longer sofas hugging the wall behind that. The grey armchairs were the most comfortable option. I sat down opposite Verbero, who ignored me.

'A drink for you sir?' The steward put down a bowl of pretzels and another of mixed nuts.

'Sure,' I answered grabbing a handful of pretzels. 'Are they free?'

Verbero rolled his eyes. The steward nodded.

'Could I have a rum and coke? I never turn down a free drink,' I said, borrowing ZakDot's line. 'No telling how they'd react to rejection.'

No one laughed. I wasn't very good at jokes. The steward smiled his professional smile and returned with a rum and coke and a martini. I noticed Verbero hadn't even had to order his. I missed ZakDot. I never did get the chance to tell him what I was doing.

The little Saab climbed up past the wispy clouds. I watched the red-roofed houses receding below, the tiny aquamarines of their occasional swimming pools sparkling like jewels in a desert. The ship-shaped cluster of tall buildings in the city centre pitched and rolled below us and we were away. Verbero continued his project of supporting the Bolivian economy. My ears buzzed with the noise of the engines and my mind whirred with images: of Maddie throwing that bomb, of Grevillea Bent and her tattoo, of Julia with her hands clamped to her cheeks. My fears and doubts and desires bubbled away.

That's why it took me longer than it should have to observe that the ocean was on our right hand side. We were heading north.

Verbero was staunching a nosebleed with a wad of tissues. 'What're *you* looking at?' he demanded, when he tipped his face forward again.

'Nothing.' I poured the rest of the rum and coke down my throat and asked the steward for another. He brought it right away. An image of the little sweat stain that had seeped out between Senior Constable Grevillea Bent's breasts floated into my mind and I got a hard-on. I imagined her leaning over her case-strewn desk at the cop shop.

Verbero hoovered up another line of coke. 'She's a beautiful woman, you know,' he rasped, making the statement sound like a threat.

For a second, I thought he was talking about Grevillea Bent.

I nodded, not sure what the appropriate rejoinder would be.

Looking out the window again, I focused on the bleached khaki hills and irregular patchwork of farmland. Billabongs stared up at us like melting blue eyes. Gradually, the browns yielded to green and the scrub to rainforest. I thought about what colours I'd mix to summon up these subtle changes on canvas. I thought about Grevillea. I thought about Maddie. I thought about ZakDot. I thought about everything, in fact, except the task ahead of me. We swung inland.

We were flying over dense eucalypt forest when the plane began its descent. There was no city or even town in sight. The top of the trees whipped about, dangerously close, it seemed, to the belly of the plane. Not a second too soon, a clearing appeared. I spotted a windsock, and a packed-dirt runway, and then we touched down. Dappled light played on ferns and trees as we taxied to a halt. The air-conditioning almost immediately surrendered to a fiercer, more humid heat. Despite a sense of foreboding, I felt on the cusp of an adventure, defiant and excited. An adventure. How many of those does an artist—or anyone for that matter—get to have in a lifetime?

'C'mon, Walker,' Verbero said. 'De-plane.'

'Is on de ground?' I ventured.

His gaze was as reassuring as a dentist's drill.

The other steward had opened up the luggage compartment and tossed out my gear. I winced as the box of paints hit the dust and rushed to grab the roll of canvas before it followed.

'No, no, please don't trouble yourself,' I said to an impassive Verbero, who stood tapping his feet. 'I'll be right.'

Clutching my case of paints in one hand, balancing my roll of canvas and pile of wood under my arm, my rucksack slung over my other shoulder, I paused to breathe in the sweet smell of rotting vegetation and overabundant life. A flock of cockatoos exploded out of the trees and swept screeching over our heads.

'We ain't got all day,' Verbero snapped.

'Yes, sir,' I said and fell into line. 'I'd salute but my hands are full. You know,' I added, 'if your face ever froze in that expression you'd have a good chance of getting Diane Arbus to take your photograph.'

'I twy and keep myself out of the limelight,' he replied.

Behind us, the VIP took off again.

Crunching on bark and stepping carefully over stones made slippery with the clear trickle of a winding stream, I followed Verbero to another clearing in the centre of which stood a large Queenslander. A gorgeous, rickety, wooden-slatted house on legs with a great circling verandah. I recalled rumours that the prime minister maintained a fortress-like residence somewhere in the north-east. The press dubbed it 'the Bunker'. I'd pictured a concrete building with gun turrets, underground rooms, massive iron doors. It was nothing like that at all.

I halted, set down my gear, wiped my sweat with my sleeve and took in my surrounds. The beautiful old house, the thick moist ferns, vine-tangled scrub and ironbark gums, the loud sawing of the crickets, the magical tinkling of the bellbirds and the hysterics of the kookaburras revived all my old Romantic fantasies. I was Turner and Constable and Blake, Géricault and Millet.

'Bloody birds,' said Verbero. 'We oughta get a cat.'

He seemed nervous as we came in sight of the house. It occurred to me that if Verbero was apprehensive, maybe I should be too.

No one came out to greet us. We climbed the rickety steps to the front door, which was open. Some bunker. Verbero showed me to a room that would be mine for however long it took to do what I'd come to do. It was plain but comfortable, with a wicker sofa and chairs, table, wardrobe and double bed with a mosquito net. One door led into the hallway, another onto a small bathroom and a third onto the verandah. Dropping my gear on the floor, I switched on the ceiling fan; groaning into action, it pushed the heavy air around. I pulled out my two t-shirts and hung them up in the wardrobe. I rattled the wire hangers. I put my toothbrush in the bathroom and washed my face. I scattered my few possessions around the room, threw my empty rucksack in a corner, tested the bed springs, went out onto the verandah and rolled a ciggie. In the background I could hear conversation, and just made out the voice of the prime minister. I'd read that British critics compared actors' voices to wine. Gielgud was a claret, and Irons a whisky. Destiny had a voice like cask riesling. Thin, cheap and a touch too sweet. I was to discover that it could be intoxicating, but the hangover vicious.

That hangover will be history in a little over one hour.

It was probably getting onto six o'clock when Verbero knocked on my door. He was accompanied by a young Aboriginal girl who he said would wash my clothes and bring my meals. This made me uneasy. When she reappeared about half an hour later carrying a tray with dinner—chops, spuds and two veg—I asked her how she came to be there. She bit her lip and rolled her eyes nervously at the ceiling. Following her gaze, I noticed the barely concealed eye of a video camera. She put down the tray and padded out on bare feet.

Unnerved, I shifted the table away from what I estimated was the range of the camera and sat down. I was too hungry to think clearly about the implications of what was happening to me. I prodded a spear of dull green broccoli with my fork. It was dead all right.

I was just wondering what the evening's entertainment would be when Verbero popped his head in the door.

'How was the tucker?' He seemed more at ease now.

'Tetsuya would be proud.'

He frowned, searching my sublimely innocent features for traces of mockery. 'Who's that?' he demanded. 'Some Jap fwiend of yours?'

I nodded. What could I say?

'And the digs?'

I said I felt like I'd landed in the middle of an Henri Rousseau painting. He gave me a blank look. I considered asking him about the video camera but thought it might be wiser not to let him know I'd discovered it.

He eased himself into the wicker chair in the corner of the room. His movements were smooth, yet there was a kind of wariness about them that put me on edge. 'She's vewy excited,' he informed me.

I looked at the floor. 'What if, you know, she doesn't like it?'

'Walker, if you're half as good as those two poofters say you are, then you're home 'n hosed. I wouldn't twy any funny stuff, mind you. None of that, whatchamacallit, clubbism.'

'Clubbism?'

'You know, weirdo stuff like that Picasso bloke was into.' He pronounced Picasso 'pick-*ass*-oh'. 'Two eyes on the same side of the nose, that sort of bullshit.'

'Cubism?'

'Yeah.' In one fluid gesture he snapped his fingers and pointed his forefinger at me. 'That's the one.'

I didn't sleep very well that night. Giant mosquitoes threw themselves at my mosquito net, trying to bash their way in. Occasionally one or two got through, just like the thoughts I was trying to keep at bay, about what ZakDot and Maddie would think if they knew where I was. I slapped and scratched, and put my hands over my ears.

The forest was noisier than an inner city warehouse full of artists. There were chirps and rustles and squeaks, rich squelchy sounds and crackling noises. The music of frogs and bats, bandicoots and bunyips. I slipped out the door that led from my room to the verandah and switched on an outside light. A moth with a half-metre-long wingspan flew out of the dark and hurled itself against the globe. My stomach churned at the sight. I turned the light off and the moth flapped around for a while, thudding into the window before returning to the forest.

I'd just managed to doze off when an explosive bark like that of a dog erupted from the trees, followed by a sound like someone screaming in distress. I jumped to my feet, terrified. Eventually I made out a pair of round yellow eyes in a nearby bloodwood. It was a barking owl. I was well and truly spooked now.

I'd stashed some whisky in my rucksack. I drank half the bottle. Above me the contracting tin roof popped and pinged like a John Cage symphony.

I was feeling seedy when, just on seven o'clock, a little Asian girl knocked on my door holding a tray with tea and Vegemite toast. I asked for a Panadol and this time it was a little Arabic-looking boy who brought me the tablet with a glass of water. Like the other two children, he looked uncomfortable when I asked him how he'd come to be working there. He didn't answer. I assumed their parents were employed by Destiny. Yet she had always been so dismissive of Aborigines and Asians and Arabs on account of the depth of their cultures and their attachment to them. Maybe there was another side to her that I didn't understand. I didn't feel up to the task of working it out at that moment. I had enough to do herding my brain cells into one paddock. I concentrated on organising my paints and brushes.

'How you feeling today?' Verbero poked his head in the door.

'My head's as furry as the inside of one of Meret Oppenheim's teacups,' I quipped.

'Who's this Oppenheim, another mate of yours then? Jewish fellow?' I'd forgotten that Clean Slate wasn't too keen on Jews either, their being responsible for such a big swathe of culture and all. I didn't say anything.

'Why doesn't he just put 'em in the washing machine?' Verbero persisted.

'I don't know,' I replied. 'I'll ask him next time I see him.'

'You can take the artist out of the slum,' he scoffed, 'but you can't take the slum out of the artist. Well, you weady or what?'

I gathered up my paints and things and followed him to a conservatory that had been built as an extension of the house. It was full of ferns and plants that gave the light a beautiful, dappled quality. It was like a miniature, safer version of the rainforest outside. Ceiling fans rotated, distributing the cool exhalations of the plants. In the centre of the room stood a brand new easel. Not a drop of paint had spilled on its polished frame. It looked like a movie prop. It faced a plain yellow sofa, not old but already faded by the sunlight.

I told Verbero I'd need a staple gun and a hammer and nails. Without taking his beady eyes off me, he punched a few numbers on his mobile. Minutes later a burly fellow in a bad suit who Verbero introduced to me as Destiny's personal bodyguard, Wayne, appeared with the tools. I set about making a stretcher and tacking the canvas to it. Wayne, Verbero, and two federal agents who'd been slouching in opposite corners of the room, huddled round, peering over my shoulder. The agents murmured observations about my activities into their wrists, cocking their heads to hear each other's answer in their earpieces. The attention thrilled me. I fantasised that I was Gentileschi or some other Renaissance master working on a grand commission for the church, surrounded by lackeys who would mix my paints and tend to my needs while I concentrated on my masterpiece. 'I'd like a coffee,' I said, without looking up. 'Black. Two sugars. Espresso if you have it.'

'You're pushing it,' Verbero muttered. He nodded at one of the others, who reappeared with a steaming mug of instant.

I suppose, when they were on commissions in the sticks, the Renaissance masters found it hard to get a good coffee as well. I put the mug down on the floor at my feet. I felt impor-tant, professional.

A hush fell over the room. I could hear the leather of the men's shoes squeak and the cloth of their suit jackets swish as they stood to attention. Deliberately, I kept at my task, though my heart was racing. High heels clicked across the tiled floor, stopping just centimetres from where I squatted. I had one more corner of the canvas to go. I pulled the cloth tight over the frame. The staple gun exploded into the silence. When I finally looked up, it was at a pair of shapely female calves encased in nylon stockings. I stood up, brushed my hands on my trousers and shook the proffered hand, which was little, smooth and soft. 'Prime Minister,' I said.

'Call me Destiny?' she said. 'I've just had highlights put through my hair? Reckon you'll be able to work 'em in?'

# Narrative
## art

Destiny was wearing a blue shirt-waisted frock with short sleeves. Her arms were firm but not muscular. Her legs were gorgeous, and her neck long and soft, and only faintly ring-barked by age. She had extremely direct eyes.

I explained my approach to portrait painting, which draws upon the formalistic techniques of the old masters and yet has strong elements of the contemporary as well. She nodded blankly; I could see she wasn't the sharpest knife in the drawer. The men exchanged glances and one of the feds whispered something into his wrist. I told her that I'd start by doing sketches in various media.

Destiny looked worried. Her forehead knotted. 'I'd rather keep the media out of it? You know, just do it confidential-like for now?'

I explained.

'Oh?' she said, biting her lip.

'I'd like to begin sketching now, if you don't mind.'

Verbero snickered at this. 'Do you want to come

up and see my sketchings?' he chortled. All the men laughed with him: 'huhhuhhuhhuh'.

'That's etchings,' I corrected. Verbero's smile dried up like gouache.

I invited Destiny to sit down on the sofa and make herself comfortable. I dragged a stool to a position about two metres in front of her and, sketchpad in my lap, studied her moon-like face with its smooth forehead, guileless eyes, thin nose and small, serious mouth. As my pencil started to move over the paper, Verbero positioned himself at my back. I could hear the breath whistling past his nostril hairs and the steady grinding of his teeth.

'Do you mind?' I said, after I could take it no longer.

'Just making sure there's no funny business.'

I put down my pencil. 'I can't work with you standing there.'

'Do something useful, V,' Destiny ordered.

Verbero scowled and retreated to a corner of the room, where he worried the fronds of a fern until his mobile rang. He scurried off to answer the call in private.

Destiny flung herself with verve into the task of posing. She vamped, she pouted, she slung her shapely legs this way and that. If she weren't the prime minister and the nation's most notorious artist-hater I'd even have said she was flirting with me.

'It's actually called *sitting* for a portrait,' I pointed out. 'It would be more helpful if you would pick one pose, something comfortable and natural, and hold it. It's not a shoot for *Vogue.*' I felt powerful. Destiny, looking chastened, settled, patted her sleek hair and stretched her lips into a smile.

'It's going to be hard to hold that smile,' I warned her. 'You might as well just relax.'

The smile melted.

At last, I could begin in earnest. As I've mentioned, the first time I saw her, she struck me as looking like Ingres' *Odalisque,* and later like Jules Bastien-Lepage's peasant girl. I'd seen her face hundreds of times since, on TV and in the papers. Now, as I studied her in person, she seemed to grow amorphous, intangible. I squeezed my eyes shut and looked at her again. Her features dissolved, reformed, dissolved again. I couldn't get a fix. I could feel beads of sweat forming on my brow and upper lip. I crumpled up the paper and started again. I mentally reviewed all the rules of perspective and proportion and the mapping of faces. I switched to charcoal, then pastels, then pen and ink.

I began to wonder if I wasn't blocking her out of political antipathy. But the truth was, while I hadn't expected to like her, I found I didn't dislike her either. I couldn't work out what was going wrong. I put my pen down with a sigh of frustration. She looked startled at this and I realised she was even more nervous than I was. I must have smiled or something, for at that instant she beamed at me. I frowned, confused, and she retreated behind her eyes. She was eerily like a sponge, soaking up every emotion I threw her way.

A veritable Thredbo of discarded sketches rose from the floor near my feet. I glanced over at Verbero, who was smirking.

It finally dawned on me what the problem was. Most of us are born into or choose some form of cultural identity. I could've easily painted a cattle station owner, with eyes used to looking straight at the horizon, the practical hands, the leathery skin. I'd have no trouble painting Maddie, the warrior princess, or ZakDot, a walking installation in search of inspiration, or the angular Lynda, or Oscar, for whom camp was a place you spent your whole life, or Thurston, big and awkward, yet shining in his armour. Destiny, by contrast, had worked so hard at denying culture—any culture—an entry into her soul that she appeared to have become the clean slate of her party's title.

To paint her I needed to understand her. I asked her to tell me something about her childhood, her interests, her life both in and out of politics. This is when she told me about her mum and dad and her own brief career as an artist, her marriage, and how she'd plunged herself into saving the nation.

She related her misadventures in parliament, the tension in the Cabinet Room, the terrifying encounters with the press, the quiet time in the Meditation Room, the way that *Cap d'Antibes* had jolted her, and how, sitting among the Historic Memorials, she'd awoken to the power of portraiture—and art. As she spoke in that cask riesling voice, her features clarified and settled, and my sketches came to life. I stopped crumpling them up. I'd sussed it.

Destiny belonged to a culture all right. The culture of the anti-culture, which had always lurked beneath our art-soaked obsessions. It was a culture which over the years had put down deep roots in sandy soil, even if people like me had been blissfully—or perhaps just stubbornly—oblivious to it. When a few years back one of the richest art prizes went to someone who'd glued a printout from the website of a real estate agency over a cheesy landscape purchased at a garage sale, I'd bristled at what I saw as an insult to true art.

The members of the anti-culture saw it as an insult to everyone. They fretted about what other people might think of our little country, forgetting that other people didn't think of it at all.

What Destiny, sensitive and spongelike, had done was to soak up our subterranean anxieties, our geographical uncertainty, the cultural cringe that was the flip side of cultural pride. She was the distillation of our collective disquiet.

I had her. I worked madly, not stopping till I'd completed half a dozen detailed studies. Laying down the sketchbook, I stood up to stretch.

'Can I see?' she asked, eager as a child.

'Sure.'

She examined the drawings with great interest, touching my arm lightly with her nails as she did so. She smelled of lemon.

I told her I'd probably do another day or two of sketching and then begin work on the painting.

By the third day I began to get used to the pattern of it, the dense jungle nights that gave me heavy, sensual dreams, the mysterious presence of the sad little children, the malignant ubiquity of Verbero and the hypnotic hours at my easel with Destiny. There was little to remind me of the world outside. Occasionally, Verbero interrupted our sessions to discuss some piece of urgent political business with Destiny, but parliament was in recess and the little country, being smack in the middle of nowhere and directly on the periphery of everything, didn't generate an awful lot of urgent political business.

The evenings were long and still. The mournful children brought up my dinner on a tray each night and then hurried away before I could talk to them. There was no television, no radio. I passed the first few evenings just smoking on the verandah, gazing into the forest and thinking. For some reason, Trimalkyo's face kept floating up before my eyes. Something nagged me about him. I also thought about ZakDot and Maddie and Thurston and occasionally even Grevillea Bent. I cursed myself for not bringing some light reading. Me and my fucking second-hand classics.

One evening, bored, I picked up the *Satyricon*. With a sigh of resignation, I curled up on my bed with the book. I was soon absorbed by it. Turning the page, I felt a chill run up my spine. I had come to a section called 'Trimalchio's Dinner'.

The narrator describes Trimalchio as a rich and uncouth man who desperately wants to be known as cultured, who treats his guests to an astounding feast, bad jokes and mis-quotations of Homer. Trimalchio's wife is present, but he's clearly far more interested in his slave boys. Could 'Trimalkyo' be an alias, I wondered. If it was, I reflected, it was an odd one for an art dealer to adopt. There was an element of self-mockery there that I couldn't reconcile with my image of Trimalkyo. I turned to the translator's introduction, which I'd skipped. It talked about the author's difficult relationship with the emperor Nero, for whom the character Trimalchio was apparently a cipher.

Thinking back on that now, my hair stands on end. Earlier, when Verbero told me that the party's theme was Roman decadence, it hadn't clicked. Didn't he say that Trimalkyo was dressed as Nero? Had Trimalkyo always intended to fiddle while Rome, or at least the *Dinkum*, burned?

One afternoon, she dismissed the feds.

'What'd you do that for?' Verbero accused. 'There are secuwity issues, you know. Stop gawping,' he added for my benefit. 'You're one of 'em.'

'Artists are sooo dangerous,' I mocked him. 'I'm surprised you're not wearing a Situationist-proof vest.'

He raised his fist.

'V?' She put a hand on his arm. I felt unreasonably jealous. 'Go devise a taxation policy or something.'

Verbero narrowed his eyes at me.

Once we were alone, she surprised me by asking, 'What do you think about culture, Miles?'

'What do you mean?' I was wary of a trap.

'Well, like, is it important to people?'

'I think so. It's important to me, anyway.'

She beckoned me over and patted the cushions of the sofa. 'Please explain?' I recalled another woman politician who had used those words. I recoiled.

'I really want to know? Please?'

'All right.' I wiped my hands on my trousers and sat on the sofa, not too close to Destiny but not too far away either. I smiled uncertainly at her. She smiled uncertainly back. Ringing a bell, she got a little Aboriginal girl to get us some G&Ts.

Maybe it was the languid environment, maybe the isolation, maybe just the sheer absurdity of it all. Sitting cross-legged on the end of the yellow sofa, sipping from a tall glass, faced with this eager listener who also happened to be our prime minister, it all poured out. I told Destiny how I felt creativity was at the very heart and soul of what it meant to be human, how culture was humanity's legacy to itself. How great art and literature and dance and music expanded the boundaries of our minds and excited our senses. I talked to her about all the artists who have had an influence on me, from Caravaggio to Frida Kahlo and Odd Nerdrum and Jenny Saville, and about other artists whose work I appreciate even though it's quite different from my own, like Howard Arkley and Andy Goldsworthy.

'Those blokes which you talk about? I ain't heard of most of 'em?' she remarked dubiously.

'That's all right,' I retorted. 'They're not all blokes. And most of them haven't heard of you either.'

Her face darkened. Now I'd done it; I'd gone too far. She reached out and, for one tense moment, I expected her to slap me. Instead, she stroked my hair; I could feel her long nails scratching my scalp. Goose bumps rose on my legs and arms. 'Fair enough, too?' she chuckled. 'You know, Miles, you're funny? And you're smart? I like you?'

'I'd better get back to it,' I mumbled, my throat suddenly dry. I jumped up and raced back to the safe place behind my easel, blushing, mixing pigments furiously.

This became our new routine. Every day, after a few hours of painting, she'd shut the others out and we'd talk. Or rather, I'd talk, and she'd listen. She was a good listener. I was flattered. No one had ever listened to me with such attention before.

She'd still occasionally come out with the most outrageous

statements. 'You know the Sixteenth Chapel?' she asked once. 'In, like, overseas? With those paintings all over the ceiling?'

I nodded. She must have meant the Sistine Chapel. I tried not to smile.

'That's one of those things about art I don't get? No one would've looked up if it weren't for the paintings by Michael, Michael…'

'…angelo?' I prompted.

'Yeah, Angelo. If it weren't for Angelo, everyone would look straight ahead and see where they're going? Art makes you look in different directions than you would normally? And sometimes it's impractical? I mean, if everyone's looking up? And no one's looking where they're going? They bump into each other?'

She had a point. 'I'll buy that,' I said.

'You can't buy it? It's just an opinion?'

Another week or so and I began to think that I had never been anywhere else. Sometimes, sitting on my verandah at night, I tried to regain my perspective on things. To remember how outraged we all were when Destiny got into power. How we'd laughed at her. My life in Sydney became as distant as the vanishing point in an exercise in perspective.

The portrait was coming along well. I was enjoying myself. I love the process of painting, the intoxicating smells, the small whispers of the brush against the canvas, the way a picture grows and blooms before your eyes. That's what it was all really about, anyway, wasn't it? I mean, who cares who the Mona Lisa was, anyway? The point is, she and Leonardo will both live forever.

Back in my room, at night, I could still detect a faint citrusy scent.

I suppose it was inevitable.

'Can I come in?' She was in by the time she asked. It was late, and I was already in bed, lights off, trying to conjure up Grevillea Bent's ankles. I sat up, pulling the bed sheets up to my neck, hoping she hadn't noticed what I was doing. Little Miles was on full alert. I brought my knees up to my chest, hoping the bugger would calm down, but he seemed happily intrigued by this unexpected visit.

To my alarm, Destiny sat down on the edge of the bed. I reached over to turn on the bedside lamp, but she stayed my hand with her own. Her skin looked luminescent in the moonlight. I realised with a jolt that she was wearing nothing but a silk nightie.

From the moment I realised it was Destiny knocking on my door, I knew it had the word 'wrong' written all over it. Not just 'wrong', either. 'Disastrous' and 'big trouble' were also etched in giant, flashing neon letters. Unfortunately, unlike his purported master, Little Miles was functionally illiterate. Little Miles was starved for attention. Little Miles had yearned to play with ZakDot and Maddie the night of the piercing lock, and with ZakDot when I got home from Oscar's that time, and with Sativa and Grevillea and, all right, I admit it, Lynda and Julia and about two per cent of the male and fifty per cent of the female population the rest of the time. And I'd always stopped him. Well, Little Miles was not going to be stopped this time. Little Miles barrelled straight past all the warning signs and saw the only word he recognised:

S-E-X. Little Miles, if no judge of character, had an excellent eye for opportunity.

And when the prime minister is pulling her nightie off right in front of you, and she pauses with her hands over her head, the nightie held as though binding her wrists together, and you can see the soft curves of her flesh and the rounded swell of her breasts and the soft hint of hair under her arms and the glistening between her thighs, and her big brown eyes are fixed on you with a look of total adoration, well, it's some sort of opportunity.

And when she lifts the mosquito netting and slips inside, and takes that nightie and puts it behind your neck and pulls your face up to hers and teases the tips of your eyelashes with her tongue and nibbles on your cheeks and when you find that your hands are roaming over her breasts and the smooth skin of her stomach and tickling their way through the curly hairs of her pubis, and she shifts her position to open her thighs wider and you slide your fingers over the slippery folds of her labia and into her warm wet depths and she is reaching for your erect cock with first her hand and then her mouth, and her hair cascades over your thighs, well, by then, it's an opportunity you are not going to pass up.

'You know,' she said in a little voice as I urged her ankles up over my shoulders, 'I've never had an organism?'

I stopped thrusting.

'My teacher at art school? The bloke which I told you about? He said that art is inseparable from desire? I reckon I've been a bit suspicious of desire ever since?' Looking down at her, I noticed her eyes had gone sad. Little Miles did not like the idea of either intellectual exchange or emotional drama at this point. He called time out.

Although I didn't actually have a lot of sexual experience, I had given the subject of sex a lot of thought over the years. It was a matter of pride to go where no man—apparently, in this case—had gone before. But when I lowered my head to her mound, she squirmed so violently and I had to bounce around so much to keep up with her moving target that the bed gave way and we tumbled with a crash to the floor, dragging the bed sheets and the mosquito netting after us. Within seconds, there was a rap on the door.

'Walker. Fuck are you doing in there?'

I froze at the sound of Verbero's voice. I was fucking the prime minister. I was certifiably insane. Outside, insects shrieked, filling the silence.

Destiny looked at me, eyes wide, finger to her lips. I took a deep breath. 'Nothing. Just, uh, rearranging some furniture.'

'Wee-a-wanging furniture? In the middle of the night?'

'I couldn't sleep.'

There was no answer. After a while, I heard his footsteps recede down the hall and his door close. It was the sensible time to call a halt to the whole thing, to say that it was all a terrible mistake and that we should just forget it ever happened. 'Now then,' I whispered. 'Where were we?'

Very quietly, we tugged the mattress all the way down onto the floor. She lay back and opened her legs. I pinned her hands by her sides, and pressed down on her legs with my body to keep her still. As she bit her lips to keep from moaning, I fattened my tongue against her swollen vulva, licking her juices, sucking on her clit. Destiny turned out to be immune neither to desire nor its fulfilment. There was hope yet for art, I thought to myself.

I'd be a liar if I said it wasn't fun. It was an incredible thrill to fuck Destiny and help her achieve her first 'organism'. And her second and third. Afterwards, I was as floppy as a Claes Oldenburg. Even as I lay there, deliquescent, one part of my brain, not the part of which I'm most proud, mind you, was standing up and hooting, 'Cor, Miles, you got your leg over the prime bloody minister!'

What happened next helped me regain my sense of perspective.

# The thing     is

'The thing is,' she said, as she lay with her head on my chest, her hair tickling my armpits, 'I don't get why youse have to get so carried away, right?'

I was just on the verge of dozing off. The tone of her voice alarmed me. 'Sorry?' I said sleepily, raising my heavy head to look at her. 'Who're you talking about?'

'You know. Artists, writers, musicians?' she said. 'If I'm looking at a picture of a fish, right? I want it to look like a picture of a fish? Not some explosion in an Eye-tie delicatessen? And, like, poetry? I don't get it. I mean, me mum always told me, if you're gonna say something, say it straight? Say it so it can be understood, right?'

I was treated to a torrent of opinion on culture and the arts and the people who practised them that ranged from offensive to bizarre and back to offensive again. The screams of the barking owl sounded sweet by comparison. Had I flattered myself that my conversations with her had made some difference to her way of thinking? Was I so needy for sex that I didn't care?

I now know that, if I'd paid more attention, I'd have realised she was testing not me but herself. I couldn't hear it at the time. I felt ill. I thought guiltily of ZakDot and Maddie and the others, fighting the righteous fight while I was sleeping with the enemy. How could I? I wished I was able to place the blame entirely on Little Miles.

'Look, Destiny,' I gulped, untangling myself from her and snaking toward the edge of the mattress. 'This isn't going to work.'

'Why not?' She suddenly looked older, tired, mean. She squinted at me and faint lines crawled down from the corners of her mouth.

How could I explain? 'No woman can compete with art for my devotion.' Jesus, I was a git. 'I'm sorry,' I mumbled, grabbing a towel and rushing into the bathroom. I barred the door and leaned against it for a moment, catching my breath. Then I leapt into the shower and scrubbed myself with a facecloth till my skin was raw. I even shampooed my hair, which was so surprised at being washed twice in one season that it stood up and practically applauded. When I emerged, she'd gone.

The sheets smelled of sex. It took me ages to fall asleep.

I woke up alone on the mattress on the floor, wretched, conflicted. I couldn't bear the thought of going to the conservatory. I inspected the bed frame and discovered that we hadn't actually broken the slats, just displaced them, so I reconstructed the bed and then crawled into it. I found a pale blue ribbon on my pillow. It was from Destiny's nightie. I wound it around my finger, over and over, trying to come up with a credible story for Verbero who, I knew, would be knocking on the door any moment now.

As he did.

From the way he stood there grinding his teeth and twisting his rings around his fingers I could see he was coked off his tits as usual. But there was something more going on. He was vibrating like one of Len Lye's kinetic sculptures.

'Fuck are you doing?' he demanded as I cowered under the sheet, sweating convincingly. 'You're supposed to be down there.'

'I think I'm coming down with a wog,' I mumbled, wiping my forehead with the back of my hand and trying to raise a cough to illustrate the point.

Verbero studied me, hostility written all over his features. 'You taking the piss?' he asked. He sniffed, and his sinuses rearranged themselves loudly and wetly.

I shook my head.

'Get one thing stwaight, Walker,' he rasped. 'You're here to paint Destiny's poor twit. That's it. Full stop.'

'Yeah, well, I don't feel well,' I countered. 'I'm taking a sickie.'

'You felt well enough last night,' he shot back.

Guilt and fear wrapped themselves around my throat and stomach like an installation by Christo. 'What are you talking about?' I croaked, now feeling genuinely sick. It struck me that I might have taken Verbero's place in Destiny's bed. I didn't want to consider the implications of that.

'Get your clothes on, you fucken pwick. We'll expect you down there in five.' He looked as though he wanted to say something else, but decided against it. He left, slamming the door behind him. I was shocked. This was the first time he'd called me a 'pwick'. Obviously, it wouldn't be the last.

I considered my options. They were not many. When I got

down there, Destiny was already seated on the sofa. Searching her face for some sign of emotion, I found none. The ideal resolution would be for me just to get on with it, finish the painting and get the fuck out of there. I was nearly done anyway. No one would ever have to know what had happened, it would never happen again and that would be that.

It seemed that these were her thoughts as well, for after lunch she didn't dismiss the others as usual. An hour or so into the afternoon sitting, she said she felt like a kip and told me to take the rest of the afternoon off.

It was hot, and I wished, not for the first time, that there was a pool in the yard. A nice, safe, chlorinated, fauna-free pool. In the forest there was that creek, which, if you followed it far enough, led to a beautiful, refreshingly cold watering hole, but you had to take salt or matches for the leeches, and the spiders and snakes made me nervous, even when I didn't see any. Especially when I didn't see any. Once a wallaby hopped out of the bush and nearly scared me sense-less. I took a walk to the landing strip and looked up, wishing for aeroplanes.

I felt fragmented, strung out: Braque meets Giacometti.

I missed my mum and ZakDot and Maddie and even Thurston. I wondered, pathetically, if Grevillea Bent ever thought of me.

There were no aeroplanes. I returned to the house. Climbing the stairs, I noticed that the door to my room was ajar, which was funny, as I always closed it when I was out. Trying not to make a sound, I crept up to the doorway. Verbero was crouching in the corner where my bag was. He jumped up when he heard me coming.

'What's going on?' I accused.

'Thought I saw a mouse,' he mumbled, crabbing sideways out of the room.

Yeah, and I *knew* I saw a rat. Well, if he were looking for anything, the joke was on him. My bag was empty. My total assets came to about twenty-five dollars, and that was stashed in the pocket of my cardie, which hung uselessly in the closet—trust me to take a cardigan to Queensland in the summer. I checked the cardie. The money was all there. It was depressing to think that, on top of everything else, Verbero was trying to steal from me. I closed the door and flopped down on the bed, blue as Yves Klein. Rolling over, I listened to my stomach growl. I'd been ostentatiously off my food all day, as part of my sick act. Now I regretted it. I could grab something from the kitchen, but I didn't want to leave my room.

There was a rap on the door.

I held my breath.

The door creaked open. I sat up.

'Destiny. I don't think this is a good...'

'Let's not talk about it now?' Plopping down next to me, she reached out to stroke my hair. I wriggled away. She looked hurt. 'I know what they say about me, you know?' she said quietly.

'What's that?'

'That I'm a philistine?'

'Now why would they say that?'

'I don't know?' she replied. 'I mean, I've never even been to the Middle East?'

I coughed.

'You really aren't feeling well, are you?' She frowned. 'Bloody Verbero? He insisted you were wagging, but I didn't believe him? I know what you need?' she said decisively, rose and walked out of the room.

A few minutes later, she came back in followed by a little Indonesian girl holding a tray with two tins of Fourex and a pile of steaming pies with tomato sauce.

'This'll set you right?' She cracked one of the tinnies for herself. 'That's what always fixed up me dad when he was crook?'

I smiled. 'Yum. Just what the doctor ordered.' I cracked the other tinny, and tapped it against hers.

As I smothered a pie with sauce, I remarked, 'Ah, the food culture of our country at its best.'

She regarded me with disbelief. 'What d'ya mean? How can this be *culture?*' She looked mistrustfully at her pie. 'I mean, it's just good Strayun tucker? Nothing to do with culture?'

I reached for another pie. 'I suppose not,' I shrugged. I refused to be responsible for the banning of meat pies.

There was a pause. 'Do you think my opinions are ignorant?' Her voice had gone very small.

'Frankly, yes.' It felt like a risky thing to say, but I wasn't a good enough liar to answer otherwise.

She nodded, biting her lips. She didn't stay long, and kept her hands to herself. There was a part of me, not solely restricted to the vicinity of Little Miles, that felt unaccountably sad at this.

The next morning, I ventured down to the conservatory in an apprehensive mood and hungry, too. There had been no breakfast. When I arrived, Verbero was pacing up and down the room, making it small. 'When's this bloody thing gonna be finished?' he accosted me. 'It's almost Chwistmas for Chwist's sake.'

It was actually about two brushstrokes away from being finished but I was perverse enough not to want to tell Verbero that. 'I'm working in oils. They dry slowly.'

'What's the good of 'em then? Haven't they invented something that dries fast yet?' He was growing splenetic.

Truth was, I was thinking about Christmas too. My mum was probably wondering whether I'd be coming home. If she'd called the warehouse, they'd have told her—shit, what *would* they have told her?

'I need to use a phone.'

'There aren't any,' he hissed.

'How about your mobile?'

His hand flew protectively to where it sat clipped on his belt. 'National emergencies only.'

'Forget it,' I said, picking up my brush and adding what I realised was probably a final touch. I painted with excruciating slowness, for Verbero's benefit. I was as keen to finish as he was to see the back of me.

I sat down in front of my easel and studied my work while waiting for Destiny to arrive. If I say so myself, it was looking good. The expression in her face was fantastic. Her eyes burned with a kind of crazy innocence. Not unlike mine, I was taken aback to realise one night when I looked in the mirror. Except for the corner that I'd left, as was my wont, at the stage of underpainting, the painting was done.

Destiny entered, looking pleased with herself. 'Thought we'd have breakfast down here for a change,' she said. 'Hope you don't mind.' Following her was a little white girl in a smart black dress and tiny Doc Martens boots, a row of tiny silver hoops piercing one ear. On the tray she carried were three mugs of coffee, a pitcher of juice and, instead of the usual Vegemite toast or Weet-Bix, a pile of croissants.

'Croy-sants?' pronounced Destiny proudly. 'Thought we'd get some more food culture around here.'

I smiled wanly, though the croissants did look good. 'Destiny,' I said. 'I have to ask you something.'

'Shoot?' She spread her butter over the top of the croissant. Verbero, observing her, followed suit.

'What's with the children?'

'That one,' she said, as the little girl closed the door behind her, 'is the child of inner-city cappuccino-sipping elite? The others are the children of ethnic minorities with long cultural traditions? We've, uh, I think *stolen* is too loaded a word? We've borrowed 'em from their families in order to try and raise a new generation of citizens unburdened by culture?'

I almost choked on my croissant.

'Maybe we were a bit rash? But it's well-intentioned? What? Don't you like croy-sants?' she asked, disappointment in her voice. 'Why aren't you eating? Something wrong?'

What was wrong was me. I'd imagined myself a court painter and found I'd become the court jester. From Last Art Hero to First Art Traitor.

I desperately needed to see ZakDot and Maddie, to fall to my knees, to beg their forgiveness, to get as far away as possible from Destiny and her stupid, cockamamie ideas. I felt more contaminated than Homebush and twice as toxic.

I leapt up and started packing up my paints. 'I'm sorry,' I mumbled. 'I have to go.'

'I see?' Destiny said coolly, putting a half-eaten croissant back down on her plate. 'And where would you be going?'

'Back to Sydney.' I pined for my mother and my friends. 'I'd like to spend Christmas with my family.'

Destiny and Verbero exchanged glances. Destiny raised her chin defiantly as she spoke. 'I'd rather hoped you thought of us as family, Miles?' The cask riesling soured, turned to vinegar.

I swallowed.

She disappeared to that spot behind her eyes. 'And how are you planning to get there then?'

'Yeah,' said Verbero, leaning back in his chair and pressing some sort of button on the wall that I'd never noticed before. 'How *are* you planning to get there?'

Two things occurred to me. One, that they were not asking in order to organise a flight. Two, that I hadn't a clue where I was. There was nothing but rainforest for miles around.

I had about three and a half seconds to consider my options before Wayne burst into the room with an assault weapon. I had a vision of myself as a figure from the volume of Gray's *Anatomy* that I'd studied for life drawing classes. I was a collection of puncturable organs and tearable flesh arranged around an easily damaged skeleton, all held in, along with my blood, by a very thin membrane known as skin. Then, for one surreal moment, I felt like laughing—Thurston and his crazy formula. I'd done it!

To be perfectly honest, I pissed myself. There's a diffeence between an art hero and a regular hero and I never claimed to be the latter. Little Miles, correctly assessing the situation for once, tried to make himself as small and inconspicuous as possible, something he ought to have done right from the start around Destiny.

Her face was a frozen mask of hurt and defiance. 'I thought you might pull something like this,' she said. 'You are, after all, an *artist*.'

I shifted my gaze to the barrel of the gun. It seemed safer.

After what seemed like an interminable pause, she told Wayne to lower his weapon. Disappointment carved itself into his dumb, meaty face.

'You'll finish the painting?' she said, her expression impenetrable, her lips quivering. It wasn't a question.

'It's finished.'

Verbero exploded in a harsh laugh. He pointed to the unfinished corner.

'That's a trademark of my style,' I explained miserably. I was uncomfortable where piss had run down my leg. 'It's a statement on the impossibility of closure.' They looked dubious but, Destiny signalled for Wayne to leave. Thank you, Cynthia. I'd never appreciated the importance of theory before.

Verbero's mobile rang. 'Yes,' he barked. He frowned, and then handed the phone to Destiny. She walked out of the room with it.

When she returned, she seemed more composed. She handed back the phone. 'Trimalkyo wants to know how everything is going?' She glanced at me. 'I said it was going good? He's invited us to celebrate with him at a party on the harbour on New Year's Eve? On the *Dinkum*?'

'You didn't accept.' This from Verbero. He looked like she'd told him he'd won a holiday for two to Kosovo.

'I did?'

'Have you lost your mind? It'll be a fucking love boat full of artists and poofs.'

Destiny drew herself up.

I looked from one to the other. I hadn't a clue what was going on.

'I said we'd go and that's that?' She'd been doing some thinking and she'd decided that New Year's Eve would be a perfect occasion to tell the world just what she'd been thinking about. I didn't know that then, of course.

'I'll have to keep me date to the wall all night,' Verbero grumbled.

As she gathered her troops and swept out of the room, Destiny turned and offered me a wan smile. 'You're invited too, by the way?'

'I hate New Year's parties,' I said.

I had no idea how much I could hate a New Year's party before tonight.

'You'll be there?' were her parting words.

That night, I tossed and turned, thinking Destiny might barge in at any moment. I dozed off, only to dream about a tap-dancing jester like the one in Barrie Kosky's *King Lear*. The taps of my dream-jester beat an insistent tattoo across the stage of my nightmare. Someone was rapping on my window.

What now?

I assumed it was Destiny, not wanting to attract Verbero's attention by knocking on the door. I didn't think I could take any more of Destiny at that moment. I pretended to be asleep. Then I heard the window open. There was a quiet thud of bare feet on the floorboards and a feral pong like I'd never smelled before. My heart raced. I forced my eyes open and, as they grew accustomed to the dark, I made out the figure of a muscular woman, probably in her forties, her skin as dark as gumnuts and leathery as an old saddle, her hair wild and dreadlocked. She was stark naked except for a roughly woven hemp belt that circled her waist and from which dangled a bowie knife and the bloody legs of a freshly killed boar.

# Primitivism

'Who are you?' I gasped. Sitting up in bed, I clutched the sheet to my chest, shivering though it wasn't cold. I'd meant it when I told Thurston that living dangerously wasn't my style.

Ignoring my question, the female savage gestured towards the window with her chin.

'Hold on a tick,' I squeaked. She stared at me while I dressed. I was self-conscious of my pale thin body, wishing she would look away, though some-how unable to ask, as I pulled on my trousers. Little Miles was doing his best to become a vagina. My visitor picked up my rucksack and bunged it over at me.

Whatever else this was all about, it looked like I was about to escape this lunatic asylum, and I was all for that. I grabbed my clothes from where they lay strewn about the room and threw them into my bag. 'I need to get my paints,' I said. She grabbed me by the ear and twisted. Mourning my beautiful new brushes, I followed her out onto the verandah and into the forest. She let go of my ear.

She moved effortlessly through the bush. Me, I was always stumbling over roots or having to untangle my clothes from where they'd snagged on a branch. The feel of a spider web wrapping itself over my face sent me into a panic. She watched, smiling, as I flailed about pulling it off, slapping away imaginary spiders. Another time, she stopped short and put out a hand to keep me from moving. A two-metre taipan slithered across our path. I decided I hated nature. I missed the bricks and concrete and bitumen of Chippo. I hoped we were headed in that direction.

Just as I thought I couldn't take it anymore, when I was so tired and footsore I felt like weeping, the sky began to lighten. She bent down and sniffed the trail. The birds chose this moment to explode into song. I was overcome with a sense of wonder.

She looked up into the air and made silent calculations. A quarter of an hour later, as dawn's grey light slowly restored colour to the world, we came into a clearing. I was startled to see another half-dozen naked Amazons, all just as crusty as my new friend. Several were still asleep, or just waking. Two had risen and were making a fire. They grunted at our arrival. My guide untied the boar's legs from her belt and flung them at her sisters, who caught them and chucked them straight onto the fire. No one said a word.

Overwhelmed, exhausted and feeling shy and useless, I sat down a little out of the way on a fallen eucalypt. I untied my bootlaces and eased my aching feet out of the hot leather. I peeled off my socks and examined my blisters, which didn't look half as bad as they felt. All the women were up now, scratching and yawning and stretching, and picking brambles out of their matted hair. There was a small, perfect creek nearby, its water delightfully cold and clear. After they'd washed their faces, I dipped my feet in and splashed my face and neck and chest. I drank from it as well. Maybe I still could be a Romantic painter after all. I stayed at the creek for a while, enjoying the cool trickle of water between my toes.

Soon the meat was done. I watched as the women pulled out their knives and carved the flesh off the bone, before stuffing huge chunks of it into their mouths. My hunger overcame my revulsion and, seeing them signal me to come over and join them for breakfast, I didn't hesitate.

Chewing on the charred flesh, trying to keep my eyes off their tits and vulvas, which their habit of squatting tended alarmingly to expose, I could feel Little Miles stirring. Down, down, I commanded him. He'd gotten us into enough trouble already.

The women looked at me, and then at each other, licking their lips and wiping their greasy hands on their muscular thighs. 'Do you mind if I ask who you are and what this is all about?' My words, slow and awkward, hung in the air like stringy pieces of bark. I started again. 'My name is Miles. What are your names?' A great roll of cackling laughter erupted from a kookaburra perched in a nearby tree.

The leader was crusty as old bread, with a tangled mane of grey-streaked black hair, but almost magnetically attractive, with fierce brown eyes and cheekbones you could—well, cut a slice of meat off a boar's leg with. 'No names,' she ejaculated, tossing back her hair.

'What do you want from me? If you don't mind my asking.'

She began to laugh, a big throaty chuckle that grew to a roar and spread like bushfire through the group. For one delirious moment, I imagined that they had kidnapped me for sex. Despite my exhaustion and misgivings—when would any of them have had a bath last, 1970?—Little Miles was priming and stretching himself. Little Miles simply did not share in my high ideals of love, or even understand the concept of a quiet, contemplative life. But not even Little Miles could keep me awake. I have a misty recollection of collapsing sideways onto the ground. The next thing I knew one of the women was prodding me awake.

My back was sore and I was covered in mosquito bites. A fat leech was hanging off my knee. I was bone tired and couldn't believe we were on the move again. This time, I had the whole tribe to mock me for my problems with invisible spiders.

I don't know how far we travelled. We tended to keep to the woods and avoid the towns, probably a wise choice given my lady friends' fashion sense. Well past midnight a few nights later, we arrived at a horse stud. I was exhausted. I was also scratched up from crawling through lantana and running through the woods. I was nervous about knocking on the door of a country home that late. The owners, two women, didn't seem fazed in the least when they opened the door to us, as if it were perfectly normal for a tribe of naked feral women to deliver a bewildered young man to their door in the middle of the night. After we waved goodbye to the No Names, and I'd splashed some water on my face and washed my hands, they made me tea and gave me Christmas leftovers. When did Christmas happen? I felt disoriented. They invited me to crash in the spare room, but I was desperate to get back to Sydney, and the bus down south, they'd already told me, picked up in town in a couple of hours. Their car was broken but we could ride to the bus stop. All the horses on the farm, they explained, were named after artists and writers and musicians. They saddled up Artemisia for me and we trotted together through the dark into town and the bus stop. When the bus came, they waved goodbye to me, Claudel and Kozic stamping their hoofs in the dust.

I can't believe that was only the night before last.

It was a long bus ride. Over fourteen hours. I intended to use the time to work through everything that had happened to me and sort things out and maybe even come up with a plan for dealing with, if not the rest of my life, at least the next day or two. I conked out the moment the bus started moving and awoke to discover we were already pulling into one of the bays outside of Central Station. The old sandstone façade of the station glowed in the soft, early evening light. It was a beautiful sight.

Slinging my rucksack over my shoulder, I headed for the warehouse. As it turned out, I wasn't the only one going in that direction.

Verbero's back. He goes into the toilet. He seems in a jolly mood. 'Thanks for bwinging this down to Sydney for me, by the way. Mucho appweciated, sucker. Ack ack ack.'

So it's true. He's got the bag. That means he—or rather, his men—returned to the warehouse after…But I've been through this line of thought. Maddie and ZakDot are on the boat, right? That means they're okay. That just leaves…

Thurston. Oh shit. Loyal Thurston. You can only surprise someone with a broadaxe once.

I beg Verbero, as best I can, to remove the gag. We don't have much time left. I begin to panic in earnest. He just laughs. Ack ack ack.

# Smash.ing

As I rounded the corner to our street, I noticed that people were looking at me weirdly. I glanced at my reflection in a shop window. My hair was an Andy Warhol fright wig in red. I had dirt in creases and wrinkles I didn't know existed. It looked as though I'd put my clothes through the shredder, put them back on and then rolled in the mud.

I wasn't going to win any beauty contests, that's for sure. All I cared about was that I was nearing home sweet home. The street, with its rickety terraces and odd businesses, looked like paradise to me. Even the sign pointing the way to The Church of Our Princess Diana evoked a wee pang of nostalgia.

'Miles! That you?' I turned to see ZakDot coming up just behind me. 'Jesus fucking Christ,' he exclaimed, looking me up and down. 'Where have you *been*? And what have you "done"? Even the police are looking for you.' He stepped back and studied my appearance. 'I'd say you looked shocking, except the latest issue of *Pulse* said that "shocking" was the new word for "cool", "cool" apparently being "out" again.' ZakDot was air-quoting so fast his fingers were a blur.

I suddenly realised what he'd just said. 'What do you mean, the police have been asking about me?' I asked. I felt guilty enough, but I wasn't sure that any of my various crimes were worthy of the attention of Sydney's finest. By now, we were climbing the stairs together. ZakDot's hand was on my shoulder, though he was keeping a space between us. I thought it was because he didn't want to dirty his clothes, but what he said next made me wonder if he didn't suspect I was soiled in some deeper sense.

'I don't know,' ZakDot began. 'It was just two days ago. Julia had stayed over—yes, that's all happening—and she answered the door with me. I said we didn't know where you were. Julia had told us how you'd gone off with that, that *Verbero* guy, how she thought he was kidnapping you, but that it also looked like you knew him. When she first told us about it, we were very worried. I remembered you wanting to tell me something that night at Club Apocalypso. I wondered if that had anything to do with it. We thought of calling the police, but Maddie didn't want them sniffing around here. You know, she's got a big collection of illegal chemicals.'

'I'm glad you got your priorities straight. Security of the arsenal over safety of the housemate.' We'd reached a landing. I stopped, shook off ZakDot's fingers and folded my arms across my chest. 'I can't believe that. Some friends.'

'Miles, you don't understand. We didn't call the police but we fucking found you and brought you back, didn't we?'

'What do you mean? I was found all right, but nothing to do with you.'

'That's what you think. We couldn't figure out how there

could be any link between you and those Clean Slate arseholes. So, we searched your studio for clues. We found Trimalkyo's card and, on the back of it, someone had written the exact date and time that you were picked up. Maddie slapped together a bomb out of a juice bottle, hydrochloric acid, and aluminium foil and we fronted up to Trimalkyo's place to demand an explanation. As you know, Maddie can be particularly "persuasive" when she's carrying explosives. We met "the man" himself. Trimalkyo told us that you were with the prime minister. Or as he put it, the "prime meeneesteero". So, I called Doppler's office and, impersonating a journalist, drew out the information that she was spending the parliamentary recess in her private residence up north.

'Thurston hacked into government data bases and came up with an address for the Bunker: Little Woop Woop, Queensland. Little Woop Woop didn't appear on any maps. This stymied us for a while. Then Maddie got on the blower to her mother, who still lives on a community outside Nimbin. Her mother's boyfriend was having a didge lesson that afternoon with someone who knew a tribe of feral women trackers known as the No Names.'

'The No Names! That's it! But how…'

ZakDot held up his hand like a cop stopping traffic. 'Almost finished. Maddie asked her mother to pass on a message via the boyfriend's didge teacher to the No Names. This was the message, and I think it fairly represents how we all felt: "Bring back that weak-brained little fuckwit, dead or alive." And so they did. And here you are.'

I went all warm inside. My friends did care about me after all. 'But hold on, did you say something about the police? Where do they come into this?'

'They don't, really. It was just that this one policewoman came and asked for you.'

'Policewoman?' My heart skipped a beat.

'C'mon,' ZakDot said. 'Let's get out of this stupid stairwell.'

'Was she pretty? Nice eyes? Good legs?'

'Jesus, Miles, you hear a policewoman's come looking for you and all you can think of is, does she have big tits. One of these days, you've actually got to *have* some sex, Miles. It'll help you get your mind off.'

'I didn't say anything about tits,' I protested as I pushed open the door of the warehouse. Inside, I caught my breath. 'What a fucking mess!'

The signboard on which ZakDot recorded his inspirational sayings had been flung across the room, where it lay splintered against the brick wall. The sofa and chairs and table were overturned, our toys scattered. ZakDot's inflatable wombat, Bazza, had been deflated and strung up from a lamp. Our pathetic collection of plates and glasses was smashed and the rack for pots and pans dangled crazily. The pots themselves were all over the floor.

'I go away and the first thing you guys do is throw a party,' I joked.

'Fuck me dead.' From the look on ZakDot's face, I knew that, if there'd been a party, he hadn't been invited either. 'I just went out a couple of hours ago,' he said, trembling. 'Everything was fine when I left. Fuck, fuck, fuck!' We embarked on a tour of the devastation.

'Do you think this has something to do with Maddie?' I asked, thinking it looked like a bomb had gone off in the place.

'That's my name. Don't wear it out.' We turned to see Maddie emerging from what remained of her room. 'Shit, Miles, you look as bad as this warehouse.'

Bacon picked his way towards us through the debris, stopping right in the middle of rock n roll. I scooped him up and hugged him to me. He mewed.

Thinking of my paintings, I raced into my studio. The others followed.

'Jesus, what a debacle,' Maddie exclaimed. The floor of the studio was littered with screwed-up pieces of paper, tubes of paint, scattered brushes and bottles of turps and varnish and linseed oil. Reference books lay thrown about on the floor. 'They've really ransacked this place,' she said.

'Actually,' I admitted, 'I think the studio's as I left it.'

We started to laugh and, once we started, we couldn't stop. I clutched the doorframe and wiped my tears.

'Oh well,' ZakDot said after a long while, 'I take it this means you did *something* right.'

Maddie poked me in the ribs with her index finger. 'Well?'

'Ouch,' I said. 'Lay off it.' I squirmed away.

She rolled her eyes and sucked on her tongue piercing. 'Did you?' she asked, finally.

'Did I what?'

'Do something right, you git. I get home to find our whole place trashed, coincidentally just before you get back. So. I was just wondering if you had anything you'd like to tell us that might explain any of this?'

Heavy footsteps pounded the floor in the direction of the studio. We braced. It was Thurston, who hurled himself at me and wrapped me in a bear hug. *He* didn't care about getting his clothes dirty. The hug went on a bit too long. As if intuiting my discomfort, he released me and stepped back a pace or two.

That's when I noticed the bandage on his forehead. 'What happened to you?'

His hand moved up self-consciously to his face. 'Nothing. I mean, it's just a little gash.'

'Were you here when this happened?'

'Yes, I was. I was sharpening the blade of my broadaxe when they came in.'

'How'd they get in?'

'Quietly. Must've had a skeleton key or something.'

'A skeleton key? What'd they look like?'

'Not like ordinary thieves. Not as I'd imagine ordinary thieves to look like anyway. They wore dark suits and sunglasses.'

'Like *Reservoir Dogs*?' asked ZakDot. 'Cool. I mean "shocking".'

Thurston looked confused. 'Sort of,' he said.

'Go on, Thurston,' I encouraged.

'Anyway, I came out of my room and stigged and tartled at the sight of them. I brandished my axe and demanded to know what they were after. They looked just as surprised as I had been. I don't think they expected to be threatened with a broadaxe. Nuk nuk.'

'It's a great axe,' Maddie affirmed.

'"You know what we want, Walker," said their leader, keeping his eye on the axe and obviously mistaking me for you. "The bag."'

'The bag?' I didn't get it. 'Are you sure they said "the bag", Thurston?'

'Yes. They said, "Hand over the bag now and there'll be

no trouble." Then they started throwing the furniture around. Oh, Miles, I didn't know where you were at that point or what you'd done, or what bag he was talking about, but if I knew one thing it was that I had to protect your art for posterity.'

ZakDot and Maddie exchanged glances that could possibly be interpreted as sardonic. I ignored them.

'So, I made a lunge at them with the axe and, after a tussle, I barricaded myself in your studio. I could hear them trashing the rest of the place but at least your paintings are safe.'

'Thurston.' My voice came out in this funny croak. I was so grateful I wanted to kiss him. 'Thanks. Thanks a lot.'

'Yeah, thanks a lot,' Maddie added.

'Anyone feel like a beer?' ZakDot asked.

Our local had changed since Clean Slate came into power. The owner had painted over the angels and classical Greek figures, and lined the walls with poker machines, which provided the only music now to be heard there. Poets avoided the place and the bartender no longer worked on his novel, in public, anyway, which was probably not a bad thing.

'You didn't, like, root her or anything?' ZakDot asked after I'd finished telling a slightly edited version of events. In this version, I had no idea what Trimalkyo and Oscar were getting me into. Once there, I'd struggled valiantly to escape, painting only at gunpoint. 'Well?' he persisted. 'Did you?'

I choked on my beer.

Maddie punched ZakDot in the arm. 'Miles wouldn't do that. Would you, Miles?'

I willed my head to shake itself.

'Miles,' Thurston informed the others, 'is celibate. He doesn't have sex.'

'Miles?' ZakDot sounded even more suspicious now.

'So what if I did?' I challenged. 'Leave me alone, all right?'

Maddie stared hard at me. 'He's kidding, ZakDot,' she said. 'Aren't you, Miles?'

I nodded, weakly. 'What do you think?'

'Bloody hell,' sighed ZakDot, slugging back his beer.

'So, what now?' Maddie drained her glass and tapped her fingers on the counter.

'Well,' I began, 'I'd like to do a new series of paintings based on the quality of light in the rainforest. It was amazing, and I need to get it down on canvas before it goes out of my head.'

'Oh, Miles,' Thurston interjected. 'That sounds beautiful. I'm sure you'll create *brilliant* work from this experience.'

Maddie put her gorgeous, fresh-shaven head in her hands. 'You're a bloody hopeless dag, Miles, you know that? But hold on, we still haven't worked out this "bag" thing that Thurston was talking about. Do you have any idea what they were after?'

I shook my shoulders. 'Not a clue. Maybe they had the wrong house.'

'Think hard. It's got to have something to do with you. They addressed Thurston as "Walker", after all.' She signalled to the bartender for another round.

ZakDot's eyes lit on my rucksack. 'That's a bag,' he observed.

'It's just my old rucksack. Why would they want that?'

'Hand her over,' Maddie ordered, sitting ramrod straight on her bar stool, jutting out her tattooed chin and lowering her eyelids in what ZakDot and I had privately labelled her 'commando look'. It was very fetching. I passed her my rucksack.

Maddie rifled through my stuff, flinging things willy-nilly as she went.

'Hey! Hey! Be gentle with that stuff,' I cried, diving for a pair of undies that had hit the floor. When I crawled back onto the stool, still grumbling, Maddie, Thurston and ZakDot were all staring bug-eyed at a zip-lock freezer bag packed with white powder that she held in her hands.

'What's this, then?' Maddie asked.

'It looks like the titanium white pigment I buy from a supplier in Balmain. But I don't remember taking that with me. It's such a carry-on to prepare. You need a mortar and pestle and...'

Maddie, checking to see no one was looking, licked a finger, stuck it in the bag, and licked it again. 'Whooo,' she exclaimed. She stuffed the white powder back into my rucksack, reached out and grabbed me by the chin. She jerked me closer, nearly pulling me off my stool in the process. 'Miles, is there something you ought to be telling us?'

Shit, I thought. They know I fucked her.

'Do you have any idea who would have put this with your stuff?' Maddie's words had sped up.

'No, I...oh, hold on.' I told them about the day I caught Verbero snooping around my room.

'Looks like you were being set up big time.' ZakDot whistled, impressed. 'Maddie, pass the blow.'

'Later!' she barked. Maddie was scary enough when she was languid. This stuff made her terrifying. 'It's not safe here.'

'But why?' Thurston scratched at his beard.

'Too many people might see, Thurston,' she replied in a patronising tone.

'No, I mean, why the set-up? Do you have any idea, Miles?'

'I dunno,' I replied, feeling very tired. 'All I know is that I've had a gutful of politics. I'm over it.'

'The question is, is politics over you?' Maddie sucked energetically on her tongue piercing. 'Judging from the events of this afternoon, I would say a reasonable guess would be no, not by a long shot.'

'I just want to get back to my painting,' I moaned.

'Miles.' Maddie slapped ZakDot's hand away from my rucksack. Holding it protectively on her lap, she aimed the hatchet of her gaze straight between my eyes. 'What did you say about Trimalkyo inviting Doppler and her gang to a New Year's bash?'

'Yeah, it's gonna be on—'

'—the *Dinkum!*' Maddie exclaimed, clapping her hands.

'How'd you—'

'Remember? ZakDot and I are working for Dinkum. We're rostered on. Quadruple overtime. That's tomorrow night, too. C'mon, gang, the night is young and we've got work to do.' She jumped up and made to toss me my rucksack, then, thinking better of the idea, slung it over her own broad shoulders.

Thurston looked at Maddie, who was practically vibrating, with a worried expression.

'You weren't planning on going to the party, Miles, were you?' Maddie demanded.

'God, no. I hate New Year's parties. There's such a ridiculous level of expectation attached to them. Besides, I can't dance and I never have anyone to kiss at midnight.'

'Do you get the feeling Miles lives in some parallel universe?' ZakDot asked Maddie. Then, turning to me, 'Miles. Mate. Darling. Sweetie. We're not talking about whether or not you can "dance". There are slightly more serious issues at stake. You've got to go into hiding.'

'Go into hiding? What are you talking about? I haven't done anything wrong. I'm not some criminal. I'm just a poor artist.'

'A poor artist who's got enough cocaine on him to light up every nightclub in the city for a month,' Zak pointed out.

I grimaced. 'That's not my fault.'

'Tell it to the judge.'

'Where would I hide, anyway?'

'You could probably borrow my olds' shack up the coast,' ZakDot said after a pause. 'I'll call them when we get home.'

As soon as we got in the door, ZakDot relieved Maddie of the bag and went into the bathroom to find a razor and a mirror. He offered me and Thurston some, but we declined. Maddie, biting the end of her pen, righted the sandwich-sign table and, sprawling across Kraft & Vegemite, began covering sheets of paper with diagrams and lists.

'Okay. This is what we'll do. We'll plant a bomb big enough to blow up the whole fucken boat, Destiny and every single arse-licking art traitor on it at midnight.'

'Fuck, Maddie,' I cried. 'That's *murder* you're talking about.'

'Don't think of it like that. Ever heard of Thomas de Quincey, Miles? Miles?'

I lifted my head from my hands. 'Uh, *Confessions of an Opium Eater*? That one?'

'Yeah, well, in his essay "On Murder Considered as a Fine

Art", he talks about how the timing, place and style of a murder are actually all components of an aesthetic.'

Recalling Destiny's insistence that I be at the party, I thought this could be my old nightmare come true—my friends were going to kill me after all. Then I told myself not to be ridiculous. I'd escaped. I was going into hiding. What was Verbero going to do, hunt me down, kidnap me, drug me, tie me up and throw me on board?

It wasn't a bad guess.

Thurston nodded excitedly at what Maddie was saying. 'That's it,' he said, 'an aesthetic of violence. That's how we approach our mock battles. If you look at it that way, it's'—his grin pushed his cheeks up like two red balls—'almost an *art* form.'

'So it is. And there's a role for you in this as well, Thurston. Will you do it? For Miles?'

An hour later, Maddie was using Thurston's computer to surf the net for new bomb recipes on the one hand, and the plans for the *Dinkum* on the other. She found the latter on a website advertising harbour cruises.

Thurston was soon on the blower to Gwydion and several other of his weirdo mates, Rodmur, Torold and Baldar. I heard him say, 'No one involved in this inkle must quatch,' and then, 'We shall come like a thode.'

ZakDot, once more abandoning irony to its own devices, sprawled on the floor, fervently penning a new manifesto. I moved around the warehouse, righting furniture, sweeping up, re-inflating the wombat. I'd slept all the way back on the bus, but I was exhausted. The following morning I was supposed to meet ZakDot's mum at her office on George Street to get the key to the shack, and then hop a train up the coast. In truth, I didn't mind this plan so much; I liked the idea of hiding away and painting. I wanted to get back into my own world. The real one had become a trifle overwhelming.

I hoped they'd all come to their senses by the following morning. If not, I'd talk them out of it somehow. I wasn't going to leave till I did.

When I woke up—this morning—they were all crashed out. I knocked on ZakDot's door and pushed it open. I went over to the window and pulled up the shade. As the light hit his face, he squeezed his eyes tight and clawed at the air like a cat, hissing and growling.

'I have to talk to you,' I said.

He pulled his sheet over his head. 'Talk is futile.'

I sighed and considered my options. I needed to pick up some new arts supplies—pastels, oils and brushes. That'd take an hour or so. I'd do that, come back, wake ZakDot and the others, talk them out of their insanity and then disappear.

Stepping out onto the street, I looked at Thurston's watch, which I still hadn't returned to him. Half past eleven, and the day was already stinking hot. I didn't even see them coming. Next thing I knew a coat had been flung over my head and I was being pushed into the back of a waiting car.

And I still hadn't asked ZakDot about that policewoman.

# Bomb shell

The VIP touched down at Canberra's Fairbairn airport. It was around one in the afternoon. This afternoon. Verbero didn't say a word to me the entire flight. I kept expecting him to ask about the bag of cocaine, which he didn't. I fretted about what I assumed was going to be a testy encounter with Destiny.

The car was waiting. We glided down the smooth, shaded roads of the little country's neat little capital. Soon we were crossing over a bridge across the lake. We'd be at Parliament House in minutes. Danger has a way of making me a little reckless. I broke the silence. 'So tell me, Verbe-*wo*, were you using me for a delivery boy or were you trying to frame me? I'd like to know.'

Verbero's eyes went to slits.

The car disgorged us onto the green green grass of, if not home, at least the House of Representatives.

'Well?'

'We haven't got all day.' Verbero strode towards the ministerial entrance, clearly expecting me to follow.

I stood my ground. 'What makes you think I haven't already gone straight to the police with it? You know, I could go on Trixie Tinkles' program and tell the world just what sort of business is being run out of the prime minister's office.'

Verbero stopped mid-stride and turned to face me. 'But you won't,' he stated.

'What's to stop me?' I wanted to know.

He snickered. 'For one thing, I'm sure you don't want your arty-farty pals seeing the home movies we made at the Bunker.'

'Home movies? What're you talking about?'

His voice turned smug. 'You're an observant little cunt. I'm surpwised you never noticed the video cams concealed in your bedwoom. I nearly laughed me hole off watching you two.'

It took me a moment to figure out what he was trying to say. Then it struck me. 'Surely, you wouldn't...' I gulped. 'I mean, doesn't Des...the prime minister have more to lose than I do if those get out?'

'Not weally. Politicians are wegularly caught in bed with all sorts of people—media moguls, big business, the whole bloody mining industwy for Chwist's sake, and it doesn't do their caweers no harm.' He slapped a pass into my hand and shoved me towards the door.

'You've gone pale,' he smirked. 'Listen to me, Walker. You've done something to her. She's losing it. She's not the leader she was. I had hopes for her. Now, they're gone. Don't think I'm not onto you, either. You and Twimalkyo and all those art faggots, you had this planned fwom the start, didn't you?' He pointed a finger at me.

'You think I'm just doing this out of self-intewest. I want what's best for our cuntwee, Walker, and the bottom line is that culture does a lot more harm than good. The citizens of this cuntwee elected us because we pwomised to do away with culture, we had a mandate. But you people, you saw your opportunity and you leapt at it, didn't you? Don't intewupt.' He lowered his voice. 'I knew that once she'd had a taste, once it was in her system, in her blood-stweam, she'd never be able to get enough. I've seen it before, you know. Before the Twoubles. People would say they're just going to one play, one dance performance. Next thing you know, it's art openings, book launches, subscwiptions to the opewa. It doesn't stop there, either. Soon they're bleeding money into collections, patwonages, sponsorship, begging the government for more festivals, wicher pwizes. If she doesn't get off this thing now, we'll be wight back where we started fwom. Twoubles. Twoubles. Big Twoubles.'

'If she's made up her mind, she's made up her mind. What can I do about that?'

'You're the cweative one. You'll think of something. Dissuade her.'

'From what exactly?'

'She's going to make an announcement tonight. She wants to weverse all of Clean Slate's policies. Go back to the old ways.'

I *was* an Art Hero. I mentally patted myself on the back. 'And if I don't?'

'Miles Walker, you're dead.'

By now, we'd woven our way down several long, blue-carpeted hallways, past the offices of the Ministers for

Payback, Travel Rorts, Spin Doctoring, Power Lunches, Networking, and Death and Taxes. We turned a corner and stood before two massive doors. He pushed them open. They led into an antechamber furnished with a sofa and two chairs, upholstered in a garish orange. There were more massive doors leading off the room to both the right and the left; straight ahead was a courtyard with a waterfall, the same one, I realised, that Destiny had described to me. The waterfall was flowing. This was her office. She was in.

'Stay,' Verbero commanded, knocking on the right-hand set of doors and disappearing inside. I sank into a doughnut-shaped chair.

A minute later Verbero reappeared. 'Go,' he said, pointing to the door. Destiny was seated in a high-backed brown leather chair at the desk on the far end of the spacious office, her back to me, contemplating the empty bookshelves along the office's back wall.

I looked around. My eye was always drawn to paintings, and I immediately noticed Churchill's *Cap d'Antibes* hanging not far from Destiny's desk. The right wall was panelled in the most luscious wood, broken in the middle to reveal a series of shelves, each one containing a single, exquisite ceramic pot. I guessed that it had not occurred to Destiny that bowls might also be art.

She swivelled around to face me. 'I think you forgot to say goodbye.'

'Never can say goodbye,' I sang weakly.

'That's it! That's exactly it!' she cried, so loudly that I looked over my shoulder. What was she talking about?

'You see, Miles, thanks to you, I've had a piphany!' she exclaimed, rising out of her seat and coming round the desk towards me. She was wearing brighter colours than I'd ever seen her in. Her hair was loose on her shoulders.

'Oh, yeah?' I said, backing up against the heavy doors.

'Culture is everywhere, Miles.' She rushed to where I was standing, took my hands and pulled me towards one of the orange disco chairs. 'It's everything. It's the music on the radio, the food you eat, the magazines at the dentist's office.' She whirled around, pushed me into the chair and plopped herself down in my lap.

'Please don't,' I pleaded weakly. 'Not here. Remember what happened to Bill Clinton.' Her eyes glittering, she twisted so that she could wrap her arms around my neck as she spoke.

'We're not like that here,' she said. 'We've got a different political *culture*.'

'Nice use of the word "culture",' I said. 'Now can I go?' She wasn't listening.

'I've got it, Miles, I've finally got it. Culture is *everything*, even the furniture we sit on...'

'Well, maybe not this furniture.'

'It's movies, cafés, even graffiti. I read all about it in a book, and there was this guy called Basquiat...' She pronounced his name 'bass-*kwee*-at'. She wriggled in my lap. Little Miles semaphored back his own unruly exhilaration.

'Yes, I know who you mean. Prodigy of Warhol.'

'Who?'

'Never mind.' I wrenched her hands off my nipples. I noticed that she no longer ended all her sentences in a question.

'It's people, like, sitting in department store windows for a week, it's rows of dried fish tacked onto a gallery wall. It's artists shitting paint out their bums onto canvas, it's big green puppy dogs outside the MMCEA!' She frowned. 'We're going to have to get that building back from those South Americans,' she observed. 'Remind me.'

'It's also painting, drawing and sculpture,' I said, tugging my shirt back down. 'Could we do this somewhere else? This is too weird.'

She grabbed my hand and pulled me out into the foyer, where Verbero was speaking quietly into his mobile. He looked up long enough to give me the evil eye. We passed straight through to the set of doors opposite. We were now in her private dining room. The room was long and thin. A stretch limo of a table extended almost from one end of the room to the other; it was fashioned from blackheart sassafras with a central panel of marble. One end of the room had doors leading, presumably, into a kitchen. The other faced out onto the courtyard. Floor-to-ceiling mirrors next to both the window and the kitchen door made the room seem even thinner and longer than it was. She backed me up against the table.

'I love the portrait, by the way.'

I tried to push her away, but my hands somehow landed on her breasts. She had the most womanly breasts I'd ever seen. Just one last, tiny feel and I'd never touch them again. 'Look Destiny,' I panted. 'I have to talk to you about Verbero. He's playing some sort of game.'

'I doubt it.' She shook her head. 'He hates games. Won't even play Go Fish with me on the VIP. Anyway, let's not talk about Verbero,' she said, sliding down my body and, unexpectedly, grabbing me by the ankles. Next thing I know, she'd hoicked me onto my back on the table and was tugging off my boots and socks. I stared up at the marquetry on the ceiling.

'You know what I did the other night?' she asked, leaning over and nibbling on my big toe. 'I ate in a *thigh restaurant.*'

'Pardon?' I gasped, trying to wriggle away. That *tickled.* 'A thigh restaurant?'

'You know,' she replied, looking up, 'with food from Thighland?'

I suppressed a chuckle. 'You mean you've never...'

'Nup,' she said. She was undoing my belt and tugging at my pants. 'Never ate thigh, never tried Chink, never even had a fluffle.'

I raised my backside so she could get my trousers off. 'You gotta be careful with felafels,' I said, as she hooked her fingers into the waistband of my daks. 'People have been known to die with them in their hands.'

She looked at me blankly.

'It's not important,' I said. Then I suggested, 'After you get through the food bit, you should try books.' I was being mean, I know. It was getting hard to think straight.

'Books!' she cried. 'Like literature 'n stuff?' She unzipped her skirt, which dropped to her ankles with a satiny swishing sound. 'Y'know, I could write a novel.' Meditatively, she unbuttoned her blouse and tossed it to one side, where it landed on the sideboard, shrouding the silver tea service. She was now wearing nothing but a lacy red bra, red French knickers, a suspender belt, translucent black stockings and red high heels; she looked like one of Egon Schiele's erotic drawings. I loved Egon Schiele. 'I might read one or two first, though, just to make sure no one's got my idea. You ever read a novel, Miles?'

I nodded, and rolled my head to the side. I could see her plump arse and the fleshy white tops of her thighs in the mirror on the end wall. I could also see the soles of my feet and my head. I stared at myself. Was this the face of an Art Hero?

'Which novel was that? Maybe I'll start with it. Write it down later for me, will you?'

'Yes, ma'am.'

'I can tell you're being sarcophagistic,' she said, raising her chin slightly. 'I think you should be pleased now that I see the light.' She liberated me from my shirt.

'You see, Miles, I'm a changed woman. I *love* culture. I love it so much.' She grabbed my feet, pulled them up so that my legs were fully extended and then pushed. I slid towards the centre of the table, my buttocks squeaking on the precious wood.

'It's gone way beyond just appreciating'—she clambered onto the table and straddled me, her knees on the sassafras, my arse on the cool marble—'*representational* painting.'

I surrendered. I reached up and drew her down to me. Little Miles drove straight past the lax French border patrol and straight into her warm wet chunnel. Little Miles was a heat-seeking missile and he had certainly found the hottest spot—in Parliament House, anyway.

Missile. The word hung in the airy space in my head where my brain had once been. She was riding me like a jumping castle. I moaned. My buttocks made a chirping sound as they bounced about on the sassafras and marble.

'You know,' she grunted, 'this is the table, ohhh, where I entertain, mmm, dignitaries?'

'Like this?' I gasped.

'No, silly.'

Missile. The word was tapping on my skull for attention.

238

Shit! Fuck! I needed to warn her about tonight. Maddie, ZakDot and Thurston. Blowing up the ship. 'Destiny,' I bleated, 'we have to talk.' I could feel my balls tighten.

She pinched one of my nipples between her fingers. 'I know,' she cooed, 'I know. You were right all along. I've decided to make an announcement tonight, at Trimalkyo's party.'

'The…party…bomb.' My syntax was in my perineum.

'It will be a bombshell,' she said, climbing off me and jumping down from the table. She grabbed me by the wrist, jerked me off the table and slammed me against the side wall, which luckily was slightly padded, covered in grey silk like an upmarket brothel.

'Destiny,' I pleaded.

Like a mad ballroom dancer, she spun us around again so that now she was backed against the wall. She raised one leg and wrapped it tightly around my waist. Little Miles had gotten over his slight disappointment of moments earlier and was now doing the cancan inside the one-woman Radio City Music Hall that was the leader of the nation.

'I see now,' she said, ramming her hips into mine, 'that culture is the life of the nation, it is the soul of the people, it is what makes life worth living. Oh, oh, I'm going to organism!' With this observation, she tipped her head back, arched her spine and screamed.

I was heading for oblivion. My balls tightened, my stomach muscles clenched. Just as I began to come, I felt a hand roughly grab my shoulder, pull me off her and, before I knew what or who or why, a big male fist slammed into my nose. I saw stars. Then I saw Verbero.

# Found objects

It feels very late. It must be almost midnight. Verbero comes in. He's changed back into his suit. He puts his stash into the inside pocket of his jacket. He pinches his nose a few times, sniffs and folds his arms in front of his chest. He tilts his head back and, looking down at me, begins to speak.

'Okay, Walker, let me paint you a picture. Kca kca kca. First, I'm going to take off your gag. And then I will loosen your wopes, but not totally. You'll still have to work at getting fwee. By my weckoning, this will take you at least five minutes. You can then do as you please. You can cheer on Destiny's new policies and even fuck her over the dessert table, for all I care. You'll both be histo-wee soon enough. You see, not long after I picked you up, my men made a second visit to your warehouse.'

So, I was right.

'You artists weally are slobs, aren't you? You'd hardly cleaned up any of the mess they made on their first visit. And you're a lazy mob, too. Evewyone still in bed, though it was nearly noon.

The cocaine was on the dining table. Most convenient. While my men were wecovewing the bag, they noticed something intewesting. It was sitting on top of a pile of papers. The papers included the bluepwints for this ship as well as wecipes for bombs big enough to blow it up. There were all manner of calculations on one scwap of paper as to how to time depth charges to go off at midnight. Natuwally, my men thought I might be intewested in these plans. They called to tell me about them while you were banging the pwime minister in her pwivate dining room.'

I feel myself going very very pale.

'As you know, I have a weal pwoblem with Destiny's new passion for culture. It doesn't fit in with my plans for this cuntwee at all. I thought about it while she was abusing me for coming in and knocking you out cold. Oh and she abused me, all wight.' Verbero paused and sniffed. 'She said some personal things which I can tell you I didn't like at all, Walker. Like you, she has noticed that I have been wunning a little business on the side, and she wasn't happy about that. But that's neither here nor there. The bottom line is, it doesn't matter anymore. You see, by the time you manage to fwee yourself, your fwiends' bomb will be going off and you and Destiny and all the west of your arty-farty poofter fwiends will be histo-wee. The culpwits will be caught by the police, and you, though dead, will be implicated. No one will know about Destiny's change of mind, and I will go on Twixie Tinkles and evewy other bloody television show in this cuntwee and talk about how she was a martyr to the cause. Widing the inevitable wave of sympathy, I will announce my own candidacy, wun for parliament and—'

A sudden banging on the door causes us both to look up.

'Open up! Police!' A female voice.

Verbero signals me to stay quiet. I rattle my chair and make strangulated noises from behind the gag.

One vicious kick from outside and the door explodes inwards. 'Freeze!' I see, as in a vision, Senior Constable Grevillea Bent, gun held out at arm's length, her left arm supporting her right wrist, just like in the movies. She is the sexiest woman I have ever laid eyes on. She winks at me. I am faint with relief and joy and lust.

'Okay, Svengali,' she says to Verbero, that tough little mouth of hers working into a sneer. 'Hands up, face the wall. No funny stuff.'

Verbero protests. 'I fucken mean it,' she scowls. I love a woman who swears.

Verbero pivots slowly and faces the toilet door. Puts his hands up. She turns to me. 'Remember these?' she says as she pulls her handcuffs out of their pouch and secures him to the sink.

I nod. Kinky.

'You just be a good boy.' She pats Verbero on the arse. Then she frisks him up and down. She finds the bag. Titanium white. Whistling, she puts it in her own pocket, making sure the top is well sealed. She also relieves him of his key chain.

'You're going to be in big twouble, you know,' he growls. 'You don't know who I am. I know my wights.'

She listens to this with her green eyes wide open and her mouth curved into a perfect little 'o' of mock surprise and fear.

'Big time coke dealers like yourself usually do, in my experience. We've had our eyes on you for a long time, Verbero. Using the prime minister's office to conduct your thriving little business. Cheeky as. Ever hear of ministerial codes of conduct? No? Well, you're no different from the rest, then.'

'You can't pwove anything. Bitch.'

'You say "bitch" like it's a bad thing,' she replies and, ignoring him, moves to my side. Gently, her soft hands brushing my cheeks, she unfastens the gag and, without bothering to wipe off the saliva, shoves it in Verbero's maw.

'How…what are you doing here?' I am hoping that she will say that she's come to rescue me, even though she couldn't have known I was here. 'This isn't your usual beat.'

'Oh, I got tired of going round busting up artists' gigs and whatnot. Didn't feel right.' She moves around behind me, unlocks the handcuffs and starts puzzling out the other knots that bind my torso, legs, and feet to the chair. 'I should tell you that meeting you was a turning point. Just didn't want to do it anymore after that.'

I was desperate to see her face. I twisted around, but only succeeded in half-tipping myself over. She caught me and smiled. 'Anyway, a few months ago, a colleague mentioned he was transferring to VIP security. Close personal protection, we call it. Thought I'd give it a go myself. Put in an application, had the interview and security check and next thing you know they're telling me I've got "aptitude". In like Flynn. Never thought I'd be protecting *her* though. The real question is, what are you doing here? I wouldn't have expected a nice artist like you to be mixed up with his type.' She throws a thumb in Verbero's direction.

'It's a long story. I'll tell you if you like, but can I ask you something?'

'Shoot.' I am enjoying the friction of her as she moves around me, untying.

'Did you come to my house a few days ago?'

She looks up. Her eyes twinkle. 'Yeah. I had your address from the time at the Apocalypso. I heard from some of my colleagues in VIP protection that Doppler had got herself a young artist in residence, called Walker. I couldn't believe it was you, so I thought of some excuse to stop by. When they said they didn't know where you were, I grew suspicious. But I thought you'd have your reasons.'

It's crazy, but this moves me so much I want to stand up. I forget I've still got both feet secured to the chair and I tumble forward, into her arms. We fall together onto the bed. She reaches behind her for support and ends up pulling the curtain and rod down on our heads at the same time as the chair flies up and smacks against the back of my legs.

'Ow!' I cry. We laugh and untangle ourselves from the curtain. 'It's Raining Men' is blasting out of the loudspeaker and someone's set off fireworks from a nearby boat. I'm almost delirious with the romance of it all. I want to kiss her and hold her and tell her how much I've been thinking about her and what a miracle this is when I suddenly remember something.

I look at my watch. Thurston's watch. 'Oh shit! It's nearly ten to twelve!'

'Just in time for the countdown,' she replies.

The pounding of footsteps causes us both to look up. Though the bare window we see, clear as day, Maddie and ZakDot racing past, down the breezeway towards the stern, discarding bits and pieces of their catering uniforms as they go.

'I remember her,' Grevillea says.

'You don't know how big this countdown is gonna be,' I tell her. 'We've got to get outta here.'

She quickly unties my feet. She runs out onto the breezeway, me stumbling behind, my legs and feet stiff from being tied up for so long. We reach the stern just in time to see a longboat rowed by what look like Viking warriors angling its bow into the 'v' of the duckboard. Maddie and ZakDot jump into the boat, rocking it perilously, then the Vikings, under the direction of Thurston, row like billyo.

As quickly as I can, I tell Grevillea what's happening. We race back up the stairs and to the deck with the party.

Imagine a Hollywood wet dream of ancient Egypt with a dash of Roman Empire thrown in for good measure. A barge fit for Cleopatra or Nero, for pharaohs, kings or princes. Billowing clouds of gold lamé cover the top deck. It looks like the floating love child of a Gold Coast motel and the bus in *Priscilla Queen of the Desert*. Young Adonises mill about in loincloths, pretending to be oarsmen or statues, their oiled biceps gleaming in the torchlight. Nubiles in silk togas, frangipani blossoms in their hair, flutter about serving the costumed guests. There is a dessert table on which are lavish trays of sweets and cakes and two enormous displays of fruit crafted to look like peacocks with spread tails.

Cynthia, Lynda and Cashie are standing by the table, plucking pieces off the peacocks' tails and sharing some private joke. Cynthia is wearing a pointy metallic bra like something out of a Madonna video, and a tall cone of aluminium foil on her head. Lynda is dressed in rags, like a beggar, and Cashie has done something quite bizarre to her hair, or maybe that's what it always looks like when not confined to a turban. Together they look a little like a feminised version of the Tin Man, Scarecrow and Lion.

'To conclude, I'd like to make a very special announcement.' Destiny taps her microphone. She looks around in despair. By her side, Wayne frowns. Everyone is facing her, but no one is listening. Even with the microphone, she can barely make herself heard over the tinkling of jewellery, the clinking of glasses, muffled snorts and the occasional stage-whispered ejaculation—'Oh, *really?*' 'He paid *what?*' It's exactly, I realise, like an art opening.

I scan the deck, not exactly sure what I'm looking for. It could be anywhere. But there it is, plain as day if you're looking for it. A bomb. Right under the dessert table. A black orb with the word 'bomb' thoughtfully lettered on the side in white texta. In smaller letters: 'This machine *really* kills fascists.' A fuse leads off to the galley.

Grevillea spots it just as Destiny notices me. Destiny drops her microphone and rushes towards me. I freeze, not sure which is the more nightmarish fate—to be blown up or clinched in passionate embrace by Destiny in full view of Grevillea. In time, I'm sure, if we manage to survive, I'll tell Grevillea all about Destiny, but this does not feel like the opportune moment. Before Destiny can reach me, though, Grevillea tackles her and wrestles her to the rail.

Destiny struggles to break free.

Oscar sashays over in a grass skirt and coconut-shell bra, waving his arms like he's hula dancing. 'Hello, girlfriend!' He twirls. 'I'm a Hawaiian princess. Can you tell? Have you been here all evening? Sorry, I must sound a little hyper, we've just been doing the *best* blow all evening. Anyway, so glad you're here. I thought you had something better to do. I've been *dying* to find out how it all went up there. Apparently, you made some kind of impression. She was asking for you *all* night.' I glance over my shoulder. Grevillea was at a safe distance. 'Goodness, your friend looks like she is about to toss her overboard. It's about time, too. Dreary woman.'

Another copper in plainclothes, this one a man, has barrelled up to Grevillea and Destiny. Grevillea briefs him in an instant. As Oscar and I watch, together they throw Destiny over the rails. She goes with a howl and a splash. The copper sends a lifebuoy spinning through the air after her.

'Woohoo,' Oscar cries, taking off one of his flowery leis and twirling it around on his finger while circling his hips. 'Quite right too. No one should ever make a speech at a party that goes for more than fifteen minutes tops. I mean, it's *New Year's,* for God's sake.'

'Oscar—'

'Ladies and gentlemen,' Grevillea has the microphone now. The authority in her voice makes everyone stop what they're doing and listen. What a woman. I almost get a boner just listening to her. 'There's an emergency. A bomb has been placed on board this ship and it is set to go off in'—she looks at her watch—'six minutes. I want everyone overboard. Jump and swim. Right now.'

A drag queen screams.

'What are you waiting for, finger bowls?' Grevillea and her partners then move about the shocked guests, helping them over the rails. The society ladies aren't too happy about getting their frocks wet but the drag queens are the worst, wailing about their make-up and wigs, and squawking like cockatoos; you'd think it was the *Titanic*. I help Lynda, Cynthia and Cashie to jump. Once they heard Maddie was involved, they knew it was no joke. I look down and see that Cynthia is having some problem righting herself in her metallic bra. She unhooks it. She's got excellent tits. They float.

I spot Trimalkyo dashing frantically about, calling for Oscar. He seems to have forgotten his accent in his panic. 'Oscar! Oscar! Where are you?' Oscar shimmies over to him and Trimalkyo clasps him to his breast. I don't think Oscar has anything to worry about in the relationship stakes. They dive over the side together, imperial gown and grass skirt flying. I guess Trimalkyo wasn't in on the plot after all.

Grevillea signals to me. Everyone, including the crew, has been evacuated. She takes my hand and we jump into the harbour.

As we break the surface, still holding hands, Luna Park grins, the Opera House gapes with all its maws wide open and the Harbour Bridge beams its upside-down smile. We swim away from the boat as quickly as possible, kicking off our shoes. The water is cold, but not too cold, and the evening is balmy. The official countdown starts and a roar of excitement rises from all around us. It echoes from Mrs Macquarie's Chair to Shell and Neutral and Lavender Bays, from the naval base of Woolloomooloo to the finger-wharfs of the Rocks, from Pinchgut to the shores of Clark and Shark Islands, from the decks of the tall ships to the low bellies of speedboats and dinghies. Some people on other boats notice our party treading water but they must reckon it's a crazy night and crazy shit happens.

Everyone, us included, faces the sky as the most extraordinary fireworks display in the city's long history of celestial spectaculars begins. Sulphuric flowers bloom scarlet and silver in the sky, candescent pompoms shake out their tassels, ringed planets of light burst in the air and great, sparkling jellyfish unravel tentacles of green and violet and ultramarine. Giant sparklers transform the Harbour Bridge into a glittering tiara. Fat golden fingers with red tips tickle the moon and Centrepoint spends itself in a shower of glittery ejaculate. The harbour echoes with the snap and crackle of the explosions and the gasps of the spectators following each fresh display of pyrotechnic kitsch.

Every boat in the harbour sounds its horn. But nothing is happening with the *Dinkum*. Several minutes pass. For one deeply embarrassed moment, I think that all this carry-on is simply the result of a paranoia I thought I'd left behind. Grevillea looks at me as if to say, well?

I suddenly realise that, whatever is about to happen, I've made Maddie into something she could never really be: a terrorist and a murderer. Where would she get explosives big enough to blow up a ship like the *Dinkum*? And in twenty-four hours, no less? What we saw under the table must have been some sort of witty installation piece. They must have gotten all hyped up on the coke and then had a big laugh working out how to scare the shit out of anyone who discovered the 'bomb'. I feel *really* stupid. I look at Thurston's watch, which fortunately is waterproof. Quarter past twelve.

Then I remember that Thurston said Maddie had taken my watch for a detonator. My watch, which took its own sweet time in getting anywhere.

Just as this occurs to me, on the top deck of the *Dinkum*, there's a rumble and a flash and an explosion. It's now raining melon balls and grapes and champagne and chocolate truffles and jellies, tarts and petit fours, mousse and cake; amongst the shower of treats, scraps of burning lamé float down like shreds of golden sky. It was a bomb all right.

As some Americans on a rented yacht duck the sweet debris, they raise their champagne glasses in a toast to us. 'We love it! World-class fireworks! World-class city!'

I laugh. Grevillea's eyelashes have clumped into dark wet spikes. She spits out a stream of water. I draw her to me, dancing in water, and that's when the real pyrotechnics begin. I love New Year's now. It's not bullshit, it's not hype. I have found my truest love. We're just getting into it when her colleagues in the harbour patrol come along and pluck us out of the water.

As we're speeding back to shore, we remember Verbero was still on the boat, gagged and handcuffed to the sink in the toilet, when the bomb went off.

# Found objects

# (2)

A new age dawned in the little country that was also a big island. Everyone came round to thinking that the original inhabitants were right after all, that the country is where it always was, under our feet, and that this is an excellent place for it to be. We stopped creating Troubles out of culture and blaming culture for our troubles, which were, we realised, much fewer and smaller than those of any other country on earth. Tolerance ruled the land.

Penelope Tolerance: the first Aboriginal prime minister. Destiny wasted no time in resigning and calling a new election. The government of Tolerance and Justice (Malcolm Justice, her deputy prime minister) led the little country through the first decade of the new millennium. The forty-first millennium, give or take a millennium or two. The Aborigines had, you see, a slightly advanced perspective on the rest of us. Asian immigrants, and Arab ones, and Europeans and even Anglo-Saxons delved into their own traditions and each other's, and the love that dare not speak its name—multiculturalism—flourished.

Tolerance reversed all of Destiny's policies. No sooner had she restored funding to scientific research than geophysicists discovered that we had developed a bulge in our heart, making the little country a few hundred square metres larger than we thought it was. Satellite photos taken at the time, however, confirmed that it was still smack in the middle of nowhere, directly on the periphery of everything. Tolerance reopened the schools and libraries and galleries and museums, and provided corporations with irresistible incentives to invest in sponsorship of the arts. Sports people were a bit put out at first, but deep down they loved the arts as much as anyone else and soon grew reconciled to the way things were. Tolerance revived all the prizes and competitions, and reinstated the body that gave out grants and fellowships.

One person who never fails to put in a grant application is Destiny. She's become a performance artist. She delivers long monologues while swinging naked from a trapeze and playing a homemade musical instrument that makes a sound like doors opening. In the beginning, when we'd run into each other, she'd throw these long wistful looks in my direction. It was embarrassing. I couldn't really blame her, though. Despite everything else, we'd had some great sex, and the thought of it still got me hot from time to time. But she doesn't need me anymore. She has every gawky shy boy within a twenty-kilometre range of the inner city hanging off her. She's a neurotic artist magnet.

Once the initial euphoria wore off, most people I know started whingeing that life wasn't as exciting as in the days of Clean Slate. The citizens of our country still come out and dance on the street when a local film shines at Sundance or a local artist makes it into a top New York gallery. But it's finally occurred to the artists that the people of the little country are generally so relaxed, easy-going and happy that they'll come out and dance on the street at the slightest provocation anyway.

Artists reminisce *ad nauseam* about those halcyon days under Destiny, when art was banned and therefore thrilling, relevant, important and real. How many parties have I been to where artists of my generation—late twenties, early thirties—spend their time lost in a haze of nostalgia, trading stories and laughing about the good bad old days, while younger artists shake their heads and plot our overthrow.

My mates graciously attributed my, er, date with Destiny to the head trauma I'd received from running headlong into Thurston's armour that evening, or as ZakDot put it, 'out into the knight'.

Speaking of my mates…Maddie fled the country before anyone could figure out the connection between her and what had happened to the *Dinkum*. We got a postcard from Iceland, and then there was no news for ages until one day the *Herald* reported that she was being deported from France for attempting to launch the Eiffel Tower into space. The Museum of the Most Cutting Edge Art (which the Colombian drug cartel returned to the city in exchange for tickets to every New Year's Eve celebration for the next fifty years—no one told them you don't actually need tickets) contacted her on her return and offered her a commission to take out the Art Gallery of New South Wales. She turned that down to accept a grant from a peace foundation to blow up old military installations all around the world.

ZakDot is still searching for meaning, though he's finally realised that the search for meaning is itself the focus for his art. He has an idea for an exhibition called '"Search" for "Meaning"—I Interrogate "Myself"' but it's not past the pre-conceptual stage. Despite the fact he still hasn't done any art, he's successfully achieved the status of 'celebrity artist', by concentrating on the celebrity side of things. He's a staple of all the talk shows and panels. They even asked him to host the new series of 'Art/Life', but he knocked the offer back. *Pulse* had just put 'Art/Life' on its 'shocking' list, 'shocking' now being the opposite of 'cool', 'cool' being cool again.

Gabe has progressed to the letter 'S'. I'm not sure what it stands for. Spot?

Julia is still taking photos. She happened to be on a yacht with a visiting troupe of Chinese acrobats when the *Dinkum* went up. Her photograph of exploding meringues made it onto the front cover of *Whirl Art*. Last time I saw her, she was with the lead singer of that Newtown band, the fellow who was reputedly even cooler than ZakDot. Apparently, they'd been lovers a long time ago.

Thurston has come out of the closet. I'm embarrassed to admit that there was some drama there in the beginning. It turns out that he was actually in love with me. I can't believe it never occurred to me: he used to follow me around and gaze at me simply because he didn't know how to express his feelings. I felt terrible. I was never attracted to him, but that's not the point. For a sensitive artist, I could be pretty insensitive at times. It's worked out okay in the end. He met a lovely bloke who adores him. Grev and I even went to their house-warming. And when we had our first child, he sent us a card of handmade paper on which he'd calligraphed the words, 'May you thrive and tidder.'

Yes, I had finally met the beautiful, refined, artistic and sensitive woman of my dreams. Senior Constable Grevillea Bennett. Put 'Bent' down to my poor hearing. We've embarked on what I fully expect will be a lifelong, passionate yet intellectual affair that will be the stuff of legend. Just like I foreshadowed to Thurston that day in the pub.

We named our first child Gaea (for she was truly born out of chaos) after the stool which prevented my flight from Trimalkyo's house that day. Gaea was followed by Calliope, Clio and Thalia. The muses of poetry, history and humour. They're a bit too energetic for Bacon's liking; he's a fat and lazy old thing, but he doesn't complain much.

Grev quit the force and started doing what she'd always wanted to do—write. She won a prize for her first novel, an erotic thriller about a sexually deviant cop. In the course of a raid, the cop comes across a quantity of cocaine and distributes it through criminal contacts, making a bundle and thereafter supporting herself and her previously poor bisexual artist boyfriend in a style to which neither ever imagined they would become accustomed.

ZakDot, who still lives in that warehouse in Chippendale, stays with us in our home in Woollahra from time to time. It's all of our fantasies come true.

And of course there was that show at Gallery Trimalkyo. In addition to exhibiting the best of 'Paranoia: Killing Miles Walker', I did a rainforest series featuring the No Names as warrior nymphs. The launch was huge. Everyone turned up, including the No Names, which was pretty special, even for Paddington. They were the only ones there not wearing black. They weren't wearing anything.

My mum came to the launch as well. She and I both got a shock when I went to introduce her to Trimalkyo.

'Trimalkyo.' She'd gone pale. 'So that's what you're calling yourself these days.'

I was astounded to see Trimalkyo blush. 'Jenna.' I was sure I hadn't told him her name yet.

'Well? Have you told him?' She asked this in a strange, high pitch.

'I wasn't a hundred per cent sure.' Trimalkyo's accent had disappeared again. He was looking flustered. Oscar looked to me for enlightenment, but I shrugged, as clueless as he was.

'You know,' Trimalkyo said to me, 'your mother could have been a great painter.'

I stared at him, and then my mother, in confusion. Those paintings in the attic. They must have been hers. But how did he know about them?

'Well, at least you're looking after your son.' She sniffed.

I nearly fainted. Grevillea, who was eight months pregnant at the time, held me up.

'I'm sorry, Miles.' Trimalkyo opened his arms and gave me a hug. And so I had my first exhibition, met my dad, and proposed to my wife all on the same evening.

The exhibition launched my brilliant career. Jean-Paul d'Esdaigne raved about the show in the *Herald*. It sold out and more favourable critiques, interviews and features on my work appeared in *Trash Art* and *Whirl Art* and *Art + Connections*.

It proved a great year for me in general. My portrait of Destiny won the Archibald Prize. The judges loved the unfinished corner. I received invitations to exhibit in New York and London and Beijing, and to represent our country at the

Venice Biennale. The Historic Memorials committee commissioned me to paint Penelope Tolerance's portrait when she retired. That's how it's supposed to be done, by the way.

I was successful *and* I was alive. I even became a minor celebrity. Kylie Minogue, who'd become Queen of England following a series of accidents to the royal family, asked me to appear in a music video. I referred her to ZakDot.

As my work went on winning prizes and honours, the story of how I won over Destiny leaked out, along with the videotapes. I was mortified, Grevillea amused, and I learned once and for all that there really is no such thing as success without compromise.

Speaking of which, Trimalkyo and I decided that it would be better for my career and his reputation if we let the father-son thing be our little secret. Especially as he is my dealer and all. I suppose I've forgiven him. Grevillea and I go round there fairly often. The kids love Grandad's furniture. Oscar and I have become good friends. I visited him in hospital every day after he had his buttocks implant. He's gone from fairy godfather to fairy stepmother, something we often laugh about, though he gets terribly upset if any of the kids call him 'grandma'. He and Trimalkyo run the trendiest, most happening gallery in Paddington, which is to say Sydney, which is to say, so far as Sydney is concerned, the world.

Oh, that's right. Verbero. A few hours after the bomb went off, the harbour police found him still handcuffed to the sink. He was hanging for a line, and had pissed himself, but was otherwise fine. As it turned out, the bomb Maddie had planted on the *Dinkum* was a simple device consisting of dry ice and water in a sealed two-litre plastic bottle. The fuse was a joke. My watch wasn't involved at all—she'd used it for something else. The thing about dry ice bombs is that you can't tell exactly when they'll blow. As it turned out, when it did go, as we all know, it blew up the dessert table neatly enough, and you wouldn't want to have been standing within range when it went off, but the *Dinkum* was a solid ship. It's now in permanent drydock at the Maritime Museum receiving hundreds of visitors each day, many of them school-children learning about the history of our little country.

Verbero went on to become a movie producer. After a series of commercial successes, he produced a film that he told the breathless press was 'his most sincere', a 'searing examination' of the Clean Slate experiment. *Destiny Days* was much acclaimed by critics and went on to win the jury prize at Cannes. Tyrone Australis, the extremely handsome young actor who played the character based on Verbero himself, was courted by Hollywood. He drifted off, never to return. Some things never change.

*Also by Linda Jaivin*
EAT ME

Julia is a photographer. Chantal edits a fashion magazine. Helen is a feminist academic. And Philippa is writing a novel. The best of friends, they haunt the designer cafes of Darlinghurst, eyeing the passing talent and swapping stories. Sexy, intelligent and predatory, these four women are creatures of the nineties, as are the men in their lives, Jake the 'slacker gigolo', Marc the wannabe feminist and Mengzhong the Beijing sword-swallower. But can we believe the wild and wicked tales these women love to tell each other about their erotic exploits?

With her brilliant wit and silky prose, Linda Jaivin has created a funny and seductive world in which she plays havoc with ideas about truth, sex and power. After *Eat Me*, lust, laughter, kiwifruit and the Big Merino will never seem the same again.

'Erotic escapism at its best, with a touch of humour and a touch of class; a blend of fetishism, fun and kiwifruit!'
*New Woman*

224pp, paperback, rrp$16.95 ISBN 1 875847 11 1

# ROCK N ROLL BABES FROM OUTER SPACE

Baby, Doll and Lati, three spunky alien babes,
are trapped on Nufon, the most boring planet in the
entire yoon. They steal a spaceship and arrive in Sydney,
Planet Earth, in search of sex, drugs and rock n roll.
When the babes abduct Jake, a minor rock star
and dred-headed charmer, and toss him in
their saucer's sexual experimentation chamber,
the global warming begins.

The babes form a band, and rocket to rock n roll
stardom. Trouble is, Jake and Baby are falling in love, a
posse of Nufonians is headed for Earth, the US military
is on the case and Eros the talking asteroid wants to dive
into the mosh as well. The babes are planning their
biggest gig, but can they save the world too?

'*Rock n Roll Babes from Outer Space* is written with the
unexpected sweetness of a writer who's on the outer
looking in at something with the sort of fascination and
attention that we envy in a child.' *Rolling Stone*

304pp, paperback, rrp$16.95 ISBN 1 875847 33 2

## CONFESSIONS OF AN S&M VIRGIN

Linda Jaivin gets a spanking as she interviews the manager of an S&M club. She steps into a kickboxing ring, and wears a penis for a week to find out how it feels to be a man. 'When I'm writing non-fiction,' she says, 'I tend to get into character.' Jaivin describes the effects of PMT and tells the terrifying story of her friend the axe-murderer. She reveals why she loves younger men and why sex makes her laugh.

She takes us backstage at a Beijing rock concert, explores the secretive world of Chinese gays and lesbians, and gives an astonishing account of what happened the night the tanks rolled into Tiananmen Square.

'This collection of essays and journalism offers a number of amusing diversions into comic-erotica. But diversions they are. Despite some very droll and occasionally hilarious forays into the subjects of genital swapping (literally), orgasm and PMT, *Confessions*' centre of gravity is fixed squarely within Jaivin's original area of expertise, China...Jaivin's writings on the '89 massacre rank amongst the finest pieces of reconstructive journalism published by an Australian.'
John Birmingham

216pp, paperback, rrp$19.95 ISBN 1 875847 46 4